THE UNIQUE MAGAZINE

Fall 1988

ISSN 0898-5073

Art by Carl Lundgren Studios

Published quarterly by the Terminus Publishing Company, Inc., P.O. Box 13418, Philadelphia PA 19101-3418. Application to mail at second
class postage rates pending at Philadelphia PA and additional mailing offices. Single copies, $4.00 (plus $1.00 postage if ordered by mail). Subscription
rates: Eighteen months (six issues) for $18.00 in the United States and its posessions, for $24.00 in Canada, and for $27.00 elsewhere. The publishers
are not responsible for the loss of manuscripts, although reasonable care will be taken of such material while in their possession. Copyright©
1988 by the Terminus Publishing Company, Inc.; all rights reserved; reproduction prohibited without prior permission. *Weird Tales*™ is a trade
mark owned by Weird Tales, Limited. Typeset, printed, and bound in the United States of America.

THE EYRIE

We are very sorry to report the recent death of **Lin Carter**, who once edited *Weird Tales*™ with distinction. He also wrote some of the most interesting letters we received during our own editorship of this magazine. As editor of the Ballantine Adult Fantasy Series, he had an enormous impact on the fantasy field. We all miss him very much. Robert Price, editor of *Crypt of Cthulhu* magazine, put it best by saying that "Lin Carter's obsessions have enriched us all."

We are gratified by the reader response to *Weird Tales*™. Many letters of praise you've sent us are simply that — praise — but while this makes your editors very happy, epistle after epistle of *"Weird Tales*™ is wonderful!"* might be a tad boring for you to read, so we will get on to letters with more meat.

For those of you who keep asking for reprints of stories from old issues of *Weird Tales*™, our feeling is that the pages of *Weird Tales*™ are too precious to use up with such reprints when many fine anthologies are appearing and when there are so few markets for first-rate *new* weird and fantastic stories, especially the longer ones.

We recommend a fine new anthology, *Weird Tales*™: *32 Unearthed Terrors*, edited by Stefan R. Dziemianowicz, Robert Weinberg, and Martin H. Greenberg (Bonanza Books, 1988). This book includes one story from each year of the magazine's 1923-54 run, with many classics and lost gems, some reprinted for the first time. Another fat volume of *Weird Tales*™ reprints will be pub-

lished soon by Nelson Doubleday, this one edited by Marvin Kaye and encouragingly titled *Weird Tales*™: *The Magazine That Never Dies*, with not only classic stories from the early years of the magazine, but stories from recent issues as well. We understand it will include Darrell Schweitzer's "The Mysteries of the Faceless King" (from our Spring 1988 issue).

The few reprints we have used are stories from obscure sources, such as Gene Wolfe's "The Dead Man" in our Spring 1988 issue, from a 1965 issue of *Sir!* so scarce that even the author didn't have a copy. And we hasten to point out that neither this current issue nor the one just before it, Summer 1988, contains any stories previously published *anywhere*.

Editor/publisher **W. Paul Ganley** writes of our Summer 1988 issue:

This is a very superior issue. All the fiction is extremely well written, though some of the stories left me wondering where the next chapter was when I come to the end. The two Lee stories are outstanding, the interview is charming, and the artwork is fully up to the standard set in the previous issue, in my opinion. I thought the best story was Brian Lumley's, however. He told me some time ago that this one had sold to you, and he was very excited about it (as if you guys were working for Farnsworth Wright or something) and considered it one of his best-ever pieces. What impressed me about it was that you could remove the hint of the supernatural (the woman's coffin could have been constructed from the wood of one of the old houses, for instance, with no mention of Haiti) and it would still have been a wonderful mainstream story. It reminded me of Bradbury stories like "The Next in Line."

With regard to the lettercolumn, I am definitely on your side in the matter of choosing fiction for a contemporary Weird Tales™. Still, there should be a way to (somewhat) placate those "hard core" fans who really would love it if you could spray that old pulp smell on their copies. You could carry a "vintage reprint" or do a "Mythos revisted" series, one new Cthulhu Mythos story an issue. After you finish the series of issues that are directed toward "special authors" you might consider such an idea, or throw it up for grabs and see what the readers might say about it.

One of my all time favorite series is Doc Smith's Lensman saga. I can still re-read them in an effort to capture the reactions I had to them in 1949. But I find that there are some modern books that are much better written that give me the very same reactions I had to the Doc Smith stories, and in this case, in particular, I am thinking of Piers Anthony's Cluster stories — intergalactic in scope, almost visionary, with convincing pseudo-science. I don't see why you shouldn't aim for the same effect in Weird Tales™ — bringing us things, today, that we react to in the same way people reacted to Kuttner, Moore, Lovecraft, Ashton Smith, et al. in their heyday.

We agree, Paul; you've stated our editorial policy quite succinctly. This is exactly why we *don't* want a lot of reprints or stories which deliberately pastiche the old *Weird Tales™* styles. Those would not give modern readers the same effect that Lovecraft and so on gave the readers of the 1930s. Imagine the reader of 1930 being confronted with reprints of the weird fiction of *1880*, or stories written in that manner. That's not the impression we want to make.

As for special "theme" issues, what do you readers think of them? We'll certainly let this idea slosh around in the fetid cauldron of our collective editorial brain for a while. Even a Cthulhu-Mythos issue is possible, but it will be hard to get even two or three really good, non-imitative, genuinely *scary* Mythos stories.

Ultimately, though, we will have to pass

John Betancourt
George H. Scithers
Darrell Schweitzer
Editors & Publishers
Leslie Smith
Dainis Bisenieks
Karl Würf
Vincent Evangelisti
Deborah Scott
Assistant Editors
Richard Kabakjian
Circulation Manager
David J. Williams III
Computer Consultant
Yale F. Edeiken
Of Counsel
Advanced Litho, Inc.
Photographer
The Twin Company, Inc.
Campus Copy Center
Typesetters
Malloy Lithographing, Inc.
Printer

SUBMISSIONS?

Like most editors, we get unsolicited manuscripts, *lots* of them. We survive, as do other editors, only by imposing Rules.

Yes, we read unsolicited manuscripts — *if* they are in proper manuscript format. Each must arrive with a self-addressed, stamped return envelope big enough to take that manuscript back to you, or with a stamped, addressed, business-letter-sized envelope *and* instructions to dispose of the manuscript if not bought. And no, we will not read manuscripts in unacceptable format.

This proper format is described in numerous reference works. One of them is *On Writing Science Fiction: The Editors Strike Back!*, by George H. Scithers, Darrell Schweitzer, and John M. Ford — which also goes into the whole art and practice of writing and selling fantastic literature. *On Writing* is available for $19.50, postpaid, from Owlswick Press, PO Box 8243, Philadelphia, PA 19101 (if you live in Pennsylvania, add $1.17 for sales tax).

from doing "special author" issues and "theme" issues to just plain *issues*. After all, we intend to be publishing *Weird Tales™* for a long time to come.

Author and poet **Joe R. Christopher** writes:

I was rather disappointed by the letters on the first issue, in one way. Surely some of George Barr's imitations of the artists extended beyond Weird Tales™. *Wasn't he "doing" Edd Cartier on pp. 18, 21, and 125 (the woman, not the detail of jewelry)? Cartier, of course, was in* Unknown. *I think I could hunt around and find the original of the linear drawing on p. 69 (Astounding in the 1950s?), and even the grease-pencil illustration on p. 81 strikes dim memories, although I'm not certain where to check for the source. While the identification of certain artists was nice — confirming my identification of the Finlays and Boks — I did appreciate the reference to Dolgov, whom I didn't know.*

The stories were nicely varied. The one I liked least — Lumley's "Fruiting Bodies" — was typical of its horror mode. Cross's "The Initiate" was a nice occult piece; Springer's "Bad Lands" was distinguished by its western setting. I appreciated that you'd use a story with typographical oddities in it — Wisman's "My Mother's Purse." In fact, Wisman's story, Turtledove's "After the Last Elf is Dead," and Lee's semi-Arthurian "The Kingdoms of the Air" were my favorites — in ascending order. Lee's "The Unrequited Glove" was not as good, I thought, but I'm probably just not turned on by the "Flayed Hand" motif, although I admit that Lee did do some variations on the type. Llywelyn's "Princess" was a clever re-doing of Snow White and the Seven Dwarfs, with touches of Brownies given the Dwarfs.

Was there any special reason you didn't do a complete listing of Tanith Lee's books? I notice that some of the Flat Earth series are not in your list — two of the five, I believe . . . or a couple of them have alternate titles.

Anyway, I'm enjoying the revival. I'd like to see an issue completely illustrated by Tim Kirk before you stop — and what about Alicia Austin?

Indeed, what about Alicia Austin? We have a lot of artists in mind for special issues. Hank Jankus is next. More will follow.

The Tanith Lee bibliography was listed as "Selected" because we didn't include any of her short fiction. But if any of the books were left off, then we are in error.

Paul A. Kesler gets right to the heart of the matter:

I wish to avoid discussions of any particular authors or stories. I wish, instead, to concentrate on this issue of content, or scope, which you raised in your Spring and Summer columns.

You say in your Spring issue, for example, that the occasional unclassifiable story will see print in the future. This is commendable, I feel. You also state, in your Summer issue, that you do not intend to make Weird Tales™ *a "Conan-type magazine." Again, commendable. But since this is all in the interest of updating and expanding the parameters of the magazine, I have some suggestions for some writers — and types of writing — that might be considered for the future.*

Take, to begin with, the matter of reprints. You say that only little-known reprints will appear, with an emphasis on quality. But why limit such reprints to the same old traditional circles: the Seabury Quinns, the H.P. Lovecrafts, or — as Mr. Forrest Ackerman suggested — the David H. Kellers and C.L. Moores? Or, for that matter, to any of the writers whose stories have so numerously populated past issues of Weird Tales™?

If you're looking for obscure reprints of quality, why not draw on the equally rich vein of fantastic fiction that stems from Franz Kafka, or the French surrealists, or the many Latin American exponents of "magic realism"?

In the line of Kafka descendants, for example, there's the work of the brilliant Polish fantasist, Bruno Schulz, whose collections The Street of Crocodiles *and* Sanitarium Under the Sign of the Hourglass *might be scanned for reprints. Or why not include an occasional piece by such Italian fantasists as Dino Buzatti, Italo Calvino, or Thomas Landolfi? Reprints from the Latin American fantasists could draw from the works of Jorge Luis Borges, Carlos Fuentes, or Julio Cortazar (to name but a few), or — going further back — Horacia Quiroga, a number of whose stories have already been translated into English. Even Kobo Abe, the Japanese novelist, has done some bizarre short stories*

— *perhaps more than I'm aware of* — *and there may well be more shorter works in this vein by his fellow countryman, Yasunari Kawabata, which have yet to be translated into English. (For a treat, see his already-translated story, "One Arm," in* The House of the Sleeping Beauties and Other Stories.*)*

And what of Russian authors? Vladimir Odoyevsky (a 19th century writer), Fyodor Sologub, Yevgeny Zamyatin, and Abraham Tertz all offer possibilities.

There are, in short, myriad authors of many nationalities who have either specialized in, or frequently concentrated on the weird and the bizarre, Then, too, there are the "forgotten" writers, such as the French master of the macabre Marcel Schwob, whose works have seen a recent translation. (See The King in the Yellow Mask, *published by Carcanet Press.)*

How many readers who generally peruse the pages of Weird Tales™ *are familiar with the above writers? Yet don't at least some of them deserve representation? If you want obscure reprints of quality fiction, I can't think of a better start than by exploring this vast realm.*

Finally, there's the area of the short-short story, or prose poem, which I feel could have a great potential in Weird Tales™. *Clark Ashton Smith did a number of minature prose poems, and of course Fredric Brown was a notorious master of the short-short "shocker." But the form really goes back to French writers such as Baudelaire, Rimbaud, and the very macabre, but largely unknown Aloysius Bertrand. Couldn't many contemporary authors be approached for miniature fictions on weird and macabre themes? After all, this field has experienced a great renascence in recent years, especially in the little magazines (appropriately enough). Barr Yourgrau's* Wearing Dad's Head *is the most recent collection of strange miniatures that comes to mind (though Yourgrau emphasizes humor as much as the bizarre or the grotesque).*

I realize that every magazine has to draw guidelines and criteria for exclusion as well as inclusion. I can't expect that all the work for the authors I've mentioned would be at home in Weird Tales™. *Nevertheless, I hope this letter stimulates some thinking regarding alternatives for future exploration. Lovecraft and Robert E. Howard were fine in their day, as are Ramsey Campbell and Gene Wolfe in ours. I will always love the old tradition. But there are many other writers out there, from the past, the present, and even the future, waiting their turn.*

We're not not sure how one gets stories from the future, except possibly by time-travel, but . . . seriously, thanks for your long, fine letter, Paul. Yes, we would like *Weird Tales™* to be more international and cosmopolitan. If a new or previously untranslated story by Borges or Fuentes or Cortazar came our way, we would snap it right up. . . . However, much of the work of the authors you recommend is already available in the United States. We would certainly like to see translations of foreign works (authorized by the works' authors, of course).

We suspect that science fiction and fantasy fans are often too narrow in their tastes, and we welcome exploration of "outside" writers. (How many of the writers you list have we heard of? Calvino, Borges, Fuentes, Cortazar, Abe, Sologub, Zamyatin, and Tertz. Not the others, alas. There is so much yet to be explored!) Certainly your listing is a guideline for any enterprising anthologist. Several excellent international anthologies exist, notably *Black Water* edited by Alberto Manguel and published by Lester & Orpen Dennys in 1983.

As for getting stories by writers outside of the usual genre-pool, we're proud to have one in hand from Jonathan Carroll, the author of *The Land of Laughs*, who is one of the best (and perhaps *the* best) horror writer living.

We have bought a couple of short-shorts in the Fredric Brown mode, and certainly would welcome more. Prose poems are an entirely different art form, except for length. Those of the Clark Ashton Smith or Baudelaire type (actually the same type, since Smith was profoundly influenced by, and even translated the author of *Fleurs du Mal*) would also be welcome. Harry Morris's wonderful little magazine, *Nyctalops*, was filled with such works a few years ago.

Our criteria for reprints remain: 1) outstanding by contemporary standards 2) not previously published in English in the United States in its present form, or at least 3) published previously only in some virtually unobtainable edition, like a $35.00 pamphlet with a print-run of 100.

And that concludes the discussion of reprints for the time being.

In order to persuade more people to subscribe to *Weird Tales™*, we send out postcards and other mailing pieces, in large batches. It is simply not practical to screen an outside list — such as the 25,000 names we recently rented from *Isaac Asimov's Science Fiction Magazine* — to remove the names of all our own subscribers. So, if you already subscribe to *Weird Tales™* but nevertheless receive some of these advertisements, we do apologize. We haven't lost your subscription — we wouldn't dare!

To check the status of your subscription, look at the pair of numbers that follow your name on your copy's mailing label. The first is the whole number of the current issue (292 for *this* issue); the second, the whole number of your subscription's *final* issue.

Thus "292 295" after your name means that your subscription is good through issue number 295.

We really *do* want to hear your likes and dislikes, so we can steer the magazine in directions that you will enjoy. Keep those letters coming!

The Most Popular Story

As we go to press, we haven't received enough votes on issue 291 (Summer 1988) for more than this preliminary report:

First place was "Fruiting Bodies" by Brian Lumley.

Runners-up were "The Unrequited Glove" and "The Kingdoms of the Air," both by Tanith Lee, and "Princess" by Morgan Llywelyn.   □

GOOD NEWS
For All SF and Fantasy Readers!

Get all the latest news about what's happening in SF, fantasy and horror in the pages of *Science Fiction Chronicle: The Monthly SF and Fantasy Newsmagazine.* Just as news weeklies bring what's happening in the world to you, so *Science Fiction Chronicle* keeps you in the know on SF and fantasy. And not just news of who bought what and for how much, but more: news of publishers and editors, of mergers and other changes and how it affects you; obituaries, market reports, letters, news from Hollywood, author signings, convention reports with lots of author photos, news of books and authors from England, a regular convention calendar, over 400 book reviews a year—more than any other publication in the field—the latest on what's new in computer games, audio and videotapes.

And still more: SFC readers get a monthly directory of what's coming up from each publisher with prices, whether books are new or reprint, and much more, months before actual publication. If you buy and read a lot of SF and fantasy, you're sure to find this will save you the cost of your subscription in only a few months. Plus occasional columns by Frederik Pohl, Robert Silverberg, Karl Edward Wagner, Vincent Di Fate.

Science Fiction Chronicle has been a Hugo Award finalist every year since 1980. A single copy is $2; 12 monthly issues by First Class Mail in the US are usually $23.40. Order now, and get a year for only $18 (new subscribers only). In Canada, add $3.00; overseas, add $6.00. Mail your check to the address below, today!

SCIENCE FICTION CHRONICLE
P.O. Box 4175A
New York NY 10163, usa

9

THE DEN

by John Gregory Betancourt

The Den is going to be a bit short this time; we had to squeeze it to make room for the Clive Barker interview. But next issue it'll be back full length . . . maybe even a bit longer, if I can manage it.

I had hoped to make this a special column devoted solely to new horror writers — the people just now breaking into the horror-book field. I constantly see novels by people I've never heard of before, and I keep wondering if any of them are any good. The packaging makes them all look alike: predominantly black covers, with lots of die-stamping and sometimes a splash of foil.

Alas, most of the publishers' publicity departments were slow in getting me books (those that sent books at all: it's far harder to get review copies of horror titles than science fiction and fantasy, I've found), and I haven't had a chance to read most of what I've selected. A few titles that caught my eye are in this batch. The rest (plus whichever ones turn up in the meantime) will be in the next issue.

Till then, a brief reminder: review copies should go to me at 410 Chester Ave., Moorestown, NJ 08057.

Valley of Lights, by Stephen Gallagher
TOR books, 276 pp., $3.95

This is the first book I intended to read for my "new writers" column. I must admit it confused me. It *seems* to be an original horror novel, published for the first time in the U.S. — but it has cover quotes from the

British Fantasy Newsletter, the *Glasgow Evening Times*, and the *Yorkshire Evening Post*. Was there a British edition that isn't acknowledged on the copyright page? Is the author British? (He doesn't seem to be: he writes the President's American perfectly, and the story is set — very convincingly — in Phoenix, Arizona.) Why aren't there any cover quotes from American sources if the book *is* an original novel by an American? Why isn't there an About-the-Author paragraph at the back to answer all my questions?

In any case, *Valley of Lights* looks like your average run-of-the-mill horror novel: a very dark cover, a pair of sinister eyes superimposed over a cityscape, with black mountains and blood-red clouds hovering on the horizon. But it's not a horror novel; it's science fiction, with a measure of suspense thrown in.

The plot device is a familiar one: a sentient creature that lives in humans and can switch from one body to another almost at will. We've all seen this sort of thing before, in books like Heinlein's *The Puppet Masters*. It's even made it to television on shows like *Star Trek* (both new and old). The only real difference here is that Gallagher's creature is not physical; it's an essence, a soul or spirit — we're never quite sure exactly what, and the creature itself says it doesn't know.

There are a few standard horrific elements: the creature can only occupy a human who is brain-dead, and it keeps a supply of bodies in remote areas as back-ups in case anything happens to the one it's "wearing" — it switches bodies as easily as a person changes clothes. Having brain-dead people lying around all the time is not really convincing: I'd think lack of hygiene and lack of exercise, then disease and bed-sores would quickly make the bodies use-less. . . .

Ignoring these technical problems and getting to the plot itself, we find a good, solid, workable story: Alex Volchak, a cop, discovers a room full of unconscious people in a motel. When they are carted off to a hospital, they are found to be brain-dead. Alex takes a special interest in the case and tracks down the man who had rented the motel room — but this man closes his eyes and dies when caught. Then one of the brain-dead men in the hospital suddenly regains consciousness and escapes.

Alex rapidly becomes convinced that some creature is moving from body to body, and he tracks it down. The creature — seem-ingly immortal — is incredibly old. It has taken to murdering humans, particularly children, for sport. It kidnaps Alex's girl-friend's daughter and forces Alex to play a cat-and-mouse game with the little girl's life as the prize.

The most horrific element is the paranoid tension that comes when you realize the creature might be anyone — even be your best friend. What if you don't notice?

It's good to see that the book didn't dis-solve into another little-girl-in-peril story. The writing is smooth. The characters are thoroughly real, from the sadistic creature to Alex and the other policemen. I have no idea whether this is a first novel, or a tenth; but if I see another by Gallagher, I intend to read it.

The Selected Stories of Robert Bloch, by Robert Bloch
Underwood-Miller, 1,128 pp. (2 vols.), $80.00 (trade); $125.00 (signed)

Suffice to say, this is *the* Robert Bloch short-story collection — 98 stories in three volumes, half a million words in all. As an overview of Bloch's writing — from the mys-tery magazines to the science-fiction pulps to the slick men's magazines — it's un-matched (and, of course, superb).

But yet I noticed quite a few stories miss-ing that I would have liked to read again. I guess they're in other collections, like the Lefty Feep books, which are still in print. I imagine there are enough of Bloch's stories out there for two or three (or more) collec-tions of this size. I hope Underwood-Miller finds the time and inclination to do them.

About the only thing missing from this collection is an introduction (but what do you say about Bloch that hasn't been said a hundred times before?) and interior art-work. Such things are purely a matter of personal preference, and this book certainly doesn't suffer without them.

You can order directly from the publisher: Underwood-Miller, 515 Chestnut St., Col-umbia, PA 17512. Be warned: specialty press books like this one tend to sell out rather quickly.

Bright and Shining Tiger, by Claudia J. Edwards
Popular Library/Questar, 218 pp., $2.95

What attracted me to this book was its cover: a man and a woman on horseback, she wielding some sort of magical power, with an intricate pattern as a border around them and a giant silver tiger poised over-head — very striking, and I don't think my description quite does it justice.

In any case, Edwards is a very competent writer. She sets up an old situation, the wanderer in search of a place in the world, and adds a bit of new fire by making the wanderer a woman named Runa. When Runa reaches the fringes of civilization, she finds a village of peasants in need of a pro-tector. She moves into Silvercat Castellum, the abandoned fortress, planning to stay only a short time before moving on. But the land's supernatural guardian, the Silvercat (the giant silver tiger pictured on the cover) decides to adopt her as the land's sorceress-mistress.

Conflicts follow: the Silvercat tries to re-vive its lands, the neighboring rulers try to oust Runa, and Runa struggles to decide what she really wants from life.

The book held my interest; the back-ground was interesting, if a bit muddled (is this the far future, or an alternate past or present?), and the characters were convinc-ingly real. It's not the best thing since sliced bread, but it's a fun way to spend an afternoon. Try it if you get a chance.

The Brave Little Toaster Goes to Mars,
by Tom Disch
Doubleday, 80 pp., $11.95

I thoroughly enjoyed *The Brave Little Toaster* (the novella to which this slender volume is a sequel) for a couple of reasons: it was a mythic story in all the best sense of the word, with a terrific if improbable hero, a quest that kept me interested, and a supporting cast that I cared about.

Most of the appliances from the first tale are back in *The Brave Little Toaster Goes to Mars*. It is written in much the same style as the first story — and it's fun . . . but nothing more than that. The mythic qualities are missing, somehow, and the science-fictional gloss stretched my sense of belief a little too far. Sentient appliances are okay in a fantasy story; but this is a somewhat militant SF tale, and the combination doesn't sit as well as it should.

Or perhaps I'm old and jaded. Children will doubtless love both Toaster books. Perhaps Doubleday will soon publish an omnibus edition . . . perhaps even with pop-up illustrations?

Zombie! by Peter Tremayne
St. Martin's Press, 182 pp., $2.95

I love this book's tacky cover. There's a hideous decaying face (die-stamped), and the blurb screams, **They Die. They Walk. They Kill . . . For them the grave is only the beginning. ZOMBIE!** Classy, huh?

I wish I had liked the book's, um, *innards* as much as I liked its packaging. But, alas, no. I quote a few lines from the first page:

> "Only the flickering of the flaming brands, which many of them held in their hands, gave their grave faces animation with the multitude of lights and shadows they caused to dance over their sweat-glistening coppery skins." . . .
> "There came the sharp staccato call of the birds which, with some uncanny sense, had awakened noisily to herald the dawn which lay just below the unseen horizon. Their countless cries

mingled with the high pitched orchestration of a myriad crickets and the awful melody of countless croaking frogs from their swampy homes."
. . .

> "From within they could hear it — the slow rhythmic beat of a goatskin drum giving shape and body to the wailing female voice, rising and falling, rising and falling."

Talk about muddled prose — and, what's more, scenes are told from shifting viewpoints. As a result, the reader is forced to jump from character to character, unable to know or sympathize with any one of them. The people in the book don't say much, either — they aver, grin, smile, return, and muse their words.

To his credit, I have found Tremayne's short fiction to be of much higher quality. There are a couple of possible explanations for *Zombie!*'s problems. It might be a *very* old work — the copyright says 1981. Since Tremayne started writing fiction in 1977, according to an article on him in *Discovering Modern Horror Fiction II*, this doesn't seem terribly likely. Another possibility is that somehow the book's editor or copy-editor interfered heavily. Or Tremayne got sloppy and nobody bothered to fix the book or to make Tremayne fix it (again the editor's fault), which is a real shame.

Zombie! is a good one to skip.

Discovering Modern Horror Fiction II,
edited by Darrell Schweitzer
Starmont House, 169 pp., $9.95 (trade pb)

Horror fiction is very much in a boom period — lots of new writers, lots of older writers reaching prominence, lots of classics being rediscovered and reprinted. The *Discovering Modern Horror Fiction* series seems to be sampling mainly from the middle group — Name writers who are now prominent in the field. Authors covered in this volume are: Peter Straub, Fritz Leiber, Ray Bradbury, Robert Aickman, Michael McDowell, Robert Bloch, David Case, Charles L. Grant, T.E.D. Klein, Ramsey Campbell, James Herbert, Joseph Payne Brennan, Michael Shea, John Collier, Chelsea Quinn Yarbro, Peter Tremayne, and the poetry of Richard Tierney, William Breiding, and Joseph Payne Brennan.

This book is, in fact, the only place I found detailed information on Tremayne when I tried to do a bit of research on *Zombie!* The articles range from fair to excellent, and at $9.95 seems a distinct bargain: most such academic books sell for two to five times as much, mostly because libraries buy them and libraries are at the mercy of the publishers.

A Rendezvous in Averoigne, by Clark Ashton Smith
Arkham House, 473 pp., $22.95

Clark Ashton Smith is a favorite of mine. He is the author most responsible for getting me into the fantasy field: I found a British paperback of one of his short story collections as a child, and the first story I read was his classic "The Weird of Avoosl Wuthoqquan," about a greedy money-lender who buys some stolen gems, only to have them roll off his table and out the door. When he follows them, they lead him to his doom.

It's not so much Smith's plots that thrill me, it's his use of language, the strange and beautiful images he conjures up. His work has a bizarre vividness which has never quite been matched. Here is a brief passage from "Xeethra":

> "Wondering and curious, the boy peered into the inviting gloom of the cavern, from which, unaccountably, a soft balmy air now began to blow. There were strange odors on the air, suggesting the pungency of temple incense, the languor and luxury of opiate blossoms. They disturbed the senses of Xeethra; and, at the same time, they seduced him with their promise of unbeholden marvelous things."

That is precisely the way I feel about Smith's work. There is poetry here, and magic. Smith was a genius, and *A Rendezvous in Averoigne* is a terrific sampler of his weird fiction. Unfortunately I already have all the stories in it in other collections and didn't find anything new (except the corrected text of "The City of the Singing Flame," which appears for the first time as

Smith originally wrote it).

Recommended, especially if you're unfamiliar with the bulk of Smith's work. □

WEIRD TALES TALKS WITH CLIVE BARKER

by Robert Morrish

Weird Tales™: Now that you've had a chance to reflect on your directorial debut, would you say that you're satisfied with how *Hellraiser* turned out?

Clive Barker: For the money and the time? Yeah. It does what it does. For the most part, the reviews have been extremely kind. The audiences seem to have been having a good time with it, which is a major satisfaction. So I would have to say yes, I'm satisfied.

One of the interesting things about watching the picture with audiences is seeing how it actually does disturb people. Of course there's the laughter, of course there's the tension release but . . . it seems to work on people, it really seems to scare them, which is great. And there's some images in the picture, like the guy with the hooks in his face, that I really like a lot. Hopefully some people will be dressing up as Cenobytes this Halloween.

WT: Maybe we'll see the creation of a whole *Hellraiser* subculture.

CB: Absolutely. That would be great. At some of the signings I've been to, people have been coming up with drawings of Cenobytes. I think it would be great if some of the images from the movie become . . . images which recur in people's heads and stick with them. So much of horror is about images anyway.

It looks like we're set to do a sequel. We'll pick up the rest of the story, Julia's story; a lot more about the Cenobytes, about their background. There

will probably be some kind of fiction sequel as well. Maybe a comic strip as well.

WT: Will you be writing and directing the sequel?

CB: It's my story, but it's not my screenplay. It's written by a guy named Peter Atkins, who's a fellow Liverpudlian. It's really his first screenplay, but it's tremendous, I think. We worked quite closely on it. The principal shooting will start in . . . about ten weeks' time, I guess. I would really like to see a *Hellraiser* series get going. I'd like . . . Julia to be the first running character in a horror series who's a woman, like a female Freddie Krueger. I think Claire Higgins does a great job as Julia.

WT: Tell us about the two films based on your work — *Rawhead Rex* and *Underworld* — that Empire produced without your involvement.

CB: As you probably know, I hated those, especially *Rex*. I had absolutely no production control. Negative in fact. Is there such a thing as negative production control? If there is, that's what I had. I wasn't even allowed on the set. *Rawhead Rex* was filmed in Ireland and they kept saying they were going to fly me over and they never did. Later on I came to believe that it was some kind of unspoken lock-out. Basically they took the screenplay from me and . . . it was set in mid-summer and they shot it in February in Ireland — wrong country, wrong season. I disliked the film rather more than other people, I

14

think because it was one of my favorite stories. I had a good time writing it; sort of a monster on the loose story. And they should have got it more right than they did. Also, there was a lack of courage to go out and make a genuinely scary, gross picture.

Horror's been going through a very funny phase where it's been getting real mild. Positively benign.

WT: Perhaps, but there are some exceptions, I think; in fiction, there are certainly splatterpunks out there.

CB: Absolutely. I consider myself part of that "school" — in certain stories. But it's much more difficult to splatter with intelligence in the movies. Cronenburg is an obvious exception to that. I hope *Hellraiser* is as well. I mean, it was a splatter picture in a lot of respects, very gory. But I hope it comes across as being done with some intelligence, some subtext. But there aren't too many films around that would fit in that category.

WT: Is Empire going to be doing any more of your stuff?

CB: I took them to court to keep them from . . . exploiting any more of my material. I won, so all the options came back to me. It's the first time I've ever taken anybody to court on a thing like that, but I thought, not only are they making bad pictures, they're trying to rip me for the next ones. So I was real pleased to get my stuff back.

WT: Aren't they available on video tape now!

CB: Yes, with "from the author of . . ." plastered all over them, which is very irritating, but you know, there's nothing you can do about it.

I genuinely don't know what you can do about that. The only reasonable thing to do seems to be what I've done. Or else you just take the money and don't worry about it; don't even go and see the movie. God knows how the imaginative genius of Ray Bradbury faces the next Ray Bradbury adaptation.

WT: *Weaveworld* is obviously quite a departure from what you've been doing previously. Was there any specific inspiration for the change, or was it something you just evolved towards?

CB: I think the latter point is exactly right. I've evolved towards this *idea* that's been in my head, that I've wanted to do for a long time. It's a very long book — about six hundred pages — very long for me, as long as I want to get.

I would like to do a lot more fantasy. But I use the word "fantasy" in the widest possible context. You and I know what we mean when we say fantasy — we don't necessarily mean elves and magicians. There's none of that stuff in *Weaveworld*, but there is a lot of darkness.

WT: What do you have coming up in the future fiction-wise?

CB: There'll be a new 35,000 word dark fantasy novella in the hardcover edition of *Books of Blood VI*. The novella will be illustrated in the English edition with photographs which I'm taking, which should be fun. I've been taking photographs for years and years and this is the first time there'll actually be an edition using them. A kind of movie on the page.

WT: And you have another fantasy novel coming out after *Weaveworld*?

CB: Yes, another fantasy novel, and I have plans for four more novels after that, all backed up.

WT: It sounds like you're moving away from short fiction.

CB: Short fiction is tough in a couple of regards . . . I think that one of the things you've got to confront when you do a piece of really outlandish fiction, like "In the Hills, the Cities," is "okay, how long can I make this work for? I know that this is a dangerous idea, I know that this is a trapeze act."

WT: It's easier to suspend disbelief for 30 pages than for 300.

CB: You got it. You just couldn't do it for 300. I think also in a sense that

15

the six volumes of the *Books of Blood* were, in a sense, an entire statement — me doing as much as I possibly could in the genre. The books were my version of a one-man circus — I juggle, I walk the wire. I tried to be as comprehensive as possible, as eclectic as possible. To do something that had erotic overtones, to do something with a comic touch, to do some very graphic things, and to be able to put it under the six covers, seemed like a lot of fun. Some of them are going to work better than others. Some people are going to like certain stories a lot better than others, but that's part of the pleasure.

WT: Sort of like the ups and downs of a roller coaster ride.

CB: Exactly. There are going to be places where you say this is my kind of story and places where you don't. The interesting thing about the fan mail that comes in is that no two letters are exactly alike in terms of their likes and dislikes. You find that people despise a certain story, and that others love that same story. And that's good.

And with a novel you're committing to nine months of work on a single idea, however rich the idea is. I enjoy tat emotional commitment, but it's a vastly different approach.

WT: A lot of your readers don't know that you're an accomplished artist as well. I understand that there are going to be prints made of the covers you did for the English editions of the *Books of Blood*.

CB: Yeah, when they did those covers, they pulled images from within the original pictures and cropped them very, very severely so that they could fit them onto the cover. Less than half of the entire pictures are shown.

I like the covers much better when all the detail is there. When they're cropped like that you miss the sense of the whole. That's a problem with the book covers.

We're just setting up limited edition lithos of them. There's been some problem getting the colors right. We're fiddling around with them, making sure that we do get it right.

I think they'll be nice editions. I want to do them really beautifully. I don't want to do them unless we do them right. I think we'll make them real limited and they'll all be personally signed. I think it's what I owe . . . my fans — to make sure that it's all good quality and a good value. That's one of the things I love about Poseidon — they brought in a 600-page book which looks extremely handsome for $18.95, which is a real good price for that size book. I'm very impressed by that.

WT: Are you still doing artwork?

CB: I did 17 black-and-white illustrations for *Weaveworld* in the limited edition in England.

WT: As I understand it, just three or four years ago, you were on welfare. That's quite a change of circumstance in a short period of time.

CB: Yes, all of this is really quite new, quite a fresh experience. Very odd. I got to the age of 30 without ever having had very much money, and not really caring that much. I was painting, writing, doing what I liked to do. Now we're talking about million dollar advances . . . that's a massive change of circumstance in a short time.

WT: Is it in the back of your mind now that now you have a reputation to live up to?

CB: Yeah, but one of the things about changing direction with *Weaveworld* is that now I've got a new context in which to be put. This isn't visceral.

WT: A lot of people would probably be afraid to take the risk of making such a large departure from what they're known for.

CB: Yes. I think that . . . part of the thing for me is I want to continue to take those risks — I'd like to do more fantasy and I'd like to do some science fiction. In the movies, I've been talking about all kinds of projects — animated projects, a musical — all kinds of projects. As far as I'm concerned, I just turned 35 and the imaginative adventures that I can have on the page or on the screen are just beginning and that's very exciting.

WT: You've obviously come a long way in the last three or four years. Where would you like to see yourself in 10 years?

CB: Doing all of the stuff I'm doing now — movies, books, art — continuing the continuum, I guess. Doing it all.

WT: You've been interviewed a lot. Are there any questions you'd ask yourself which you've never been asked, any things which you'd like to express your views on which you've never been able to?

CB: That's a tough one. Give me a couple seconds . . . the thing which I think finally excites me most and which is very difficult to express totally . . . is the thing about making all of this work a continuum of some kind or other. So that however it's described — horror fiction, fantasy fiction, science fiction — and however it's expressed — in paintings, movies, novels — it's part of a cohesive whole. And that's a difficult thing to address.

Even though *Weaveworld* is in many ways a departure — because it's a much more optimistic book, because it's a fantasy, because it's not visceral — it's still another valley in the same country.

I think a lot of people like to label things and in turn a lot of people are automatically turned off by labels, and that bothers me, that disappoints me. Anything that demands a sense of wonder to embrace — I want very much for the people who read this kind of fiction, who see these kinds of movies to go and and understand how pervasive the fantastique is.

And not just people in the genre community but outside it — make *them* understand just how pervasive the fantastique is. You can go to see fantastique artifices in churches across Europe. One of the greatest novels of American literature, perhaps the greatest — *Moby Dick* — is a fantasy book. There are great fantasy novels and images from fantasy movies shaping culture in the sense that they are part of our iconography.

The "imaginative life" is part of us all as children and . . . our dreams are still full of that imagery as adults. It's not like the people in these stories are so distant from us, because our lives are full of a sort of "casual surrealism."

I also think that horror fiction — at least good horror fiction — deals with adult anxieties and adult fears. I try real hard to marry up adult anxieties with this kind of fiction, rather than simply making it be about the monster in the closet. There's no reason why one can't write about these kind of fears and obsessions in an adult context. There's no reason why the freedom that literature has to address adult feelings in an adult way should not be exploited by the genre. I try to do the same thing in *Weaveworld*. Fantasy books are all too often sexually repressed books, it seems to me; chauvinist books, in fact. I tried real hard for that not to be the case with *Weaveworld*.

WT: You've said in the past that you don't like leaving things up in the air at the end of a story, that you like a definitive ending. Is there any particular reason for that?

CB: It's about statements. You stand or fall by the statement that you can make. It's important to what you say. I believe this. And at the end of a story, people should know clearly, I think, what you meant. ☐

17

THE ORDEAL STONE

by Keith Taylor

"Drive her out of the way!"

The old man's voice was harsh and forbidding as his countenance, the words dragged roughly from a throat used to providing a channel for orders — yet the hearers, men of his own household, did not move to obey. Shuffling their feet, they looked at each other, while the entourage he had stopped on the road to his family's dun took instant, bristling offence. With a cry of "Renegades!" the old man strode towards his visitor's litter alone.

A stalwart young Briton sprang into his path, eyes snapping like blue torches in anger. Without breaking stride, the old lordling dealt the Briton a buffet which knocked him dazed to the ground, and continued to approach the litter. From combined loyalty and shame, the old man's household men followed him. The visitor's escort drew together in their path, and in an instant the situation threatened blood.

"Wait," commanded a clear voice, steadied by its owner's will. The hangings of the canopied litter were drawn back by a white hand. Two beautifully shod feet swung out of the shadowed interior and down to the wet grass. Above them shimmered a gown of azure silk with a vermilion border, and finally the speaker's face emerged to know the kiss of sunlight.

Clarity. That was the first impression one received of Vivayn, princess of Hamo, whether one heard her voice or saw her visage. Bards averred that hers were the most lucent grey eyes in Britain, and young though she was those

eyes saw most things without flinching. Nothing touched her, men said, she was dispassionate as the air. Certainly no feelings were evident as she confronted the aged chieftain who loathed her, save a faint, detached amusement.

"Why am I to be driven out of the way, my lord Kinernus?"

"Because traitors are not welcome in my dun, and my kindred pay no tribute to sea-wolves. Go back and tell Cerdic that."

"No, my lord, I will not," Vivayn said calmly. If the word traitor caused her pain, she betrayed no sign. "Nor can I believe you would truly want it, knowing Cerdic as you do. None of the kindred you claim as supporters are eager to have that boast repeated, but the road is no place to be speaking of such things. We can discuss them under your rooftree if your spearmen will show us the way."

"We discuss nothing, woman," Kinernus said, his contempt like a hedge of knives. "God himself would blast my house to ashes if you entered it. You stand in garments drenched with your father's blood, and to such as you the mist of darkness is reserved forever."

"None of which," Vivayn said patiently, "makes Cerdic less avid for a tribute you can well afford, or diminishes the number of war-men he can lead to battle. Send me back empty-handed and your next visitor will be even less pleasing to you, nor will I have anything to say about it."

"Also," said the young Briton Kinernus had knocked down, his speech

18

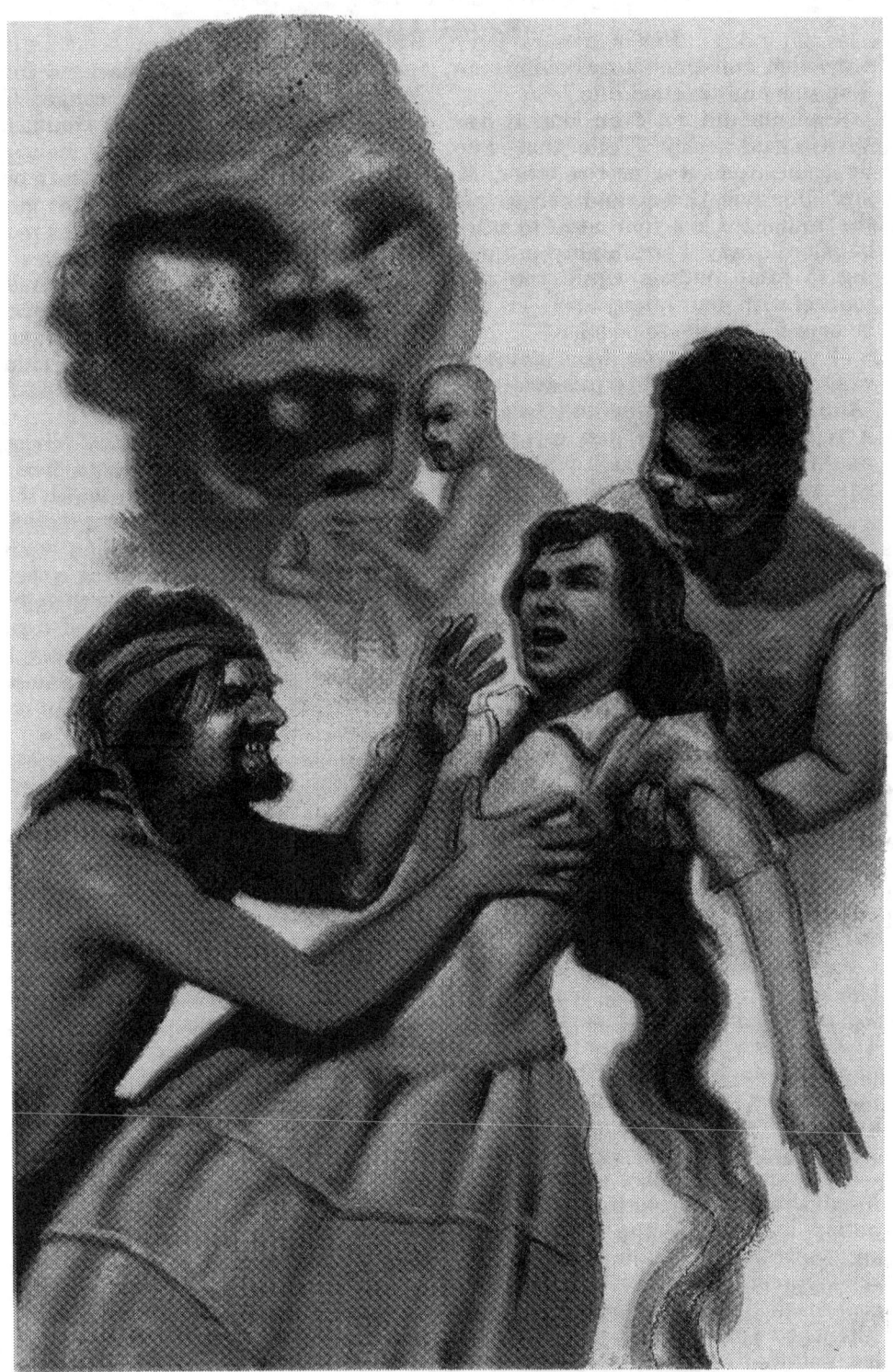

somewhat indistinct as he held his jaw, "you're a foul-tongued liar."

Kinernus did not even look at him. Vivayn said gently, "Teilo, that is not important, one way or the other. My lord Kinernus, God is not likely to take the trouble to blast your house to ashes, but Cerdic may. For tonight I am willing to camp outside while you take counsel with your family and — it is to be hoped — decide to be wise."

"I cannot stop you from camping where you please," Kinernus answered. "And Vivayn's time is her own to waste. A friend, though, if you have any, would advise you not to loiter here long. Farewell."

"It's likely that I shall not, Kinernus." Vivayn omitted to call him lord, since he had not addressed her once as lady although she outranked him by birth and marriage. "Meanwhile there might be some profit for you in giving ear to the advice of your own friends and kinsmen. Until we meet again."

Tall and straight as a Roman column, Kinernus spoke to his followers and led them back to the stockaded farmstead on a nearby rise. His iron-colored beard was too stiff to blow free in the rising wind, but his undyed garments fluttered like the rags of some ancient prophet stalking out of the wilderness to cry doom upon sinners.

Angry redness suffused the normally placid skin of Vivayn's face as she looked at Kinernus's departing back. Traitress, harlot, and other names even harsher had been applied to her by many since the sea-wolves had conquered her father's kingdom, because she had married one of the invaders — as if she could have effectively refused! Vivayn dealt with such condemnation by showing the world a face enigmatic and aloof, faintly amused by self-righteous antics — but wearing a cool mask did not make phrases like "drenched with your father's blood" any less painful to hear.

She replaced the cool mask as Teilo approached her, having arranged his clothes in the best order he could. *He* was not given to hiding his feelings, even with their barbarian masters, one reason Vivayn liked him. Just now Teilo's cheeks burned crimson as a rooster's comb.

"Lady, you cannot kick your heels outside that madman's dun at his whim!" he protested. "You are who you are, while he's no more than a cattle-chieftain. In your father's time he would never have dared."

"Indeed you are right, Teilo," Vivayn said; "and he's more foolish to dare it now, in Cerdic's time; but after all that is his affair. The purpose for which we were sent here is ours. Why do you and Liudhere not set about making a camp while I give this matter some thought? After all, we avoided a pitched fight, which is always a promising way to begin negotiations. I commend you for not starting a brawl under the provocation of that blow."

Liudhere, a cineritiously grey seawolf of the Jutish tribe, grinned ironically through his beard to hear Vivayn's compliment. He would have slain Kinernus instantly had the old lordling struck him, but what one Briton did to another scarcely mattered from Liudhere's point of view. As his master's daughter-in-law, Vivayn had some status in the aging pirate's eyes, so he clapped Teilo on the shoulder and hustled him away to begin work. The Briton went amenably enough, although not ceasing to frown.

Vivayn walked in her graceful, swaying way to the cart which had creaked along behind her litter. Perched beside the driver sat Eldrida, the only other woman in the party, a full-bodied girl with grey-green eyes, yellow braids and a look of being gamely ready for anything. She had been gazing pensively at the long thatched roof rising above the nearby stockade.

"Well, now," she said in a rich voice which slurred the British tongue with suggestions of North Sea accents, "I'd like to be a fly on the wall in yon sheep's pen tonight."

"I intend to be," Vivayn answered. Her own voice made the hearer think of cool light wine. "If Kinernus's family is wise, they will depose him at once in favor of a chieftain who can be sensible. If they are not wise —" She smiled with remote, wicked playfulness. "We must lead them by the hand."

Before long, Vivayn's tent had risen on the summer grass and the two women were installed within. Teilo stood before it with a long British spear in his hand, more in honor of Vivayn's rank than for any real protection he would be if one of the wild Germanic warriors in the party decided to harm her. Teilo might be brave and was certainly loyal, but Liudhere and several other Jutes present could have eaten him for supper. Their master's commands restrained them, not a single British guard. Barking laughter filled the air as they devoured smoked meat around camp-fires, exchanged their obscure riddles, and told stories of pillage and rapine, lying mightily about the feats they had performed.

In the precious tent of Cordovan leather, Vivayn took a fine golden chain from around her neck. At the end of the chain hung a shining phial in the shape of an acorn, twirling in the light of a scented wax candle, the cost of which would have fed a hundred dispossessed families for a year. With no discernible qualms, Vivayn let the candle burn while she drew forth the tiny phial's stopper. A more pungent fume mingled at once with the candle's fragrance.

Detachedly, Vivayn said, "Clarice warned me against taking this save in extreme need. A master sorceress can do what the potion provides with only the discipline of her mind; but I have some way to travel before I am that skilled; and Clarice, alas, has lost too many of her faculties to do much besides teach. Do not allow anybody in, Eldrida, no matter what you see or hear."

"If it's that dangerous a brew," Eldrida said hotly, "pour it on the ground and let these strutting idiots take their own chances! They wouldn't thank you if they knew what you are doing for them!"

"Come, my companion, it is not solely for them. I've made no grandchildren for Cerdic. Unless I atone for that lack by perfect success in occasional missions like this one, he may cast me out before I'm ready to go."

"Cynric wouldn't discard you because his father commands!"

"No? He married me at his father's command." Vivayn lifted the phial to her lips and drained it, her long throat working through a difficult swallow. Fingers moving with precision, she fitted stopper and vessel together again before lying down on a green coverlet, her bronze-red hair spread about her. Eldrida watched with a thundering heart.

Whirling dizziness assailed Vivayn. Her head arched backwards until the cords of her snowy throat rose beneath the skin, and her eyes stretched wide open in preternatural distress. Her entire body rose like a drawn bow, supported now on the heels and crown of her head alone, while her mouth opened to its widest extent and a long, croaking cry emerged. Eldrida made an involuntary sign to avert evil as a humming blue-green dragonfly with wings a-shimmer flew from Vivayn's mouth, borne on the breath of her anguished cry. As the creature flew from the tent, Vivayn's arched body slowly relaxed until she lay supine, breathing at a rate many times slower than normal. White with terror, her friend placed questing fingertips on Vivayn's throat and waited for anxious moments until she detected a pulse-beat, appallingly slow yet steady.

Teilo had heard the muted shriek and was demanding to know what had gone amiss. Cursing his conscientiousness, Eldrida arose, thinking swiftly of a tale to keep him on his own side of the tent's entrance and thanking her pagan gods that he was greatly in awe of Vivayn's magic.

The dragonfly sped through the dusk, following the road to Kinernus's dun, rising high above the stockade of seasoned logs which had been there fifty years before Jutish sea-wolves had swarmed up the southern estuary to plunder Hamo. Even the stockade represented a reversion to cruder ways of the ancient Celts in the face of barbarian depredations; a century before it had been built, Kinernus's forebears lived in a Roman villa with stone walls, a tiled roof and heated baths, of which nothing remained now but waist-high sections of wall. Yet the clan still called itself Roman and saw nothing incongruous in that.

The bright insect whirred closely over the backs of domestic pigs grunting in a yard paved with fragments of stone from the former villa, then shot like a blue-green dart through the hall's doorway to hover above the gathered clan. Some wore tunics in the Roman fashion, others breeches and cloaks, while all the women went clad in long gowns of varying quality. Kinernus, a grey-bearded patriarch with fanaticism in his heart, occupied the central position in the council. He never observed the shimmering insect which clung to a beam directly above his head.

"Not one cow are we to pay those less-than-men!" he declared. "They have taken too much from Britain as it is."

"Granted," said a milder-looking man in a black tunic, his scalp shining pink in the glow of a lamp. "I cannot see, though, how it will restore a fairer balance if Cerdic's devils set fire to our gables one fine night and add our blood to the freshets already set flowing. He hasn't asked for our allegiance, but only a tribute in kind. Let's give it to him and keep our roof intact."

"So you say, Gwyn," Kinernus answered with the scathing contempt he had shown to Vivayn. "So say half the kings of this blind and feeble isle, while the other half prey upon their own folk before the sea-wolves can reach them — and without the excuse of knowing neither civilization nor God! The Saxons and Jutes are our punishment for sloth, yet not on that account can we justify submitting to them. They are not human, enemies of all the good and decent things you and I know."

"And shall we stop them with eighteen fighting men?" asked Gwyn. "You spoke of kings. Well, Vivayn's father gave battle with all the strength he could muster, and we fought on his side, but now he is dead and the nearest ruler is Agloval of the Atrebates. Will he send his riders south to help us if we defy Cerdic? I doubt it. We cannot fight him alone and win. To try would be suicide, which the priests tell me is mortal sin. Let us pay the tribute and wait for a better time to resist."

"There is the counsel that slays souls!" Kinernus thundered. "Sit down, instrument of Satan, and tell me no more of priests, for they are as bad as the rest of our diseased flock in this island, impious and unperceiving. The black fire of perdition rages for all who betray the Lord of the Tree." Flinging a knotty, powerful hand towards a crucifix on the hall's main pillar, he roared, "There is our only master, and so it shall be while I head this clan! Let those who would acknowledge the kingship of a heathen robber go to him, and swear your unclean oaths on his altars of blood!"

Gwyn, although he flinched from the old man's fury and the sheer volume of sound, did not appear impressed by his argument. Rising to his feet, the bald man declared in a hotter tone than before, "Cerdic has not asked us to worship his gods, either. So long as he leaves us our faith it is a case of rendering Caesar his due. *You* are the one threatening to destroy the clan, when you gibber of defying a thousand Jutes with barely eighteen men. Tell me not of the Christ! I defy not him, but Kinernus!"

"You defy Kinernus, eh?" the old man said in a dreadful voice. "Then let God judge between us now! Since you have challenged me for the honor and existence of our clan, let us both submit to the testing of the stone, he who survives to be chieftain. Beware, Gwyn, for as surely as you refuse I will bring you to judgement and have you made an outcast!"

The volume of that terrible voice rose to the ceiling-beams, making the wings of a certain dragonfly quiver. Gwyn whitened slowly with shock, and his silence grew lengthy while Kinernus's sneer of disgust became more blatant. The old chieftain could do what he threatened in law. Gwyn knew that. Hesitating, he looked about him, finding appalled looks in plenty but no signs of protest or support save in one quarter.

"Kinernus, this is foul!" a woman declared. "You call the sea-wolves godless heathens, but what do you become when you invoke the testing of an idol old as the forests?"

"It never was an idol. God sent it from Heaven to try the chieftains of our line, that they be worthy to head the clan. If Gwyn is true of soul and my better in judgement, no harm will come to him. If I am wrong, let the blight of the stone fall on me. Vorcant, go to the shrine and bring hither the stone of testing." When Vorcant hesitated, the old man thundered, "Go!"

Vorcant departed. Above, unnoticed, the dragonfly rubbed its antennae. Subdued murmurs ran around the table, not one escaping the insect-shape which was Vivayn's spirit in a convenient form.

"It's the tradition —"

"— long since it was done. Only Kinernus in living generations has ever seen it."

"— what if he prevails? Even with Heaven on my side I won't defy Cerdic. It's madness no matter what oracles say differently —"

"— divine judgement —"

The man named Vorcant came back to the table from the clustered shadows at the far end of the hall, a short, heavy-limbed figure with drooping moustache, staggering under the weight of the cumbrous carved stone he held in his arms. Shaped like a grotesque, bestial head, it showed a yawning gape of mouth beneath the broad snout. Vorcant lowered it reverently to the table, whereupon all present signed themselves with the Cross or made older gestures of worshipful awe. In Vivayn's eyes the object was hardly worth so much respect, being as crude a carving as she had ever seen, and ugly besides. Still a cruel, ancient might seemed to reside in it, and shadows clotted about the thing where it glared on the table. Kinernus rested his hands upon it, looking more diabolical than godly himself.

"Strength of our clan!" he addressed it passionately. "Strength of our clan, destroyer of sin and weakness, this house stands in danger again, less from foes without than from the unworthy within. Show us our true chieftain in the way accustomed since Britain was peopled, when Brutus led his people hither after the Flood. Judge between me and the one who would rival me, as we place our heads in your power. There can only be one chieftain. I, Kinernus, submit myself to your testing first. So."

The old man knelt, not humbly but like a king for his anointing, and thrust his head into the carved stone mouth. It vanished as far as his shoulders, further than any observer would have guessed it could be swallowed, for the stone carving did not seem large enough. Kinernus remained in his odd, somehow frightening position while his heart beat a score of times — and that of the watching Gwyn a hundred.

When Kinernus withdrew his head from between the basalt jaws, his relatives sucked in a shaken, anticipatory breath as though they would not have been amazed to see it changed to the red-eyed head of a wolf, or behold a ragged torn stump of a neck as proof of supernatural decapitation. Both stories had been told of the ordeal stone for generations in their clan.

"Behold, I am vindicated," Kinernus said, glowing with triumph. "Now it is your turn, Gwyn. Yours! Come forward."

The bald man stared with horrid fascination at the head, with its carved sightless eyes, wrinkled snout and cavern of a mouth. One step, and a second, he took towards it before his nerve broke. He shook his head in mute denial.

"Too late for other thoughts," Kinernus said. "You must do as I did. Vorcant! Eiro! Show this recusant how to be steadfast!"

The old man had named two of his most faithful supporters. As though the iron in his voice had entered their souls, they seized Gwyn's arms and, twisting them behind his back, forced him closer to the stone despite his furious struggles. As his face neared the carven monster's gape, Gwyn vented a long, gurgling scream, which ended as his tormentors thrust him into the fanged hole. The watching dragonfly's wings quivered.

Dense yellow vapor gouted from the stone mouth in a silent belch, to coil around Gwyn's neck like tresses of smoke. Kinernus's two bully-boys, star-tled, let go their victim's arms and stepped back. Gwyn remained on his knees, his hands feebly stroking the wood of the table, while the sulfur-hued fumes vanished into stone nostrils as though inhaled by a living creature.

Gwyn's head fell gracelessly out of the carven maw which had contained it. A basalt fang scored a red groove in his scalp, and his forehead struck the table's edge with a loud crack before he collapsed to his hands and knees. A little, frightened whimper sounded. The man who had faced Kinernus with dignity at the council table now turned around on all fours like a bewildered child, mewing softly. The muscles of his face had slackened mindlessly; he blinked milky eyes which saw nothing. Without pride or awareness, he uttered a frightened wail.

Vorcant and Eiro themselves looked at the results of their action with horror. The latter signed himself unconsciously, and Vorcant nearly followed his example before remembering that Kinernus watched the scene.

"Blind and crazed," the old man said somberly. "Such is the judgement of God this night. Who questions it? Who still advocates paying Cerdic to leave us alone?"

None spoke. Gwyn's youngest nephew began a desperate, outraged lunge forward, but his brothers seized him while his mother hissed, "Still, for your life! Do you wish to be next?"

Not wishing that at all, the youth covered his face with both hands.

"Then we must deal strongly with the band of traitors he sent forth as his tax-gatherers!" Kinernus roared. "All of them, and particularly the traitress Vivayn! She it was who plotted with the heathens against her own father and king, calling them in to burn Hamo because of lust for a pirate chief's son. She it was who encompassed the murder of her sire, as all men know, and now rules jointly with the father and son. She —"

He ranted on, making foul accusations against Vivayn until sheer lack of breath forced him to stop, his description of her sins and crimes showing an equal division between two categories — the wildly exaggerated and the wholly untrue.

"Vivayn must be taken and put to death," he concluded, "or the Lord's displeasure will lie upon the land until it is wasted and barren, while the sea-wolves, his scourge for sin, eat it bare of what little is left. Only if we act in righteousness will they be removed from us!"

His clan raised an **amen**, some enthusiastically, some reluctantly, but all of them responded — even Gwyn's mother, with tears on her cheeks and her mouth twisted as though she choked on something hideous. She had other children, and the mouth of the ordeal stone remained open to swallow them.

Gwyn made his tiny noises, groping about like a lost child.

None noticed a shimmering dragonfly dart through the room, to vanish out an unstopped chink in the wall and flash to the sea-wolves' camp where Eldrida waited beside her dormant friend. When the Jutish girl saw it wing into their tent, relief flooded her heart like a torrent, and she poured a goblet of strong wine for the moment when Vivayn should awake.

Vivayn's white hands lay open, palms upward, beside her. Hovering above the right one on wings like slivers of gemstone, the creature landed delicately, its exquisite legs crossing Vivayn's line of fate. Her fingertips twitched. Slowly her hand curled shut over the jewelled form, tightening until it was crushed, upon which it gave back the independence of her body which she had granted for a brief while.

Her snowy eyelids flickered, then opened so suddenly and with so wild a look in them that Eldrida was frightened. Blindly, Vivayn clung to her friend, quivering in every fiber of her sensitive form — no longer a princess or a witch but only a young woman who had forced herself too far beyond normal boundaries. Eldrida rocked her gently back and forth, murmuring comfort while a tempest of sobs remained locked away behind the aching tightness in Vivayn's throat. She could have shed tears in streams, as Eldrida knew; but not once had the yellow-haired girl seen her friend cry.

Nor did she now. When Vivayn's tremors ceased and she drew away a little, her disconcertingly clear grey eyes were dry as Eldrida had always known them. A deep sigh came from her throat, but no words.

After waiting too long with as much patience as she possessed, Eldrida demanded, "What happened? By all of Freya's drowned lovers, *what?* Has the old man called in the Warlord of Britain to attack us?"

"Nothing so extreme, Eldrida, but bad enough . . . bad enough. That old man, that lunatic, has cowed his clan so that it will obey him in anything. He plans to wipe us out and hang me for my many sins. By sorcery he destroyed a kinsman who disagreed with him. The poor fools think he has God on his side . . . most of them. The others are afraid to raise their voices."

"He's going to attack *us?*" Eldrida said. "Our men would eat his British yokels alive! Wait. I was forgetting. Here's wine, Vivha; you need it."

Vivayn drank, grateful for it and for the use of her pet name and Eldrida's comforting arm around her shoulders.

"You are right, dear. We have nothing to fear, that way; it would be a slaughter, and that's what I would avoid. We have to plan — but not yet. Not yet."

"What is it?"

"Nothing . . . the old story, with fouler trimmings. Kinernus was raving that

I brought in your father to conquer the kingdom, and aided him with sorcery." Vivayn had been fifteen at the time of Cerdic's invasion, and known no sorcery worthy of the name — then. "Vivayn the traitress. All Britain believes it, and that is the tale men will remember."

"Not all," Eldrida said stoutly. "They are not all simple-minded, you know." She held the other woman closer. "You'd help yourself if you would weep."

Vivayn shook her head. Ripples flowed through the great mass of bronze-red hair she wore because it pleased her lord, although she found it a cumbersome trouble. "I'll weep on the day I am free to smile or weep as I please. Meanwhile we must carry out Cerdic's will, and save this farrow of idiots from destroying themselves on Jutish spears — whether they wish to be saved or not. That will take some ingenious scheming."

"Better to rest first," Eldrida advised.

"I cannot rest!" Vivayn snapped. "Not unless I empty that flagon, and this is no occasion for a wine-filled head. Had you seen what I saw you would not be thinking of rest. Kinernus has a stone of enchantment which is supposed to test the true chieftain of his clan, the one favored by God. So *he* says. Surely it can destroy, and I have seen that he's immune to its power, but I will never believe it is because God favors him. The notion's blasphemous! Besides, magic is not like that. It works as a knife works, effective for any who knows which end to hold and how to cut. I wonder, I wonder . . ."

Vivayn walked back and forth in the tent, restless and absorbed, her pain thrown aside as she pondered the riddle. As swiftly as she had begun, she stopped, clapping her hands sharply once as she reached a conclusion.

"There is a secret to that ugly stone head, a knowledge which makes it possible to face the testing without fear.

There must be — and Kinernus has it! He's the oldest man in that family, so it stands to reason that he would remember something all the rest have forgotten." Vivayn closed her eyes, casting her mind back to the scene in Kinernus's hall, trying to retrieve every detail she had witnessed through the dragonfly's begemmed organs.

"Kinernus placed his hands just *so*," Vivayn murmured, raising her arms to demonstrate. "It may mean nothing, and yet . . . there was a line of faded writing carved on the throat of the head, like a necklace of words. It wasn't Latin or Greek, or even the Hibernian cipher they call ogham. Maybe it's the older ogham, the true ancient script invented when Don's children ruled the earth. I must see it again, in my own body."

"Tomorrow," Eldrida said firmly. "Tomorrow is time enough; tonight you must rest. There are few enough hours until dawn, and that soul-transformation has cost you dearly. Lie down, for the body you're speaking of is tight as a harp-string. I'll rub some looseness into it, and then perhaps you will sleep. Never fear. I'll be here if dreams trouble you."

Any dreams which haunted Vivayn had been discarded before she emerged from her tent the next morning. She wore a black and jade gown with a pearl-adorned cincture, while the shadows beneath her eyes had been artfully hidden, whether with paint or magical illusion remained her secret. The auburn hair fell to her calves in brazen, gleaming waves, brushed by Eldrida till it shone in the sunlight, for Vivayn did not intend to face Kinernus looking other than her best. To outward seeming she was again the cryptic, tranquil princess with an enigmatic trace of a smile lifting the corners of her mouth, confident and remote. Teilo bowed to her, and even her escort of savage warriors treated her with rough respect, clashing spears on their hide-covered shields in greeting.

"Ready my litter if you will, Teilo." she said. "I am going to visit the chieftain Kinernus, and this time he will listen with more care to what I say. It's my desire that only you and the litter-bearers shall accompany me, therefore groom yourself to shame the men of that rough dun. We may serve Cerdic, yet in my mind this has become a matter for settling between Britons, and we will not invite our barbarian friends to partake of it. Let them fire the dun and steal whatever remains unburnt if we should fail. It's what they do best. And you should know that we probably will not live to criticize if it comes to that."

Teilo had served her for two years. He knew that Vivayn had just offered him a chance to refuse what could prove to be a three-furlong journey into great danger. With a smile he said, "Give me an hour, lady."

The Jutish warriors in their cross-gartered breeches and heavy beards were harder to persuade, particularly their leader, who wanted to take a tree-trunk and batter down the Britons' gate. Vivayn reminded him patiently that Cerdic his king had personally advised him that Vivayn's commands were to be obeyed on this mission, and with many a Germanic grumble the man finally came to accept it. Teilo, his dark hair resplendently coiled, moustache trimmed and clashing bracelets of enamelled copper on his arms, appeared within the promised hour, his spearhead polished to a dazzle like sunlight on water, a merry strut in his walk. He might have been going to a tryst with a girl whose smile made him feel seven feet high.

No smile was displayed on Kinernus's face as he came to the rampart of his family's stockade to stare down at the litter. Righteous, intransigent, he scowled at Teilo and said curtly, "Be-gone, traitor."

"I'll answer that if you will take a spear and come out to meet me," Teilo said. "If you will not, my lady must answer, though you are not deserving of the honor."

Vivayn descended from the litter. Her shoes, sewn with smoky British pearls, flashed as they emerged from between the curtains. When she stood upon the ground, her girdle and shoulder-brooches shone with like splendor, and as she lifted her head to meet the gaze of the man above her, Vivayn's famous eyes reduced the pearls to drabness.

"Greetings, Kinernus," she said. "You are free with the word 'traitor'."

"And you're lavish with the actions of one," he retorted. "All I had to say to you was said yester-morn. My family and I are one in this matter, so your dogs carted you up this rise for nothing."

"Your family," Vivayn said distinctly, "is cowed and terrified by your evil sorcery, you who are so hypocritically swift to accuse me of that very thing. Else would they have kicked you out of their dun last night and paid my lord Cerdic's tribute as the lesser of two ills. For risking their destruction at his hands it is you who are their betrayer. I who would see them live and prosper am a better friend to them than you! If you would dispute that with me, Kinernus, you have only to open your gates that I may enter — and you see that I come with only one armed man to do me honor."

Behind the blazing stare of the fanatic, Vivayn saw other, more calculating thoughts a-move, thoughts which she herself had stimulated so that Kinernus would admit her. *She is the child of our last British king,* those thoughts went. *If she is destroyed, one influence of moderation and kindness towards Britons will vanish from our conqueror's house; and brute that he is, Cerdic will oppress them more greatly, while his son will seek vengeance for his bride. The Britons of Hamo will be driven to revolt against the heathen! All this if the witch is destroyed — and here she stands, begging to enter my gate without guards!*

"Enter, then," Kinernus said sonorously. "You cannot prevail, yet I would be just."

As would I, Vivayn thought. *You who defamed me owe me requital.*

The gate of adzed logs creaked wide, and her litter-bearers carried her across the mud of the yard, through a rout of pigs, clamoring dogs, and squawking hens. Stopping before the door, bemired to their knees, they waited while Teilo lifted their mistress across the muddy threshold, into the smoky hall with its many odors. Vivayn advanced to the wide communal hearth, treading the carpet of rushes with the most costly footwear ever seen in that dwelling. Men and women alike stared at her, some with the desperate ghost of hope.

"Kinernus, I come for justice," Vivayn said before them all. "You have named me traitor, parricide, and apostate, I who am none of those things. If you regard justice in any way, you will make your words good or cease to be chieftain of this household. Thus do I challenge you, I, Vivayn, Natanleod's daughter — or do you not possess a chief's honor?"

"Where fitness to lead the clan is questioned, men of my line have a sure recourse," Kinernus said, "and that is the testing stone of which you may have heard. We settle doubts of our honor in the same way, but beware, woman! Those who place their heads in the gape of the stone receive true judgement according to their deserts. Dare you endure that?"

"I dare most things, old man. Bring in your stone."

"Vorcant, you hear our guest," the chieftain said. "Eiro, fetch Gwyn that the witch may see the results of defi-

28

ance."

Neither sight came as a surprise to Vivayn, but when Eiro led in the stumbling, whimpering figure which on the previous day had been a man, Vivayn found it easy to present her loathing as astonished horror. How vile of Kinernus to display his victim as though he were proud of what he had done, to daunt Vivayn's spirit!

"And this was done to him by your testing stone?" Vivayn asked, dissembling. "How do I know? Every clan has its lackwit born, and you have cause to wish me frightened away."

"Here is the judgement stone of ordeal," Kinernus told her. "Place your head between those jaws, and in a moment you can grope and dribble with Gwyn."

"Supposing that I deserve it," Vivayn said coolly. As Vorcant set down the basalt image with a grunt of relief, she walked with birch-slender grace to examine it. Seen through human eyes, it was no more lovely than when she had beheld the thing with the myriad facets of a dragonfly's orbs. Yet around the carved throat like a collar ran the band of writing none could read any longer, unless he had teachers as strange as those who had instructed Vivayn.

The script flowed in curious patterns. Time had worn it to partial legibility, and Vivayn had never mastered that writing fully, as she had Latin and Greek. Concentrating intently, she asked, "What do these marks mean?"

"They declare, 'Divine vengeance to the unrighteous'," Kinernus said harshly.

He lied. As nearly as Vivayn could discern, the inscription read, **My eyes award destruction; my nostrils breathe healing; my mouth is below both.** The last phrase baffled her powers of translation. It might signify, **My mouth is subordinate to both,** or **My mouth is the channel for both,** or a number of other things, none with a clear and unmistakable meaning. Yet it *was* clear that Kinernus could not read the script at all. He only knew what had come to him through his family tradition, by the spoken words of his father. Vivayn had information he lacked, and the first two statements were unequivocal.

My eyes award destruction.

Vivayn closed her own eyes, the better to visualize that dreadful scene of the previous night. When Kinernus had knelt before the image, he had raised his hands — yes — but not merely to rest them on the stone monster's brow, as she had thought. *He had covered its eyes.*

The eyes which awarded destruction.

If Vivayn did likewise, she would be safe; but that was insufficient. She had come to defeat Kinernus, not simply to match him. An idea burgeoned in Vivayn's mind, yet she dared not carry it out before she knew more.

"There is the stone," she said. "Let my host set the example."

"Gladly, mocker," Kinernus said.

Gwyn whimpered in his personal darkness.

Watching, Vivayn saw the chieftain sink to his knees. Yes, he was raising his hands; and now he covered the eyes of the monster. Her guess had been correct. Kinernus's grizzled head vanished into the stone maw, remained there for a long moment, and then withdrew unharmed.

"Dare you do the same, woman?" he demanded.

"I have a better way," Vivayn said. "Divine judgement to you means destruction, for that is all you have in your heart — but it may be mercy and healing too. Last night Gwyn here was stricken blind and witless; let us see if there is not a cure."

The fierce eyes of Kinernus narrowed in suspicion. Vivayn saw her mistake; she had been told that Gwyn's condition was caused by the power of the stone, but none had told her how recently it happened. Kinernus was asking how she knew, and drawing his own conclusions.

"I would take Gwyn and restore him through the same stone which left him bereft," Vivayn declared. "Have I his near kin's leave to try? He cannot be worse afflicted."

"That he cannot," Gwyn's sister conceded, harsh-voiced in her bitterness, while her sons cried out in favor of trying and Gwyn's aged mother nodded weakly before turning her head away. When Kinernus opened his mouth to forbid it, his entire clan opposed him with looks so hostile that even he shrugged in acquiescence, though he swore that Heaven's anger would light upon an attempt so impious.

Vivayn led Gwyn gently by the hand and coaxed him to his knees, where he began to tremble and sob like a little child. She said quietly, "Teilo, this will not be work to your taste, yet I ask it. When I command you, thrust his head into the hole." Swiftly she covered the glowering stone eyes with her hands. "Now."

My nostrils breathe healing.

Teilo's warrior limbs handled the helpless man easily — at first. Then visions of his fate at the hands of Vorcant and Eiro flashed through Gwyn's muddled mind, and even in blindness he sensed the confined, stony space around his head. With a shattering squeal that rose to a pitch of terror unimaginable, Gwyn heaved his shoulders back from the stone image against all Teilo's efforts to hold him there, ripping free of the younger man's grip. Vivayn sprang aside as the ordeal stone toppled to the floor, while Gwyn stood blinking foolishly.

"I . . . I . . . what has happened?" he asked. "I passed the test . . . but it is daylight, and . . . how are you here, lady?"

"Gwyn!" his sister screamed. "You

29

see?"

Vivayn thought, *Manifestly he sees, and he has uttered the first sounds of meaning since the stone swallowed his wits. You are the enemy now, Kinernus, not I.*

With a dreadful roar, the old man descended upon her. Seizing her in a grip of irresistible strength, he bent her to the ground, thrusting her head towards the fallen stone. Wild with sudden terror, Vivayn struggled frantically, until the hands on her neck weakened and Kinernus reared back, croaking thickly. The shaft of Teilo's spear stood out of his body, between two ribs. Gagging blood, Kinernus fell forward. His head, lolling loosely on his neck, dropped into the hollow stone on the rushes, with a neatness that suggested supernatural intent.

Kinernus's people gathered about the corpse, including the bewildered Gwyn. Each face showed awed reluctance to pull the body away from the ancient stone, though not one — even those of Vorcant and Eiro — betrayed intense grief. At last two men gritted their teeth, heaved the body clear and rolled it over.

Then it was that Vivayn's nerve failed her at last, and she fled the hall leaning on Teilo's arm. The young spearman had gone white as well, in common with half Kinernus's clan, who cried out and shuddered until someone had the presence of mind to throw a cloak over their slain tyrant. The face of Kinernus lacked features altogether; it had turned to blank blind flesh from hairline to chin, while beside it the stone beast's head grinned at the rafters.

□

COMING IN OUR WINTER, 1988 ISSUE!

Our Special Avram Davidson Tribute, Featuring

3 New Stories and a New Article by Davidson —

Knox's Nga

The Odd Old Bird

Nothing Like a Clean Weapon

Adventures in Unhistory: The Great Rough Beast

— plus —

Kaeti and the Village
by Keith Roberts

Message from Hell
by Robert Sheckley

The Frog Prince
by Jay Sheckley

Don't risk missing an issue — subscribe today! Turn to page 7 for details.

PROFILE: KEITH TAYLOR

by Cherry Weiner

Keith Taylor had been writing long before I met him. He published four short pieces in *Fantastic Stories* in 1975 under the pseudonym Dennis More because he didn't feel that "I was good enough to publish under my own name." He is a shy man.

We were introduced at a science fiction party by Merv Binns during one of my yearly visits to Australia. I think it was 1980. We spent a little time talking, and arranged another meeting to talk seriously about Keith, his plans, and his writing.

After our meeting he was ready to get back to the typewriter and write . . . under his own name. His first project was to take the stories that he had written for *Fantastic*, bridge them and turn them into a novel.

While Keith was doing that, I came back to the States and started talking to editors about him and his work. At one of my editorial meetings I was telling an editor about Keith and his plans for *Bard* when Terri Windling, then editor at Berkley, became very excited. She had read the stories "a long time ago" and had been trying to find the author ever since.

Thus came *Bard*, soon to be followed by *Bard II: The Return of Felimid Mac Fal* ; *Bard III: The Wild Sea* ; and the recently published *Bard IV: Raven's Gathering*.

While he was writing the *Bard* books he was keeping himself even busier. There were stories that he did for *Void*, an Australian imprint anthology, and also a couple of novels for Void Publications.

Now he's working on a new series: *The Danans*. Books I and II have been written and handed in. Beyond that, there are many more projects on the desk and in the typewriter.

Keith won the top Australian SF Award, the Ditmar, for Best Fantasy or Science Fiction Novel of 1986, for *Bard III: The Wild Sea* (thanks for this information *Australian SF News*). The award was presented to him in April 1987.

He is now rediscovering and enjoying the short story.

Weird Tales™ asked for his work and you can see the results here. His short stories will also be appearing elsewhere, and, Keith tells me, "I am just thrilled that *Weird Tales*™ wants to do a special issue of my work."

I don't see Keith that often, maybe once a year. It's hard to get to know him. He's a quiet man. A shy man. At parties (I've only seen him at two) he stays in the background. On a one-to-one he's a delight to talk to.

Keith, I think this issue will help you to know just how much you and your writing are loved by people on this side of the world. □

by Keith Taylor

THE HAUNTING OF MARA

The lithe boy of thirteen with the black hair and the brilliant, sea-blue eyes stood alone in a circle traced on the winter grass so harsh with frost. All that covered him was a linen tunic, and all he held was a yard-long stick, while four grown men faced him across a distance with frowns on their brows and several iron-headed spears each. Nor did the circle allow him much room to dodge.

His stance was light and easy, his smile insolent.

"By Padraigh, if they kill him —" his friend Lurgan began.

"You will do nothing," the dark-haired man beside him said grimly. "Neither will I, youngster, though it's I have far more claim than you, for he swore away his right to be avenged by kindred when he issued this challenge. Aye. He made his choice and did not consult me."

"And you his father!" Lurgan dared to say, for the anger of poets was feared in their land. Yet Lurgan belonged to the conquering clan of the uí Neill, which made him sure of himself. "He did this for you."

"Quiet!" the other said urgently. "Would you distract him with your braying when the spears are about to fly?"

Lurgan shut his mouth, rebuked. It was true. He'd spoken too loudly, while Fergus the poet had held his voice low by an effort the boy would never appreciate. He stood as though solitary in the world, his harp cradled in one sinewy arm, all his faculties concentrated upon the lone figure in the circle.

Srem, the injured party, made the first weapon-cast. His spear flashed in the winter light as it hurtled towards the youth named Fal, who twisted aside without moving his feet and struck the shaft of the flying missile with his stick. It veered from its course to bury itself in the whitened ground yards away. Srem, dogged and black-bearded, took

a second spear in his hand while two of his kinsmen raced from his side to position themselves on the other side of the circle. No notion of mercy entered the cattle-chief's head, for his family had lost a hundred and fifty cattle to raiders led by the black-haired demon's whelp now facing their spears as a recompense. That herd represented vital food for the winter, vanished and gone.

Fiercely Srem hurled two more spears at his living target, who deflected one above his head with the stick and dodged the next — no easy task while remaining within the circle, as he must by the rules of his ordeal. Scowling, Srem rested on his two remaining spears while his kinsmen cast their weapons in a steady rain from two directions. Fal spun, ducked, and sprang, constantly turning, plying his stick in a humming blur to parry the spears until the **thwack** of wood upon wood became a constant sound and over a dozen thwarted javelins grew from the earth around him at strange angles like the plants of a mad, undisciplined garden. Then Srem lifted a hand and the assault ceased.

"Is he satisfied?" Lurgan asked in wonder.

"Not he," Fergus answered, his face bleak of expression. "They make Fal wait to unnerve him." His jaw closed with a determined snap, shutting in what other words he might have said. With a dozen kinsmen and some of his son's friends beside him, Fergus might have ended the harsh testing then and there, save that many of Srem's family were also present and to rescue Fal by force would precipitate the blood feud this was intended to avert. Having the powers of a bard to inflame — or destroy — the fighting spirit of armies, Fergus was still helpless. And that was his only son awaiting the next flight of iron-beaked birds given wing to rend his flesh. The poet clamped his teeth together until his jaw creaked, lest he groan aloud.

Fal was laughing at his assailants. Not for him the silent endurance of his father. He suggested that they bring substitutes to cast spears for them if they, supposed warriors, had grown so pathetically weary, and told them he would appreciate the gift of a few sheepskins on which to lie while they gathered their strength anew.

"Laugh at this, then, thief in the night!" yelled Srem's cousin Brian Black Knee, and poised his spear but did not throw it. The real cast came from his brother Deargal, on the far side of the circle, and Fal barely dodged it in time. Deargal's was the first spear actually to fall within the circle Fal could not leave, and he threw it out swiftly; the space was confined enough. Then his enemies settled down to gnaw at his nerves with a waiting game again.

They had only five spears left among them, but Srem carried the notorious Long Wing, with its five barbs and collar of heron feathers for a charm. When cast at a mark, Long Wing infallibly struck its target — so men said. Srem breathed on the weapon's fearsome head and muttered encouragement to it.

"And that superstitious yokel has the right to throw weapons at Fal — and him unarmed!" Lurgan said, unable to resist. "I'll slay him if he draws blood. By my people's god I swear it!"

"Be quiet," Fergus ordered. Sweat covered his back and a vein beat constantly in his temple.

Srem gave a signal, and one of his kinsmen threw at his target's side. Fal made an error of judgment, using his stick to parry the flying death instead of leaping aside. Now two missiles rushed upon him at once, and in desperation he fell flat, rolling, which nearly took him out of the ordeal ring. No longer laughing, Fal bounded to one knee, his stick poised, toes almost touching the mark he might not cross.

A narrow-headed javelin with the murderously hurled weight of a long ash shaft behind it came driving towards his spine, and in the same moment Srem stepped forward to launch Long Wing. The heron feathers fluttered, whispering curses in the frosty air.

Fergus's guts cramped. Appalled, he gave his son up for dead, for Fal had made a great salmon-leap into the air so that the first spear passed harmlessly beneath him — but now he was directly in the path of Long Wing's evilly barbed head. Eyes intent, hand already moving, Fal brought his stick around in a humming blur. It met Long Wing's driving shaft and snapped with the sound of a tree cracking on a night of deep frost. The spearhead snagged Fal's tunic, ripping half of it away, and for a dreadful instant the watching Fergus thought it had gone through him. Then the boy landed on his feet, skin bare yet unmarked, while the dreaded spear skidded away through the white grass until it came to a halt, spent and unfulfilled. With an exultant war-cry, Fal raised the remnant of his stick like a trophy.

His kinsmen roared. Fergus, his eyes brimming, ran down the slope to seize Fal in his arms and embrace him in love and pride. Never had he felt so great a relief. He felt his son's heart pounding like a hammer on an anvil as Fal returned the hug, and the tears overflowed his eyes despite all his efforts to contain them within bounds.

"Cuchulain!" Lurgan whooped, thrusting forward among the press of Fal's kinsmen. "Cuchulain reborn are you, Fal! Four men, twenty spears, and none of them could touch you! They won't live this down quickly, and they can't start a feud because you've given them the satisfaction they called for! O—ho—ho!"

Srem and his relatives gathered their weapons and sourly acknowledged that the honor-debt had been paid, before marching home in dissatisfied gloom. Left in possession of the ordeal ground at Mara, Fal's kinsmen and friends prepared a meal while Fal himself mounted a horse and set out in search of his mother, riding swiftly. She had not been able to endure watching him face the spears; and while it was known that she could foretell the future, it remained as dubious and misty a country to her as anybody else where her loved ones were concerned. Thus Fal urged his fleet brown mare to her best speed, the sooner to ease his mother's mind.

Turning at the sound of racing hoofbeats, Umai saw her son rushing towards her, with his breath and the mare's forming twin flags of pale smoke. Scarcely drawing rein, he sprang from the horse's back to bound forward impelled by his own momentum and hold her closely. Beside them, a grey memorial stone incised with ogham lettering cast its ancient shadow across the grass.

"Son! Oh son of mine, you prevailed!"

"Of course!" Fal laughed. "Why, none of them approached me! You grieved your heart for no reason, Priestess of Sinann."

They were greatly alike in looks, Umai the famed priestess, poetess and seeress, and her son who was too young as yet to have any achievements save reckless mischief ascribed to him. Had a tuft of Umai's shining black hair been cut in secret and then displayed in daylight, none could have sworn it was not Fal's. They possessed the same sea-blue eyes which announced with their deep color that here were two who carried the blood of Lir's children, the sea people, mingling wildly with their Earthly ancestry. Pure bone structure and skin like new milk gave both an exceptional, eerie beauty. Intense in their feelings, turbulent, wayward, they had always been as closely kindred in spirit as body.

"No reason," Umai murmured, resting her head on his shoulder to weep a little. "No reason! Vow me an oath there will be no more of this, Fal. Nightriding with Miach, faring abroad on Samhain Eve, giving mad challenges, raising trouble at Suibni's college —"

"None of that makes me different from any other man my age," Fal said cheerfully, "save maybe the second." For an unguarded moment he gazed through his mother's face at a memory he loathed, but then his defences rose firmly in place once more. "You would never wish me to vow you an oath I'd be sure to break, and never would I swear one. Miach is my own father's brother — foster-brother, then, and outlawed these two years; but he was in the right. I couldn't deny him aid when he and his men would have starved without it."

"Now they are eating lifted cattle in the south and you pay a heavier price than facing twenty spears." Umai's oval face lifted to her son's. "There is almost a madness upon you since that night. None of your friends will speak, and I know geas-bound men when I talk to them. Did a night spirit enter you, or did you see the Antlered God riding behind his pack? Fal my darling, I can tell besides that *you* are not geas-bound, and can free your voice to speak of this matter if you wish. Else it may drive you to destruction."

"No, my mother, nothing so evil," Fal said, concealing his inner horror. "I lifted some beasts for Miach, the owners called for satisfaction and now have received it, all they could have wanted and more than they deserved, since not one of their clan was so much as injured. That ends it. Come, let's return to the camp and celebrate that I still adorn the ridge of the Earth, to the chagrin of all our foes!"

Knowing that Fal's bravado was intended to cheer her, Umai allowed him to lift her upon the brown mare's back and carry her down to the camp-site

35

where twenty men and women of their clan were preparing a feast. It might have proved a wake for this lone son of her body whom Lurgan had compared to Cuchulain in the heat of his joy. Umai saw certain resemblances herself: rash, prideful, self-willed, handsome, exceptionally gifted, astonishingly young, a born fighter and leader — and likely to meet an early death for his audacity. Yet he had survived the dangers of this day. Riding before him on the brown mare's back, held secure by a strong young arm, Umai felt the knowledge seep through her soul like a transfiguring dye. Her son lived.

Because she knew Fal so well, Umai remained close to Fergus while the clan celebrated, leaving the boy to enjoy his triumph free from a mother's fussing. While he enjoyed making a bold gesture and liked glory, Fal had an essential realism hard as the rocks of the seashore. Tonight he would receive extravagant praise from many — but his head could withstand it.

"He'll outgrow making trouble," Fergus predicted, "and make a poet for Erin to remember, so."

Umai doubted it. Gently she said to her husband, "He has the gift, surely, but it may be that he hasn't the desire or the need that a poet should have. None urged you to become a bard and then an ollamh, my dear. None could have stopped you! What if Fal's teachers say he is not destined for the craft, and he should confirm them?"

"It's impossible," Fergus said, rejecting the notion out of hand. "Descended from Ogma himself, with us for parents, what else would Fal be? Our line consists of poets and bards for eighty-one unbroken generations! Fal will not turn around and say, 'No, I don't wish it.'"

"He's capable of just that, if it should be that his heart rejects it," Umai warned. "Fal has said nothing, even to me, yet more and more I believe he's remained at the bardic college a year

now because he loves you, and not the craft Suibni teaches him. That may even be the thing which makes him wild."

"No," Fergus said dogmatically. "Suibni would tell us if that were so. This isn't a time to be considering the worst, my heart! Our son is alive, and it's my belief he'll be chief poet of Erin one day."

Umai didn't pursue the matter, telling herself that there would be other times for discussion, yet finding an apt time was not the problem. On this subject, Fergus never listened.

With a troubled heart, Umai watched her son lead the dancing among the fires. Something was wrong there also; at an age he should laugh with all the girls and cry with none, Fal had become remote, holding them at an impersonal distance. While he glided through the measures with his usual flair, he barely touched fingertips with his partners. When his cousin Maolmhinn, pretty as a blossom, laughed and offered Fal a kiss the muscles of his back sprang out in rigid relief, their tension visible through his tunic. Something was wrong, something which had happened on the haunted night of Samhain, and Umai took that knowledge to sleep with her.

Fal rested badly, too. In his dreams he saw the frosty stars of Samhain, heard hoofbeats creaking on the frozen ground, and saw a monstrous hag with the strength of a dozen men barring his path. She stood before him whichever way he turned, leering, hideous, one eye flaming yellow, the other like a corpse's, while the smell of a grave emanated from her skin. At last she trapped him, reaching scabbed hands to clutch him to her, but in the instant of contact she turned to a slender woman of astonishing beauty. Yet even then she remained inhuman, with blind-appearing eyes and the coolness of leaves in skin far too perfect. Touching her robbed Fal of his power to move, rooting him to the ground. Loathing and helpless vengefulness caught like a logjam in his throat, and he awoke in the frosty night with perspiration like slime upon his skin.

A dream. Black gods of the endless night, a mere dream! Fal lay unmoving while the fog of sickened horror blew away from his heart.

Something snickered in the tent, so close to Fal's ribs that he believed for an instant it was in his bedding. Mastering reaction, he remained completely still and pictured in his mind the exact position of his spear, as near on the right side as the presence at his left. It snickered again. Fal received an impression of something little, like a weasel, yet indescribably malign. He felt an urge to crush it into the ground and listen to its bones break.

Quietly, he reached for the spear. As his fingers closed about its seasoned ash shaft, Fal rolled upright out of his enveloping cloak, needing a moment to shrug free of it. Something chittered malevolently as it darted between his feet, and Fal turned towards the laced tent-flap as his cloak's last hindering fold dropped to the ground.

The she-monster of his dream stood there, huge and real, gloating over him with her lone useful eye and reeking like a cesspit. The hands which had destroyed two of Fal's friends reached for him lustfully. Remembering what she had made him do upon Samhain Eve, Fal voiced an inarticulate sound and drove his spear at her heart. The point jolted home, to grate upon a massive breast-bone as Fal twisted it, but no spurt of blood followed as the weapon was drawn back. The wound closed without a trace.

Grinning hideously, the hag turned her back, to bend from the waist and waggle her vast buttocks at Fal. Derisive insult combined with childish lewdness in the gesture. With his hands

closing on the useless spear until blood oozed from his nails, Fal cried, "Why do you haunt me?"

Lurgan of the uí Neill and two cousins of Fal's shared the tent with him. His outcry awoke them, and they too yelled in shock to see the dreadful hag rip open the tent-flap and depart — particularly Lurgan, who had ridden with Fal on that luckless Samhain Eve and recognized the apparition at once. Tumbling out of the tent on Fal's swift heels, they roused their kinsmen and instigated a swift, furious search which achieved nothing but to make them all blue-fingered with chill. Building up the central camp-fire, they discussed the matter by its comforting light, turning for advice to the wisest among them where things supernatural were concerned — Fal's mother, Umai the seeress.

Tiny and exquisite in her blue-bordered shawl, she listened to her son's account, hearing in his stance, tone, and manner how much he was leaving unsaid. Lurgan, though he knew all the truth, had been sworn to silence by oaths which the worst of men would scarcely dare take under false pretences. After hearing him confirm what he had seen, Umai did not even try to question him more closely. Fal was the one who must tell her.

Fergus, an earthy skeptic despite his calling, pointed out that no tracks had been found. "Belike you were dreaming, son."

"So I was," Fal answered, composed and unoffended to outward seeming. "The dream awoke me, and what happened afterwards was real. If you doubt it, father, ask the others what they saw."

"*I* require no such convincing," Umai said. "Come with me, Fal, for we must talk more of this."

In the privacy of the tent where it had happened, Umai seated herself on some tumbled bedding and smiled as her only son continued to stand, masking his thoughts with a look of politely ironical inquiry which sat incongruously on so young a face. Even so, his expression would have deterred many.

"First sit by me," Umai said tolerantly. "You should know by now that you cannot gain an advantage over *me* that way; not when you once slept curled beneath this heart." Although Fal smiled in return, it was no more encouraging than his assumed indifference had been. Still, he lowered himself to a neighboring pallet. "It appears that you are haunted. Do you not wish to know why, and how to be rid of the specter?"

"Mother mine, it's of little moment whether she stays far away or stalks groaning into my chamber every night of my life. Her mark is on me and I will not be the same again. Yet she did say that she would never return." Fal's young mouth twisted. "It's clear she lied."

"The beautiful folk do that, as much or more than we," Umai conceded, "but unlike us they generally lie for a reason. If we knew what the hag wants of you there might be hope of seeing the last of her."

Fal laughed bitterly. "Small chance, I'd think. The more of that she gets, the more she will be back. And once was enough for all time."

Umai saw his muscles flutter briefly in a spasm he could not control. It would not take long for Fal to learn, though, at the rate he was progressing towards impenetrability — and that Umai wished to prevent, because she loved him.

"You met her at Samhain, not so?" The question was gentle. "The same cattle-raid which brought you to face Srem's javelins today brought you to her attention also. A costly little foray, that one."

"It succeeded," Fal replied. "Miach

and his band are eating because of it, and he'll survive to exact his vengeance one day."

"Do you truly think Miach would want those cattle at such a cost to you? Son, son, he would have driven every head back to the owner had he known what was happening today! As for the other thing, that hag slew two of your friends, did she not? They never died by weapons. And then . . . she forced you to lie with her. One day I will do her great harm for that, if I can."

"You're guessing, my mother, but guessing very shrewdly. Yes, it happened so. She would have destroyed all my comrades if I had not done her will, and a foul coupling it was. Afterwards, on my life, she became a woman beautiful in a most eerie fashion! She said I had freed her from captivity in that disgusting form, as if it could restore Cahal and Ebenár to life. I tried to slay her, and failed." The bitterness of that failure echoed in Fal's voice. "She had the effrontery, she, to offer me a boon. I asked for the favor of never seeing her again in any shape, but even there she has been false." He released a weary, sighing breath. "Now what's to be done?"

Umai rested a hand on his arm. "You are to recognize that you have had the wisdom to let go your pride and ask advice. Indeed and truly, you strayed into the Otherworld that night, and the mark of it will remain, but it need not destroy you. Hear me Fal. The first thing is to know what we are dealing with. Tell me now, in plain words, all that happened tonight."

The boy told her, as he would have told no other living creature on the ridge of the Earth; and Umai listened with her whole body. When the tale was finished she considered the whole of it, her eyes bright with sparkling tears.

"Now I have more to say," she declared. "Do not try to prove yourself invincible, prowling the camp's edge with weapons in your hands as Fergus and the others are doing. My advice is to rest; sleep if you can. I'll weave a tiny sorcery to make it possible, and stay by you until morning. There's so much murky in this that I must wash clear in the sea of my vision. Say nothing, my son. Lie down and trust me. None of you trampling, battling men can fight this with spears, but it may be that I can catch it in a net."

Fergus, an hour later, came quietly to his son's tent and drew back the flap, a worried frown on his countenance. Within, he beheld Fal asleep on a pallet, twitching faintly in a restless slumber, while Umai sat beside him, her brilliant eyes wide in the trance of a seeress. Fergus had seen her thus before. In such a state Umai thought widely and deeply, with access to more hidden knowledge than most folk (even poets) touched in a lifetime. Letting the tent-flap drop softly into place, he walked away from there, head lowered in thought.

In the morning he listened to Umai in a council circle of his kinsmen as she, the only woman present, addressed them in the unique, dulcifluous voice which contained such hidden power.

"I believe we should not return to our homes until this specter has been laid," she said, "for who knows that it will not follow us there? It is not confined to this place called Mara; Fal has encountered the hag before, and it has followed him."

"What if it haunts Mara till the stars fall out of the sky?" Cirgaich of the Burnt Leg demanded. "Are we to wait?"

"I'll wait," Fergus said with determination. "Remember, all of you, that Fal faced twenty spears only yesterday because his other choice was to embroil us in a feud. Who is eager to bear the disgrace of being the first man to desert him because it is a little cold out? I'll lay no satire or curse upon him. Let him speak now."

Men looked at each other, and at the ground, but none moved. Cirgaich of the Burnt Leg shifted his feet and eventually sat down with a muttered self-justification. Fergus smiled slightly.

"I'm for Fal!" shouted Lurgan. "Who of his own blood says differently?"

The men of Fal's clan vied to out-roar the stranger in support of their own, and he stood to accept their loyalty with the arrogant lift of his head less pronounced than formerly.

"But what if she returns?" he asked his parents later. "Weapons are no use, and walls can't keep her out."

"Softly, my darling," Umai cautioned. "This will astonish you, but I believe now that what entered your tent here was not the same being you encountered at Samhain."

"Not the same?" Fal sprang to his feet, incredulous. "Lir of the wide green sea! Mother, I saw her, and worse than that, I smelled her! She was the same!"

"Yet there are spirits who can assume any form they will. The shape means little — and I will tell you both why I am so sure this is a different being. She of Samhain Eve is a woman, no matter how uncanny; and she was lately freed from the prison of a body hideous and foul. Not for the Rulership of Faerie would she take that form again. Trust me in this! I'm a woman too, with faerie blood in me, and I know."

"But then what does this specter *want?*"

"That we must discover when it returns, as I think it will." Umai watched her son more closely than she appeared to do while speaking those words, and saw his eyelids narrow fractionally as though from an urge to flinch. Her heart went out to him. "I can see you still doubt, Fal. But why would the original hag come to you when she now *has* what she wants? Her true form! If lust moved her, surely she would approach you in the guise of a lovely woman, and why should she hate you?

39

This being is malign."

"And my creature of Samhain is not?" Fal spoke with bitter intensity. "Twice a manslayer, the evil she did me aside; and let's not omit to wonder what crime of hers merited being transformed so horribly in the beginning. I rejected her and said outright what I thought of her when I could not punish the wrong she had done me with death. That's reason enough."

"You have much to learn about the beautiful folk," Fergus interjected. "Stop trying to know more than your elders a moment, son. If you strip leaves from a plant to cure your sickness, and its thorns scratch you, do you pursue vengeance against the plant? That is how *they* view us. Listen to Umai, for in these matters she is wiser than both of us together."

A young, tormented boy and a prideful leader of armed bands simultaneously, Fal struggled with his fixed opinion.

"You fear her most in the world, do you not?" Umai asked.

"Yes," Fal owned, "but I've no desire to speak of that. What must I do?"

"You must face the hag and bid her depart from you forever, with entire sureness of your right and power to do so, calling her by name."

"Is that all? How do I learn her name?"

"That is both the simplest and the hardest thing to do. If you can but look your haunter in the face, seeing what she is, not what you have determined she is, the name will come to you. Fal, some part of your own soul has attracted this haunting. The name you must have to end it can be found within that same soul. Otherwise — I fear the haunting will follow you from Mara wherever you go."

"No," Fal said harshly. "The haunting started at Mara, and it ends here, or the sods of my grave can be upturned at Mara."

In one way, Umai felt cheered to hear it, for determination was better than collapse at any time, yet in another way the words touched a deep fear of her own. Fal committed himself to extreme positions so easily, and then for pride's sake would not retreat. That fault might one day be his death. She expressed her dread to Fergus when the two of them were private.

"He cannot be other than himself, and we all die," the poet said. "It's a fine thing to know that our son won't meet his end disloyal or forsworn, however else he goes, yet you are right. I've left it overlong to put normal sense into him, and that will be mended once this haunting is over."

The third night at Mara proved as sharp with rime as the first. Waiting in his tent beside a little fire of coals, Fal rubbed his hands impatiently. Finally he left the tent to stalk like a young wildcat around the camp's perimeter. As he walked, his father joined him, giving his silent company as they sought Fal's enemy. The boy was moved. Fergus did not speak much except in his poetry, yet he sensed when his son preferred not to be alone. Passing the naked trees one by one as they creaked in the chill, the kinsmen heard a wolf howl far in the distance. Apart from that doleful sound, the night might have been empty. Rough grass crunched under their feet; a few frozen puddles showed a lined, ice-wrinkled visage to the stars. Fal remembered that it had been very like this on that luckless Samhain Eve.

Something moved with a stir and a rustle, scuttling out of their path with a baleful whistling which raised echoes of memory in Fal's mind, and hairs on his forearms. The horripilation spread to his neck as he recalled where he had heard such jeering beast-noises before. Fal stopped, drawing his knife. The frightening rage he sometimes unleashed stirred in his mind now.

"What is it?" Fergus asked, tense.

"Nothing, maybe — or maybe the hag has a familiar. I never saw it, yet I've the certainty it was in my tent with her last night. *Gods* — *!*"

A bulky shape crashed through a thicket to confront them with its crazed, appalling grin. Distorted teeth pushed the flabby lips far back from the gums, and yards of horny wattled hide showed naked in the night, hanging in pendulous folds. The entire ghastly apparition lurched upon mismatched legs.

"My lover comes to meet his darling!" it guffawed in its loathly voice. "O—ho—ho! He brings his sire to witness the courting! Shall I break your back this time, my handsome young one?"

She — *it* — lifted breasts like masses of spoiled dough in a vile parody of allure. Fal tasted bile at the back of his mouth and spat to clear it. In a voice like metal he said, "Enemy to me and all my kin, take yourself . . . take yourself far away and never return to affright man or woman of the Corco Baiscinn na Sinann, until the sky breaks and all the stars fall! Go!"

"No, Fal mac Umai, it is not so easy! Shall I run from that? This time we shall sport the night through, ride the Moon down and the Sun up, or all your clan shall lie broken and dead here at Mara. You are mine and I have come to claim you. Remember our delights? We shall repeat them ere long, many times!"

"Enough!" Fergus gripped his son's shoulder in outrage. "Enough! Unless you depart as you have been charged, I'll make a curse that will swallow you whole and never disgorge so much as a nail of your putrescence. I, Fergus, am a poet of the fifth rank and able to do what I say. Leave us in peace!"

"The brains of poets," wailed the specter, "look best spattered among the bits of their skulls, and so shall yours be displayed. My darling here shall be seen again, when none accompanies him!"

The words drove through Fal's ears into his brain like awls. Vividly he remembered how Cahal and Ebanár had died, smashed by this monster's bare hands, and the endless horror of coupling with . . . it.

The she-monster turned away with a noisy cackle. Fal heard her stumble through the leafless bushes, knocking them aside. Then the racket ceased, and only a perhaps-imagined crackling drifted to his ears as some small being scuttled for cover, terrified by the fiend's passage.

"It is she," Fal said from a bone-dry mouth. "Father, it *is* she."

"You saw her before. . . . You ought to know." Even Fergus, who had seen a deal of supernatural, was shaken. "Brigid's fire, what a thing, what a phasm! That's every man's nightmare!"

The final words started an idea forming in the deeper reaches of Fal's mind, but it vanished before he could identify it.

"Not every man's," he said. "Mine."

"But be certain," his father urged him. "Can you swear that is the creature you met? I have seldom known Umai to be wrong."

"No," Fal answered at last. "I can't be sure. Yet everything about her is the same, the same . . . what if I have to go with her lest all of you die?"

He wrapped his arms about himself and began to shake.

"You may forget that," Fergus said flatly. "Entirely. We are all with you. We'll trap her in a pit and burn her if there is no other way." He nodded grimly. "And tomorrow night you will be in the midst of us all after we have finished digging it. *She* shall not catch you alone or with one friend again, Fal. It's on that she seems to thrive."

"Indeed." Once again Fergus's words struck a wild spark of intuition in the boy, although it no sooner flared than

vanished. They retraced their steps together, and through the remainder of the night no man in the camp slept much. They talked, planned, and boasted; stopped to wet their throats; then exercised their voices some more before snatching a little rest, generally to be awakened before long by another excited schemer with a new implausible idea for dealing with the hag. Through it all Fal kept his own counsel and sorted through his thoughts behind firmly shut lips.

Beginning after sunrise, his kinsmen worked throughout the day on a deep pit lined with fuel. Fal joined in the labor for appearance's sake, even though he had partly formed plans of his own, for he did not wish to betray his intentions. In the early evening he slipped away through the rattling trees, breathing air milder than that of the three previous nights. Some might have been cheered by that. Fal was not, being cynical where omens were concerned. He trusted Umai's wisdom and his own resourcefulness, and little else. His smile was not pleasant as he contemplated the meeting to come.

In a tree-rimmed depression rustling with dead leaves, Fal waited. A dreadful anticipation sang through his nerves, and he found it simple to allow a certain unease to emanate from him in the twilit wood. That his guest was coming he felt sure, and he must serve fare of his own choosing at the banquet if he desired to be found sane in the morning.

With the patience of a hunter, he waited, listening. Many small noises filled the woods, as always, and Fal recognized most of them. The inconsequential ones he ignored. An hour went by.

Then it came, the furtive crackling he had known before, at the edges of his hearing. Now that he concentrated, alert for it, Fal recognized the sound — and the leering chitter that accompanied it. *Welcome, little unclean beast,* he thought, yet fear welled from the depths of his soul as he considered the possibility of his being wrong. Nearby, the thing tittered.

At the periphery of his vision, Fal witnessed an upheaval of leaves, as a grotesque shape surged into view. Yellow eye, mismatched legs, horny, wart-stippled hide, all the familiar ugliness was there. Terror sought to topple the pillars of Fal's mind, but he made himself walk forward. The shape before him bellowed crassly.

"So my night's pleasure comes to meet me! Welcome, smooth mortal skin, fine blue eyes, come to my arms and never hope to escape them!"

"Welcome," Fal answered in a deadly voice, "little impostor."

The she-monster threw back her repulsive head and inflated her chest.

"Welcome," Fal continued, "leech of the Otherworld who battens upon every sort of terror, shape-changer, *dreadtick*. Welcome, trader in empty threats. Glad am I that you came, but now it is time for you to go."

"Go I will, with you tucked beneath my arm! How foolish it was of you to come here tonight, Samhain's lover!"

Fal's nerve grew stronger with every extravagant threat the creature uttered, for none of it was like the savage power of the one he had known at Samhain. *That* mighty harridan would have acted without wasting more than a moment on bluster. His mother was right — and now Fal knew what he was dealing with.

"Do that if you can," he challenged, *"srigha."*

It reached for him with blackened nails. Fal conquered his urge to flinch and smiled in the hideous face. The haunter of Mara stopped short of closing its hands upon Fal, and vented a wild bubbling scream which must have been heard a mile. Watching with a steady, probing gaze, Fal saw the wattled skin fall into even looser folds and

bags, as though a wax image was melting, or the hag shrinking from within.

Triumph surged in Fal. He had faced his pursuer and called it by name, and this was the result. Vermin of the shadowy world, a *srigha* maintained itself on a nourishment of mortal fear, which it induced by taking the form of whatever its victim dreaded the most. If fear was withheld, the being could not continue in its false shape.

"Shrivel, you foulness," the boy said with hatred. "Wither to nothing!"

The grotesque features flattened like an empty sack. In moments, little remained of Fal's nightmare but a repulsive, untenanted skin among the dry leaves, yet something inside it evinced a twitching motion. Claws ripped through the scabrous hide. A sinuous, pale grey shape the size of a ferret squirmed out, the *srigha* in its true form. Fal stamped on it ruthlessly with his heel before it could scuttle away.

Fragile bones snapped, and the thing vented a piteous squeal. Fal stood above it where it lay writhing, judged his moment, and stamped again, his mother's advice to permit the *srigha* to depart forgotten. Nor would he have heeded it even if he had remembered. This thing had caused him anguish; he wanted revenge. As the srigha's last writhings ended, he obtained it.

Kicking off his befouled shoe, Fal left it beside the tiny, shattered monster. He wanted nothing that its touch had sullied. Then, as he prepared to go, he saw torches in the hands of kinsmen approaching through the trees, and heard familiar voices call his name. Raising his own, he answered. Within moments he was surrounded by friendly faces.

"It's over," he said, gripping his father's hand. "There lies the culprit, what remains of it — all this time, a skulking thing no larger than a rat! The haunting is over."

"A *srigha!*" Fergus cried. "Those things are rare."

"Not nearly rare enough for my liking," Fal assured him.

"And didn't I tell you to remain among us?"

"And didn't *I* tell you," Umai added, "to face your enemy, but to let it depart alive lest ill luck dog you?"

"You both did," Fal admitted, "but do not scold me. Confronting us all, it would have had the fears of us all to sustain it. As for letting it go — not I, mother mine! It had done too much harm and would have done more. I feel better knowing that it is dead. The ill luck I will risk."

"Father Lir, but you are stubborn," Umai sighed. "Well, it does not matter beside the joy that you are haunted no more." She passed her arms about him while Fergus came to his other side. "Come back to the camp with us now, and tomorrow we will go home."

Fal kissed her. The dancing torches followed them out of the glade, leaving the broken corpse of the *srigha* to the darkness which covered it. □

MEN FROM THE PLAIN OF LIR

by Keith Taylor

They came from the sea, the green flowering plain of Lir, five desperate men with the marks of privation and fighting upon them, ill memories in their hearts, and weapons in their boat. Nasach the escaped slave led them, as he had to lead them or be murdered by the others for the possession of that very boat, a poor battered thing but a treasure above jewels to him because it changed the impassable ocean to a highway on which he might journey home. For the present he had no other purpose.

"That's land!" Geban cried in shrill excitement. A smallish, quick, restless man, usually the first to observe something, he stabbed a finger towards the dark mass on which waves broke whitely. "Land!"

"So it is," Nasach agreed. For once he smiled broadly instead of thinly, ironically showing the edges of his teeth. "Steer for the place, Rogh. Are any of you knowing it? We've come far enough south for it to be the mainland of Ulster, maybe."

"Never the mainland," Conary said disparagingly. Always the one to disagree, he sneered at Nasach's ignorance and the distant bit of land with equal contempt. "That's some little patch of an isle, so — probably Rathlin of the Axes. It'll do to walk on and rest."

"Why Rathlin of the Axes?" Nasach looked speculatively at the shore. A leanly muscular man of the black-haired, swarthy Firbolg breed, though taller than most, he felt more concerned with whatever might await them there

than with Conary's manner. "Are they such warriors?"

"Warriors?" Conary fairly hooted in scorn, his mouth opening wide below his heavy yellow moustache. "You don't have to be frightened, runaway. Nothing lives there but fisher-folk who couldn't fight anything more terrible than a codfish. There'll be food and water, and women — all easy to take. Better jump to the sail."

"Then why is the isle known for its axes?" Nasach persisted, showing no celerity in jumping. "Does any man here know?"

Rogh, massive and calm at the tiller, shook his shaggy head. The gangling Dhumu grunted a negative, while Geban admitted he had never before heard of the place, and after a moment's thought Nasach shrugged his tough shoulders.

"So be it. We'll go ashore and learn."

Gripping the lines, Nasach trimmed sail to the gusty wind, causing the ox-hide curragh to ride over the waves towards the land like a skimming petrel. With Rogh handling the great rudder-paddle in the stern, their boat grounded on coarse sand before the sun had lowered much further, and all the men threw their backs into dragging the craft beyond reach of the next high tide. The moment he had finished that work and taken his hands from the gunwales of flint-hard oak, Conary reached into the curragh for his weapons.

He never touched them. Approaching the yellow-haired pirate from behind with two quick strides, Nasach kicked

45

Conary's feet from under him and bleakly watched him roll over in the sand, to rise covered in gritty powder with his heavy face reddened.

"Stay down, boyo, and listen," Nasach advised. "There'll be no trouble here unless the islanders make it for us, since we're making none for them — and you may forget about their women unless you find one who's willing. We eat, we rest, we behave ourselves, and then we depart. Right?"

Conary hurled himself at Nasach's legs with a snarl, craving to bring him down and commence the task of breaking his bones. The swarthy man dropped his hands speedily within the sides of the boat to seize a heavy coil of rope, which he swung two-handed at the side of Conary's head. The brutal impact dropped Conary prone with his face in the sand for a second time, yet Nasach followed him, beating him relentlessly with the rope until he could only cringe from further blows and croak, "No more!"

With a furious grunt, Nasach hurled the rope into the curragh. Folding his arms, he glared from one tattered seathief to the next, thinking that he would have chosen the companionship of none of them except perhaps Rogh. While the giant had very little to say, there was something steadfast and dependable about him.

"Enough, is it?" Nasach repeated. Glimpsing movement at the boundaries of his vision, he said harshly, "Stand you still, Dhumu, it's late to help your comrade now! No trouble, no killing; let you all understand that! The man who begins any answers for it to me."

"I'm willing," Geban said, folding his hands in a facetious attitude of prayer. "I'll be as gentle as a monk! But why this concern for strangers, just tell me?"

"Maybe for the reason that I'm a fisherman's son myself," Nasach rasped. Taking a long spear and a tough round shield from the curragh, he added,

"Rogh and Dhumu, you guard the curragh. Geban, Conary, you come searching with me and see what we find. If we're not back by sunset you may take it that we're dead."

Gripping the spear as though it was his only certainty in the world, Nasach strode across the sand to the wind-stirred grass beyond, never looking back at the man he had just beaten into submission. Sea-birds mewed above him; tough salt herbs scratched at the stiff wrappings about his calves; the smells of salt and kelp and his own gamey clothes were sharp in his nose. Wiping blood from his face and blinking, Conary followed, armed now with shield and axe, while Geban trotted after him on short bandy legs. Nothing tangible prevented the blond man from trying his luck with Nasach again now that he bore weapons, yet he did nothing. The dispassionate savagery of the other's assault had unnerved him.

Tramping over ling and vetch, Nasach scanned the island, noting that its highest trees were stunted, wind-bowed survivors less than seven yards high. The signs of man's habitation were small, although at the western end of Rathlin a memorial mound bulked against the reddening sky, oval in general form with a crescent-shaped addition at the entrance. The points of the crescent faced outward like claws, giving the entire earthwork the semblance of a vast crouching lobster. Nasach did not like the look of it, and with the superstitions of a fisher-child thick within him he turned his face away from the ancient mound.

"Woodsmoke yonder," Conary said. He normally talked almost as much as Geban, and more loudly, but after the beating he had received from Nasach he was unusually subdued. That would not last, of course.

"There *are* men on this forsaken place," Geban commented, as if he had doubted it. "We have time to reach

them, talk to them and still return to the curragh by sundown, Nasach. I suppose we may defend ourselves if they prove unfriendly?"

"You follow my lead in that," Nasach warned. "I'll not have you deciding for yourself unless someone comes for you with a weapon. They should be friendly — and eager for news from outside, withal. You may talk to your heart's content, Geban."

"Talk?" Geban echoed, running a hand through his dandelion-puff of mousy hair. "Why, there's a time and a place . . . how much I gab will depend on what these fisher-girls are like, for we've all been at sea a long time. Are you telling me you're made of stone and have no interest?"

Nasach scowled and made no other reply. Although he felt the same desires as any man, a nigh-crippling blow between the thighs in a recent fight still caused him pain, and he had no idea how lasting the effects might be. While the thought frightened Nasach, he said nothing about it, since Conary for one would roar with laughter and never stop jesting on the subject.

Striding towards the source of the smoke, he looked as grim as he felt, a tall man in a leather kilt and lambskin vest, long-limbed, hard-muscled, with the sea-wind combing his tangled beard. Torn from his family by raiders when his voice had barely broken and traded as a slave in Caledonia to eventually escape, Nasach appeared older than his one-and-twenty years. Yet emotion stirred deep within him at the prospect of being with his own kind of people again, even briefly as a transient guest.

The stone huts of the village were solidly made, as they had to be on an island exposed to the fury of sea-storms, with stays of twisted rope holding down the thatched roofs lest the wind blow them away and seaweed caulking the chinks in the walls. Nets hung drying on frames of crooked wood, while curraghs very like Nasach's own had been drawn ashore and turned upside down. The people too were dressed very like him, in leather and heavy undyed wool, but apart from a sudden outcry by one boy none spoke or did more than look towards the strangers.

Having looked, most continued to stare while Nasach and his companions drew nearer. Something in that intent collective regard caused Nasach's brows to draw together, cutting the frown lines deeper in his swarthy forehead. These people responded — or failed to respond — most oddly to the sudden appearance of three armed men, which might portend a pirate raid for all they knew. Not one woman drew her child protectively closer, and no man stepped forward between his wife and the strangers to ask their intentions. They seemed to lack normal apprehension, and even a normal view of the trio as men.

If three trees uprooted themselves and came walking into my village, Nasach thought, *maybe I would look at them in such a way.*

Other villagers came unhurriedly from the shore where they had been mending boats or gathering seaweed, to look at the trio of outlaws in the same avid yet remote way as their fellows. Still nobody spoke. Glancing at the one boy who had cried out and pointed, Nasach saw him standing a little apart from the rest, watching the strangers as intently as they yet with none of his elders' detachment. Becoming aware of the tall man's attention, the boy shrugged, bent his head and kicked a stone before turning away. Somewhere a ewe bleated, her cry seeming as loud as a thunderclap in the silence.

"Are they half-witted?" Conary demanded, hiding his unease with overbearing contempt. "If these are your precious fisher-folk, a plundering might be good for them! It would shake them to life."

48

"Something here is not right," Nasach agreed. "Now be quiet while I talk to them."

Clasping his spear against his shield, Nasach raised an empty weapon-hand in the universal sign that he came with peaceful intentions.

"It's a good day that I give you," he said, as pleasantly as he could with the scarred, somber face he wore. "We're placeless men on our way to the south, no bringers of harm. I am Nasach. Who speaks for your folk here?"

"I do; I, Shieran." The speaker's husky, phlegm-filled voice punctuated his words with a brief spasm of coughing as he trod forward. His hands were a fisherman's, swollen and hardened from years of handling nets, though a certain softness about his body caused Nasach to suspect that he hadn't worked much of late. The rheumy cough no doubt was the reason. Shieran continued, "You're welcome if you come peacefully. Are there others with you?"

"Yes." Nasach didn't state their number. "They stayed with our curragh in a small bay yonder, and we promised to return with news before sundown."

"Hunh." Shieran squinted his red-rimmed eyes at the sun. "Best you hurry to them with the word, then, stranger. One of our men can go with you and help you bring your boat here if you wish. He knows these shores as well as I could teach him." Another bout of coughing almost bent him double. Straightening, he wheezed, "My own . . . sister's . . . son. Innlair!"

A short fellow with a brutish face grunted a brief answer. Nobody else moved or spoke, not even the young children, which Nasach found the most disconcerting thing of all. Surveying the congregated villagers, he observed one comely woman giving Conary a full-lipped smile, while the yellow-haired pirate inflated his chest and struck a fighting cock's pose for her. That at least was normal, and Nasach felt it

reassuring despite the possibility of its leading to trouble.

"My thanks indeed," he said. "As you say, we'd best make haste if we're to return hither tonight, and Innlair is welcome."

Innlair, scratching himself, said nothing to that. As they made ready to leave, Nasach found an opportunity to speak in a low tone with Geban.

"You are a good talker, man. Fall behind Conary and me with this pilot we've been given and hold his attention, for I want some unheard speech with our friend."

"It's done," Geban said with a confident grin.

Striding ahead across the ling with Conary beside him, Nasach spoke from the corner of his mouth. "For such a sad gang they are over-friendly. Shieran invites us in without asking how many we are, and gives us a hostage too, not even wanting one in exchange. We'd best take care."

"Afraid of them, Firbolg?" Conary jeered.

"It's a short memory you have. I fear neither them nor any loud-mouth named Conary, and I'll leave you on this isle if you prove more trouble than use. But I'd rather you stayed alive while I am deciding. Don't go too far away with that woman who smiled at you so kindly. She might have an accomplice who would knife you for your shoes."

"Ah! It's jealousy, not fear." Conary chuckled in jocose good humor. "When we return to that village you can watch me deal with her and maybe learn something."

Nasach snorted with sour amusement. As he walked, though, the sick gnawing ache in his groin began again, a reminder of the blow which had forced him to crawl out of a recent affray on hands and knees. Clamping his teeth against the pain, he strode on in silence. No, he did not feel jealous of Conary's luck, since it would have been

49

wasted on him at present, and the last thing Nasach wished to do was confide the nature of his injury to such a one. How Conary would roar with laughter!

Returning to the curragh, Nasach explained the situation swiftly to Rogh and Dhumu. They too felt doubtful of such instantaneous friendship as Shieran had shown, yet a rest on land was necessary for them all and it was better to be among the islanders of Rathlin than apart from them, inspiring still greater mistrust. Directly the tide permitted, Innlair took the curragh out through the small waves and guided it along the rocky coast whose every configuration he knew, in the dark or in daylight.

They passed close to the high memorial mound overlooking the sea. In the purple evening it appeared more sinister to Nasach than before, and he made a sign against evil towards it. Innlair saw, and smirked knowingly.

"Old," he said. "Old and strong, made in the days of the Axes."

"So?" Geban's curiosity pounced upon the hint. "What axes are those?"

"Dark stone axes from when Earth was new. Sacred things kept in fortress to protect us."

"So that's it,"Conary scoffed. "A few stone axes from old times. Likely they aren't even good weapons any more, and this flea-bitten isle is named after them!"

Weary of the other man's endless contentiousness, Nasach made no reply. When they splashed ashore on the firelit beach below the village, a feast of sizzling roast mussels in their shells awaited them, with dulse and a kind of thick white ale. Eating heartily beside Shieran, the outlaw leader saw Conary's yellow head bent close to a woman's dark one and recognized the latter. Casually he asked Shieran her name.

"Oh, that is Ciand," came the careless answer. "The sea widowed her five seasons past. She should marry again, but she likes doing just as she pleases and there is no law to compel her." Grinning broadly, Shieran displayed a gap of several missing teeth. "Your friend is in good hands."

"Let's hope Ciand says the same of him." Nasach drank the last of his ale, liking its effect better than the taste, and found the boy who had been first to react to his band's presence waiting at his side holding a brimming earthenware jug. "One more, then," he said, and with an eager nod the boy poured.

I've glory upon me, Nasach thought ironically. *Because we come from beyond his little shoreline with weapons of iron he fancies us heroes.*

Later, sleeping beside his curragh with a cloak wrapped about him and a folded sheepskin under his head, Nasach forgot the boy entirely; but proof arrived soon enough that the boy had not forgotten him. Even as Nasach turned in his sleep to release a mussel-flavored belch, sand whispered grittily under bark-shod feet and a lean form went to one knee beside the outlaw. With a wild beast's awareness, Nasach threw off his cloak and cast it around the intruder's arms, seizing him then to hold him helpless.

"Not a sound if you want to live," he growled. "Not a loud one, anyhow. Whisper, you hear me? Now! Who are you?"

"I — I — I'm Munro, lord!"

Nasach did not know the name, or care, but he recognized the boy by the voice and the thinness of the frame he gripped. "Munro, is it? And why do you sneak to my side at this hour? Quickly!"

"I w-want to ask if you care about the life of the yellow-haired man. He isn't here! He went with Ciand."

"Why should that endanger his life? Is Ciand a thief ?"

Munro shook his head mutely.

"Well then, speak! Tell me what threatens him!"

"It's an ill thing to talk of, lord."

*Lord, he calls me! Only a pimply yokel
f Rathlin —*

"Talk of it nevertheless," Nasach said
rimly, "for you have started now and
wish to know. Speak plainly; don't
hink of fear."

The boy swallowed. "We sacrifice
nen here. To the Bowed One In The
Mound. He lived long ago and was bur-
ed long ago, but he doesn't die, and if
he's not fed he sends disease and death."

Nasach had heard it all before, when
he and his brothers told tales in winter
round the fire. Like a wolf with a bone
he sprang upon the one matter which
had importance for him. "And strangers
are better for sacrifice than your own
people? So. I understand that. Now tell
me why you are taking this risk." When
Munro hesitated, he shook the boy and
hissed, "You wish me to act upon your
words? Then answer!"

"I, I, I could be next," Munro gulped.
I could, lord! My father was drowned
and my mother coughed out her life
with the same sickness Shieran has
.. they say I'm unlucky. I want to
leave Rathlin. If I've helped — will you
take me? The Bowed One can't cross the
sea."

"If all is as you say, we'll take you."
Nasach reached a decision. "If it isn't
— you and I will talk further about this,
Munro. Where is Conary now? What
happened to him?"

Munro snickered. "Ciand told him a
story to make him follow her to the
mound. He'll be trailing her like a ram
now. She can make men do that; every
wife on the isle hates her."

"I know the kind." Nasach knew
about gossip, too. "Munro, if you are
lying I'll beat you until you sorrow for
t. Now get ready to come with us. Hsst!
Rogh! Wake and make no sound, you
big stot. We may have to seek Conary
all over this isle."

A sound sleeper, Rogh grunted and
turned before he was successfully roused.
Crawling around to the far side of the
curragh, Nasach shook Dhumu and
Geban out of their cloaks, finding no
sign of Conary in or out of the boat; not
that he had expected to.

"Look around the beach," he told his
companions as they yawned and swore.
"He may be somewhere near, with a
woman, and if he is we can all sleep
again — but don't look too hard and
arouse our hosts. Munro, help us."

"You will find nothing here, lord,"
the boy protested. "Don't you believe
me? They have gone to the mound!"

"So will we if we don't find them,"
Nasach promised, "but we'll make a
swift search here first, to be sure. Get
on with it. We cannot waste the night
in debate."

Dispersing among the rocks and hol-
lows, they sought the missing pirate
and found nothing. As each man returned to the curragh, he shook his
head or spread his hands to show his
efforts had been fruitless.

"He could be swiving in one of the
village huts," Geban offered.

"Maybe, but we cannot look there if
Munro has given us the true tale, and
we'd best not leave the curragh either."
Nasach was harshly realistic. "It matters more to us than Conary. We'll go
by water to visit this mound of theirs,
even if we haven't a pilot. Muffle the
oars."

"I can help, lord," Munro offered.
"I've been out setting lobster-pots by
day and night here. I can guide you to
that point in the dark."

"Then be quiet and do it," Nasach
growled, "and help us launch the boat,
too."

The light, oxhide-covered boat left a
wide track in the sand as they pushed
it down to the sea's edge and set it on
the wave-tops. Gripping the oaken gunwales and rolling inboard with experienced skill, the crew seized their
sacking-wrapped oars to row out of the
cove where Munro's village stood.

"From now on we stay quiet," Nasach

51

said in a low voice. "You know how noise carries across water at night. The first one who speaks with nothing of moment to say will eat the edge of a shield."

None of them said very much on their way to the sinister mound. Young Munro crouched beside Rogh in the stern of the boat and whispered instructions from time to time, while Nasach occasionally went aft to hear his directions and hope they were true. On a night of cloudy murk like this one even a native of Rathlin might miss his way.

Waves chuckled derisively beneath the curragh's hull, and contorted clouds moved writhing across the stars. Munro's words echoed in Nasach's mind even as he pulled on the narrow-bladed oar to drive them closer to their destination. "He was buried long ago, but he doesn't die." Deeply as he wished to dismiss such talk as nonsense, the fisher-child and escaped slave could not. He'd encountered his present companions on an island cursed with eternal silence, and had stood with them upon the deck of a ghostly ship from the shadows of time. Worse things might yet stand between him and his home. With a silent snarl he put his back into the oar-stroke, battling the fear that prowled at the edges of his mind, sniffing for weakness.

They all needed Conary's strength and fighting prowess. Like him or not, the five men had only each other to depend upon, in a world where outsiders were always suspect and a little band of obvious rogues such as they could be slain on sight without causing a ripple of concern. Maybe Conary deserved abandonment for being such a woman-craving fool — Nasach had warned him — but they had to stand together.

Wind shredded the clouds apart for a moment, and a lone bright star shone on the point of land which had given Nasach such a feeling of dread from the first time he beheld it. Munro pointed

mutely landward, and the tall Firbolg heard the boy's teeth chatter in the dark. Rowing in below the menacing bulk of the ancient mound, Nasach hoped the man he sought was there, for instinct and intuition wailed that evil was certainly present.

Scrambling ashore with weapons ready, the band left its curragh unguarded to climb through the rocks. Each boulder and scrubby bush looked like a man, but as they gained the flat eminence above the sea and strained their vision towards the long earthwork, they saw human shapes that were undoubtedly real. Vague, work-gnarled figures moving in the darkness with bundles in their arms might have been tricks of vision, but not sounds of driftwood being dropped or exchanges of words.

So, they are here. Now we must learn if Conary is here too.

Leaving his axe and shield, Nasach squirmed forward on his belly with no weapon but his spear, holding it clear of the ground while using his elbows and knees for purchase. As he stopped in the cover of a gorse bush to watch the fisher-folk of Rathlin at a closer vantage, a tiny flame came to life below the mound. Flaring and growing, it cast distorted shadows through the night, making the ragged, work-bent figures seem monstrous. About a dozen had gathered within the embracing horns of the earthen crescent piled up in a forgotten age, their backs to Nasach and their attention fixed upon the entrance to the mound. Hearing a nasty, bubbling cough and seeing one of the firelit shapes bend double with fists pressed to his mouth, Nasach thought, Shieran. He pronounced the name like a curse in his mind.

The crackling driftwood fire grew, battening upon its salty food to send up flames tinged with blue and green. The grotesque figures shifted, and between their bodies Nasach glimpsed a low flat stone upon which a bound shape squirmed helplessly. Although shadows hid the hair, Nasach didn't doubt it was Conary struggling there.

"Greetings, Bowed One!" Shieran cried in his congested voice.

"Greetings, Bowed One!" his people echoed together, as they repeated each utterance of their leader's thereafter, bawling like cattle.

"We praise you, Strength of our Isle!"

"We praise you, Strength of our Isle!"

"We praise you, Master of the Axes!"

"We praise you, Master of the Axes!"

"As we give you this man's blood, give us good catches and spare us the wasting sickness! Rest without stirring in the house that was made for you! Rest without stirring!"

"REST WITHOUT STIRRING!" rose the desperate howl, repeated often as the worshipers capered into the darkness to dance frantically about the mound, their yelling scarcely human now. Shieran's head sank low as he leaned on the long curved handle of some tool which resembled an axe, gathering his strength.

Nasach saw clearly now who lay upon the stone, glaring at the fisherman-priest standing over him. Conary lacked the power to move much, bound as he was in mariner's cord, but he could curse to the extent of his heart's desire, and as Nasach crawled closer he heard the blond captive raving his invective. Conary's voice rose to a hoarse shriek as he expressed the hope that a weasel might eat Shieran's bowels gradually, beginning at the lower end, while the ragged priest raised his instrument high in both hands to end his victim's malisons forever. Now Nasach beheld it clearly, an axe of polished blue stone giving back the firelight dully in the moment before it was to fall with head-cleaving power.

Leaping upright with a shatteringly resonant war-yell, Nasach charged the older man from behind to strike him savagely in the side with the butt-end of his spear. Ribs cracked as Shieran went down, his shocked breath whistling in his throat, and Nasach kicked him hard in the body for a sequel. He'd no scruples about striking an ailing man senior to himself when that man bore an axe with indications of lethal skill. Shieran fell against the flat stone of sacrifice to rebound into the grass, where he lay unmoving.

"Rest without stirring!" wailed someone who had as yet observed nothing amiss, and Shieran obeyed.

"Rogh, Dhumu, all of you!" Nasach bellowed. "Drive these fools away!"

Without waiting to see how they followed his order, he bent over Conary to slash his bonds. The yellow-haired man sat, then stood, to lurch and topple to all fours as his limbs protested the sudden demand he made upon them after hours of confinement. Struggling to rise, he saw Nasach stand before him to meet a pair of fishermen armed with cudgels. The long spear drove and jabbed; one man fell with a gurgling cry which the other soon echoed, though he remained able to depart at a limping run. Conary by then had managed to stand.

"Thanks!" he growled. "Let's go from here!"

"Not yet."

Several strong men had come out of the dark with clubs and spears in their hands. In a line they pressed forward, lunging with their nastily bone-barbed weapons, forcing Nasach to retreat. Conary as yet could be of no help because his limbs remained stiff and slow-moving; he had barely been able to grasp Shieran's fallen sacrificial axe. Grinding his teeth in agony as circulation returned to his swollen, purplish hands, he withdrew beside his leader. The shadow of the mound covered them both.

Nasach felt his blood thicken with cold as he sensed the ancient mass of piled earth behind him, exuding a stench like that of mildewed cloth. Standing fast rather than draw another step closer to that sinister tumulus, he prepared to fight and die, thinking hatefully, *For the sake of a wild boar like Conary I am to perish away from all my kin!*

With a cry of battle from three throats, their companions arrived, hewing into the fishers of Rathlin. Nasach saw the shaggy hulk of Rogh pitch a man headfirst into the fire, while lanky Dhumu plied his spear in a deadly circle, his straight tress of hair flying. Geban slipped like a shadow through the fray, striking with his knife, until their adversaries melted before them and a way of escape lay open before the two formerly trapped outlaws.

"Well, come out!" Geban said peremptorily. "Do you love it in there so well?"

As though in affronted answer, the mound shuddered and split open between the points of its crescent. A howling wind blew out of it, scattering the fire across the ground, making Nasach and Conary stagger towards their friends. Reeling, almost falling, Nasach came face to face with young Munro in the light of a blazing thorn bush, and saw the boy's visage twist in unmasterable fear. Wrapping his arms about his lowered head, Munro fled into the darkness which had already swallowed most of the fisher-people who were still able to run.

With that unnatural wind still buffeting his back, Nasach took his courage in both sinewy hands and turned about, with his mouth dry as ancient ashes. Looming hideous against the fires he had scattered abroad stood the ancient inhabitant of the tumulus, buried ages before. Offered a man for sacrifice and then cheated of his blood, The Bowed One had emerged to demand his due.

Stooped almost double from its weight

54

of time and dreadfulness, the shape advanced. Teeth showed grey and dry as pebbles thought a thicket of beard, and the ponderous body creaked as it moved. Each footstep left a deep print in the earth.

"Run!" Nasach snapped, and set the example. Reeling, staggering, gripping the ancient axe, Conary followed, still stiff from his hours of being tightly bound. Glancing back, Nasach saw him stumble, and shouted to the vanishing Dhumu.

"Back here with you, man! Conary needs help. Are you his friend or not? *Back and lend him your shoulder, or by the black gods of the sea I will geld you!* So. That is better. I'll ward your backs, never fear."

Matching his action to his words, Nasach watched the dreadful shape from the mound shamble closer, slow yet tireless. When it had come within half a chain of him, Nasach backed away without raising his glance to meet its unalive stare. Somehow he believed that if he looked into whatever it used for eyes, he would fall on his face to lie gibbering until it trampled over him with those unnaturally heavy feet. Merely thinking of it, he could feel his mind spin into madness and his bones snap one by one.

Perhaps Conary had similar thoughts inspiring him to move, for each step he took grew more agile until he was fairly legging it when he reached the shore. Nasach crossed the sandy beach hard upon his heels, in time to hear Geban's yell of despair.

"They wrecked the boat! Mad dogs bite them all! We're dead men!"

"Not yet," Nasach snarled. "Wrecked it how?"

Geban showed him with a frantically stabbing finger. The leather of the hull had been opened with a yard-long slash, and the boat would sink as soon as it was set afloat. While they had tanned oxhide, needles, awl, and thread with which to repair it, there was no time. Death lumbered inexorably towards them, leaving deep footprints behind it.

"We'll stand together," Nasach said. "We'll hew it apart if we can, or bind it helpless. Geban, you're the quickest; run to yon flaming bushes and bring us fire to burn the thing if other ways don't succeed. Go! And come back, or any of us who survive will hunt you down. Munro — where is Munro?"

"He ran like a cur," Dhumu answered, and spat. "If I catch him —"

"Get rope from the boat,"Nasach interrupted. "All of it. And none of you look the Bowed One of the Mound in the eyes! Watch its feet or hands."

The instruction was given none too soon. Shaking the ground with its ponderous tread, the Bowed One came in all its stooped hunched monstrousness, bringing a musty odor which impelled live men to gag. Now was the time for Nasach to pay the cost of leading. With a clay-like chill in his marrow, he charged against the being from the grave while a lone twisted tree creaked above the beach in the sea-wind.

Nasach drove his spear at the Bowed One's leg. It encountered a resistance like that of dense clay and barely penetrated a finger-joint's length. Dragging back his spear, Nasach struck again and again, darting about the horror like a wolf, seeking some vulnerable spot — throat, stomach, or back. Nothing availed. Although he could strike the slow-moving lich where he would, he could not harm it, and suddenly it smote him for the first time.

A fist armored in the layered horn of centuries came around like a mace. Nasach lifted his shield, which broke like a barley-cake at the impact of the unbreathing thing's hand. The outlaw sprawled on the sand, wondering if his arm was shattered, while the Bowed One waded towards him, sinking knee-deep in gritty sand with every step.

Rogh and Conary moved against their enemy, striking in unison. The ancient stone axe Conary had snatched from his would-be slayer's lifeless hand swung powerfully at the Bowed One's hip while Rogh smote with greater power yet upon a dead shoulder-blade. Both blows, delivered by the strongest men in Nasach's band, penetrated to the bone before rebounding like straws, and both men tottered. Conary, who carried his heavy body on thin shanks, slipped to one knee before regaining his feet.

The thing from the mound barely shifted under the murderous double impact.

It can't be destroyed, Nasach thought, his blood running cold.

Then he thought of the pirates who had carried him away after striking down his father, of seven years in slavery, and all he had suffered since his escape; his torment upon the hungry grass, the silent isle and the ship of lost, accursed men. None of it had stopped him, or shaken his determination to go home.

Nor will you, dead thing. Not even you.

Anger came to Nasach's rescue, anger crammed, packed and layered in him through seven long years, burning as stubbornly as peat. He rose, shaking the fragments of his shield from an arm made wholly of agony below the elbow, and returned to the fray.

"Don't try to kill," he rasped. "Keep it occupied . . . until Geban comes back with fire."

They surrounded the undead being, feinting, jabbing and cursing. Whenever it attacked one of their number, that one would retreat while the others struck it from behind until it turned around. None of their weapons had any discernible effect; they might have been battling a mountain.

When Geban rushed onto the beach, bearing a smoky torch and an armload of fuel, they rallied their strength for

55

a long, frustrating attempt to burn their foe. Fire would not catch upon its resistant body save briefly, to smolder and wink out. One by one it trampled their brands into the sand.

Nasach led a concerted effort to bind it. They cast ropes about its limbs again and again, risking dismemberment to draw them tight, cords of flax and ropes of twisted leather, yet always the Bowed One broke them.

By then they were desperately weary, while their foe continued tireless. They had retreated from the beach to the tough, gnarled tree which had witnessed all their struggle, and still the being advanced, its feet sinking into the earth.

"The Earth," Nasach whispered in a dazed croak. *"Yes!"*

Ordering his men to hold the thing occupied, he took their last intact coil of rope and fashioned a loop in it. If this desperate inspiration did not work, they were lost, for he hadn't strength or presence of mind to devise anything else. Casting his loop over the Bowed One's head and shoulders, he dragged it tight, then hurled the other end over the tree's strongest branch, to catch the rope in desperate haste as it fell.

"Rogh, Conary, help me . . . pull it . . . from the ground. Its strength comes from the Earth. We have to lift it away from the earth!"

They stumbled to help him, two powerful men putting their backs into a task which meant their lives. All three strained until their muscles shrieked. Dhumu joined them at last, while Geban remained to distract the Bowed One, and the combined strength of four men swung the stalking terror clear of the ground at last.

The monster weighed tons. The anchor-rope hummed like a harpstring as they belayed it around the tree-trunk and knotted it fast. Turning, kicking, swaying in the wind, the Bowed One turned his fearsome gaze upon Geban,

who finally met their foe's eyes against Nasach's oft-shouted advice. With a gurgling shriek he fell prone, and none of his comrades could come to aid him. In sweating fear lest their rope should break, they cast other bits of cord about the monster's limbs until he hung from the tree like a spider's victim, enwrapped and dangling a yard above the ground.

"We have him!" Dhumu croaked. "But what are we to do?"

"Get his head off," Nasach answered brutally, "but never look him in the face! You see what has happened to Geban?"

The sharpest wit in their band grovelled on his knees, mewling and croaking while he slowly drove his nails into his face and pulled them out again. Dhumu looked, and shuddered. With hatred in every motion, he tore off his shirt to wrap it around the Bowed One's head, then hacked at the nigh-impenetrable neck. Through the long haunted hours until dawn they struggled with the task, and felling a centuried oak with wood seasoned hard as flint would have been easier. The work blunted axes, broke knives and daunted hearts, until in their frenzy of frustration they almost turned upon each other while Geban watched drooling; but Nasach held them to their grisly task.

As the sun rose, the Bowed One had grown weaker and only his exposed cervical bones held head to body. With a wild, screaming exhalation, Nasach struck three times swiftly with his edgeless axe, smashing through the white vertebrae and catching the head as it fell bloodlessly clear. The body spasmed slowly, while with a monstrous cracking half the trunk split away from the tree and crashed to the ground, boughs, leaves and undead corpse. Although it touched the ground, it never moved, and Nasach wanted to sob in relief, yet he could not release a tear. Instead he kicked the inert mass.

"No more sacrifices to you," he prophesied.

"I wouldn't be so sure," Dhumu said, staring in morbid fascination at the body. "These island scum will go on worshipping their lich, even though we have finished it. They have done so for generations; they won't stop now."

"Man, they are welcome,"Nasach said, "and I care not. Come on! Let us mend the curragh and be gone from here."

"Well, now," Conary said, looking past his leader. "Well, now. See who has come crawling back. I claim the right to kill him."

Munro the fisher-boy stood there in the blue sunrise, trembling.

"No killing," Nasach said. "He saved your life by warning us."

"And then he ran!"

"I'm not forgetting. Still, I'll deal with this. You spring to work — and help Geban, if you can." Weary in every bone, Nasach moved forward to confront the fisher-boy. "What now, Munro?"

"Lord, you have killed the Bowed One of the Mound." So might Munro have addressed a god, and even in his exhaustion, Nasach felt sourly amused. "Now I would leave Rathlin with you, for I too will be killed if I stay here. My people know what I have done."

"You ran away when the mound opened and *he* came out." Nasach stood as rigidly straight as his own spear. "Why should I trust you?"

"Lord, *he* made me afraid."

"So were we all. Listen, Munro. If you come with us you must be one of us, boy or not. That means no running, no deserting us in the face of any terror we meet, and if there's fighting on our sea-path, it's fighting I want done. You cannot ride in my curragh for nothing."

"I d— don't know how to fight."

"Nor did I, once. Learn. Or remain here."

Nasach strode back to the curragh while Munro loitered disconsolately where he was, watching the outlaws mend their battered vessel. At last he approached them. Conary rose from cutting a leather patch with a malign grin, but Nasach gave him a long, winter-black stare and he reconsidered. The others paid no attention.

"So you've decided," Nasach said. "Stand lookout for us, then. When we are ready to sail, I will call you. Do you care where we go?"

Munro shook his head vehemently, "So long as it's away from here!"

"Amen, boy," Dhumu growled, looking at the demented Geban. "Far away from here."

Munro scampered to take his watchman's post. □

PSYCHE IN THE NIGHT, CUPID BY LAMPLIGHT

Her sisters' whispers are an ocean that hisses,
A wind on the water to dampen her dreams,
So she walks without waking in a tidepool of lamplight
And tastes old frustrations on a salt tongue that bleeds.
Her husband's a serpent, a monster who holds her,
Writhing and licking like a wave of the sea.
But feathers are a snowfall on the flesh of his shoulders,
Tumbling and wisping with each wish she breathes;
His face is a tangle of long summer mornings,
Where Psyche wakes drowning in fear of her need.

— Ace G. Pilkington

Emma's Daughter

by Alan Rodgers

Emma went drinking the night after the cancer finally got done with her daughter Suzi. Suzi was eight, and she'd died long and hard and painful, and when she was finally gone what Emma needed more than anything else was to forget, at least for a night.

The bar Emma went to was a dirty place called the San Juan Tavern; she sometimes spent nights there with her friends. It was only four blocks from home — two blocks in another direction from the hospital where Suzi died. A lot of people who lived around where Emma did drank at the San Juan.

It made her feel dirty to be drinking the night after her daughter died. She thought a couple of times about stopping, paying up her bill, and going home and going to sleep like someone who had a little decency. Instead she lit cigarettes, smoked them hard until they almost burned her lips. She didn't usually smoke, but lately she felt like she needed it, and she'd been smoking a lot.

The cigarettes didn't help much, and neither did the wine. When she was halfway through her third tumbler of something that was cheap and chalky and red, Mama Estrella Perez sat down across from her and clomped her can of Budweiser onto the Formica tabletop. Emma expected the can to fall over and spill. It didn't, though — it just tottered back and forth a couple of times and then was still.

Mama Estrella ran the bodega downstairs from Emma's apartment. She was Emma's landlord, too — she owned the building. Her bodega wasn't like most of them; it was big and clean and well-lit, and there was a big botanica in the back, shelves and shelves of Santeria things, love potions and strange waters and things she couldn't figure out because she couldn't read Spanish very well. Emma always thought it was cute, but then she found out that Santeria was Cuban voodoo, and she didn't like it so much.

"Your daughter died today," Mama Estrella said. "Why're you out drinking? Why aren't you home, mourning?" Her tone made Emma feel as cheap and dirty as a streetwalker.

Emma shrugged. She knocked back the rest of her glass of wine and refilled it from the bottle the bartender had left for her.

Mama Estrella shook her head and finished off her beer; someone brought her another can before she even asked. She stared at Emma. Emma kept her seat, held her ground. But after a few minutes the taste of the wine began to sour in her throat, and she wanted to cry. She knew the feeling wasn't Mama Estrella's doing, even if Mama was some sort of a voodoo woman. It was nothing but Emma's own guilt, coming to get her.

"Mama, my baby *died* today. She died a little bit at a time for six months, with a tumor that finally got to be the size of a grapefruit growing in her belly, almost looking like a child that was going to kill her before it got born." She caught her breath. "I want to drink enough that I don't see her dying like that, at least not tonight."

Mama Estrella was a lot less belligerent-looking after that. Ten minutes later she took a long drink from her beer and said, "You okay, Emma." Emma poured herself some more wine, and someone brought Mama Estrella a pitcher of beer, and they sat drinking together, not talking, for a couple of hours.

About one a.m. Mama Estrella got a light in her eye, and for just an instant, just long enough to take a breath and let it out, Emma got a bad feeling. But she'd drank too much by that point to feel bad about anything for long, so she leaned forward and whispered in her conspiracy-whisper, "What's that, Mama Estrella? What're you thinking?"

Mama Estrella sprayed her words a little. "I just thought: hey, you want your baby back? You miss her? I could bring her back, make her alive again. Sort of." She was drunk, even drunker than Emma was. "You know what a zombie is? A zombie isn't a live little girl, but it's like one. It moves. It walks. It breathes if you tell it to. I can't make your baby alive, but I can make what's left of her go away more slowly."

Emma thought about that. She knew what a zombie was — she'd seen movies on television, even once something silly and disgusting at the theater. And she thought about her little Suzi, her baby, whimpering in pain in her sleep every night. For a minute she started to think that she couldn't stand to see her baby hurting like that, even if she would be dead as some crud-skinned thing in a theater. Anything had to be better, even Suzi being completely dead. But after a moment Emma knew that just wasn't so; life was being alive and having to get up every morning and push hard against the world. And no matter how bad life was, even half-life was better than not being alive at all.

Emma started to cry, or her eyes did. They kept filling up with tears even though she kept trying for them not to. "I love my baby, Mama Estrella," she said. It was all she *could* say.

Mama Estrella looked grim. She nodded, picked up her beer, and poured most of it down her throat. "We go to the hospital," she said. "Get your Suzi and bring her home." She stood up. Emma took one last swallow of her wine and got up to follow.

It was hot outside. Emma was sure it was going to be a hot summer; here it was only May and the temperature was high in the eighties at midnight.

The moon was out, and it was bright and full overhead. Usually the moon looked pale and washed out because of the light the city reflected into the sky, but tonight somehow the city was blacker than it should be. And the moon looked full and bright as bone china on a black cloth.

They walked two blocks to the hospital, and when they got to the service door Mama Estrella told Emma to wait and she'd go in and get Suzi.

Mama left her there for twenty minutes. Twice men came out of the door carrying red plastic bags of garbage from the hospital. It was infected stuff in the red bags: dangerous stuff. Emma knew because her job was cleaning patients' rooms in another hospital in another part of the city.

After ten minutes Emma heard a siren, and she thought for a moment that somehow she and Mama Estrella had been found out and that the police were coming for them. But that was silly; there were always sirens going off in this part of the city. It could even have been the alarm on someone's car — some of them sounded just like that.

Then both sides of the door swung open at once, and Mama Estrella came out of the hospital carrying poor dead little Suzi in her arms. Emma saw her daughter's too-pale skin with the veins showing through and the death-white haze that colored the eyes, and her heart skipped a beat. She shut her eyes for a moment and set her teeth and forced herself to think about Suzi at the picnic they had for her birthday when she was five. They'd found a spot in the middle of Prospect Park and set up a charcoal grill, and Suzi had run off into the trees, but she didn't go far enough that Emma had to worry about keeping an eye on her. Just before the hamburgers were ready Suzi came back with a handful of pinestraw and an inchworm crawling around on the ends of the needles. She was so excited you'd think she'd found the secret of the world, and Emma got behind her and looked at the bug and the needles from over Suzi's shoulder, and for just a moment she'd thought that Suzi was right, and that the bug and the needles *were* the secret of the world.

Emma forced her jaw to relax and opened her eyes. Suzi was special. No matter what happened to Suzi, no matter what Suzi was, Emma loved the girl with all her heart and soul. She loved Suzi enough that she didn't let it hurt, even when her eye caught on Suzi's midriff and she saw the cancer that made it look like she had a baby in her belly. Emma felt a chill in spite of her resolve; there was something strange about the cancer, something stranger than just death and decay. It frightened her.

"You okay, Emma?" Mama Estrella asked. She looked a little worried.

Emma nodded. "I'm fine, Mama. I'm just fine." When she heard her own voice she realized that she really was fine.

"We need to get to my car," Mama Estrella said. "We need to go to the graveyard." Mama kept her car in a parking garage around the corner from the San Juan Tavern.

"I thought we were just going to take her home," Emma said.

Mama Estrella didn't answer; she just shook her head.

Emma took Suzi from Mama Estrella's arms and carried the body to the garage. She let the head rest on her shoulder, just as though Suzi were only asleep, instead of dead. When they got to Mama's car she laid Suzi out on the back seat. She found a blanket on the floor of the car and by reflex she covered the girl to keep her from catching cold.

The drive to the cemetery took only a few minutes, even though Mama Estrella drove carefully, almost timidly. When she came to stop signs she didn't just slow down and check for traffic; she actually stopped. But the only thing she had to use her brakes for *was* the stop signs. Somehow the traffic lights always favored her, and whichever street she chose to turn on was already clear of traffic for blocks in either direction.

There was no one minding the gate at the cemetery, so when they got there they just drove through like they were supposed to be there. The full-bright moon was even brighter here, where there were no street lights; it made the whole place even more strange and unearthly than it was by nature.

Mama Estrella drove what felt like half a mile through the cemetery's twisting access roads, and then pulled over in front of a stand of trees. "Are there others coming, Mama? Don't you need a lot of people to have a ceremony?"

Mama Estrella shook her head again and lifted a beer from a bag on the floor of the car that Emma hadn't seen before. She opened the can and took a long pull out of it.

"You wait here until I call you, Emma," she said. She got out of the car, lifted Suzi out of the back, and carried her off into the graveyard.

After a while Emma noticed that Mama'd started a fire on top of someone's grave. She made noise, too — chanting and banging on things and other sounds Emma couldn't identify. Then she heard the sound of an infant screaming, and she couldn't help herself anymore. She got out of the car and started running toward the fire.

Not that she really thought it was her Suzi. Suzi had never screamed as a baby, and if she had she wouldn't have sounded like that. But Emma didn't want the death of someone else's child on her conscience, or on Suzi's.

By the time Emma got to the grave where Mama Estrella had started the fire, it looked like she was already finished. Emma didn't see any babies. Mama looked annoyed.

"I thought I heard a baby screaming," Emma said.

"You shouldn't be here," Mama Estrella said. She stepped away from Suzi for a moment, looking for something on the ground by the fire, and Emma got a look at her daughter. Suzi's eyes were open, but she wasn't breathing. After a moment, though, she blinked, and Emma felt her heart lurch. *Suzi. Alive.* Emma wanted to cry. She wanted to pray. She wanted to sing. But something in her heart told her that Suzi was all empty inside — that her body was just pretending to be alive. But her heart wouldn't let her stop pacing through the steps, either; it wouldn't let her back away without showing, one last time, how much she loved her baby. Emma ran to Suzi and grabbed her up in her arms and sang in her cold-dead ear. *"Suzi, Suzi, my darling baby Suzi."* When her lips touched Suzi's ear it felt like butchered meat. But there were tears all over Emma's face, and they fell off her cheeks onto Suzi's.

Then, after a moment, Suzi started to hug Emma back, and she said, "Mommy," in a voice that sounded like dry paper brushing against itself.

Emma heard Mama Estrella gasp behind her, and looked up to see her standing over the fire, trembling a little. When she saw Emma looking at her, she said, "Something's inside her."

Emma shook her head. "Nothing's inside Suzi but Suzi." Emma was sure. A mother *knew* these things. "She's just as alive as she always was."

Mama Estrella scowled. "She shouldn't be alive at all. Her body's dead. If something happened to it . . . *God*, Emma. Her soul could die forever."

"What do you mean?"

"Emma . . . you were hurt so bad. I thought . . . if I could make Suzi's body pretend to be alive for a while it would help you. I could make a zombie from her body. A zombie isn't a daughter, but it's like one, only empty. But if her soul is inside the zombie, it could be trapped there forever. It could wither and die inside her."

Emma felt herself flush. "You're not

going to touch my baby, Mama Estrella. I don't know what you're thinking, but you're not going to touch my baby."

Mama Estrella just stood there, gaping. Emma thought she was going to say something, but she didn't.

After a moment Emma took Suzi's hand and said, "Come on, child," and she led Suzi off into the graveyard, toward home. There were a few tall buildings in another part of the city that she could see even from here, and she used the sight of them to guide her. It only took a few minutes to get out of the cemetery, and half an hour after that to get home. She carried Suzi most of the way, even though the girl never complained. Emma didn't want her walking that far in nothing but her bare feet.

When they got home, Emma put Suzi to bed. She didn't seem tired, but it was long past her bedtime, and God knew it was necessary to at least keep up the pretense that life was normal.

Twenty minutes after that, she went to bed herself.

Emma woke early in the morning, feeling fine. She went out to the corner before she was completely awake and bought herself a paper. When she got back she made herself toast and coffee and sipped and ate and settled down with the news. As she'd got older she'd found herself waking earlier and earlier, and now there was time for coffee and the paper most mornings before she went to work. It was one of her favorite things.

She let Suzi sleep in; there was no sense waking her this early. She kept expecting Mama Estrella to call; she'd really expected her to call last night before she went to sleep. All night she dreamed the sound of telephones ringing, but every time she woke to answer them the bells stopped. After a while she realized that the real telephone wasn't ringing at all, and the rest of the night she heard the bells as some strange sort of music. The music hadn't bothered her sleep at all.

At nine she decided it was late enough to wake Suzi up, so she folded her newspaper, set it on the windowsill, and went to her daughter's bedroom. She opened the door quietly, because she didn't want Suzi to wake to a sound like the creaking of a door on her first day back at home. Suzi was lying in bed resting with her eyes closed — probably asleep, Emma thought, but she wasn't sure. The girl lay so still that Emma almost started to worry about her, until her lips mumbled something without making any sound and she rolled over onto her side. In that instant before Emma went into the room, as she stood watching through the half-open door, she thought Suzi was the most beautiful and adorable thing in the world.

Then she finished opening the door, took a step into the room, took a breath, and *smelled* her.

The smell was like meat left to sit in the sun for days — the smell it has after it's turned grey-brown-green, but before it starts to liquefy. Somewhere behind that was the sulphury smell that'd permeated Suzi's waste and her breath — and after a while even her skin — since a little while after the doctors found the cancer in her.

Emma's breakfast, all acidy and burning, tried to lurch up her throat. Before she knew what she was thinking she was looking at Suzi and seeing something that wasn't her daughter at all — it was some *dead* thing. And who gave a good Goddamn what sort of spirit was inside? The thing was disgusting, it was putrefied. It wasn't fit for decent folks to keep in their homes.

Then Emma stopped herself, and she felt herself pale, as though all the blood rushed out of her at once. She felt ashamed. Suzi was Suzi, damn it, and no matter what was wrong with her she was still Emma's baby. And whatever else was going on, no matter how weird and incomprehensible things got, Emma *knew* that Suzi was the same Suzi she'd been before she died.

She tiptoed over to her daughter's bed, and she hugged her good morning — and the smell, strong as it was, was just Suzi's smell.

Which was all right.

"Did you sleep well, baby?" Emma asked. She gave Suzi a peck on the cheek and stepped back to take a look at her. There was a grey cast, or maybe it was blue, underneath the darkness of her skin. That worried Emma. Even just before the cancer killed her Suzi hadn't looked that bad. Emma pulled away the sheets to get a better look at her, and it almost seemed that the tumor in Suzi's belly was bigger than it had been. Emma shuddered, and her head spun. There was something about that cancer that wasn't natural. She couldn't stop herself from staring at it.

"I guess I slept okay," Suzi said. Her voice sounded dry and powdery.

Emma shook her head. "What do you mean, you guess? Don't you know how well you slept?"

Suzi was looking down at her belly now, too. "It's getting bigger, Mommy." She reached down and touched it. "I mean about sleeping that I guess I'm not sure if I was asleep. I rested pretty good, though."

Emma sighed. "Let's get some breakfast into you. Come on, out of that bed."

Suzi sat up. "I'm not hungry, though."

"You've got to eat anyway. It's good for you."

Suzi stood up, took a couple of steps, and faltered. "My feet feel funny, Mommy," she said.

Emma was halfway to the kitchen. "We'll take a good look at your feet after breakfast. First you've got to eat." In the kitchen she broke two eggs into a bowl and scrambled them, poured them into a pan she'd left heating on the stove. While they cooked she made

63

toast and buttered it.

Mama Estrella finally called just after Emma set the plate in front of Suzi. Emma rushed to the phone before the bell could ring a second time; she hated the sound of that bell. It was too loud. She wished there was a way to set it quieter.

"Emma," Mama Estrella said, "your baby could die forever."

Emma took the phone into the living room and closed the door as much as she could without damaging the cord. When she finally responded her voice was even angrier than she meant it to be. "You stay away from Suzi, Mama Estrella Perez. My Suzi's just fine, she's going to be okay, and I don't want you going near her. Do you understand me?"

Mama sighed. "When you make a zombie," she said, "when you make a real one from someone dead, I mean, you can make it move. You can even make it understand enough to do what you say. But still the body starts to rot away. It doesn't matter usually. When a zombie is gone it's gone. What's the harm? But your Suzi is inside that zombie. When the flesh rots away she'll be trapped in the bones. And we won't ever get her out."

Emma felt all cold inside. For three long moments she almost believed her. But she was strong enough inside — she had *faith* enough inside — to deny what she didn't want to believe.

"Don't you say things like that about my Suzi, Mama Estrella," she said. "My Suzi's *alive,* and I won't have you speaking evil of her." She *knew* Suzi was alive, she was certain of it. But she didn't think she could stand to hear anything else, so she opened the door and slammed down the phone before Mama Estrella could say it.

Suzi was almost done with her eggs, and she'd finished half the toast. "What's the matter with Mama Estrella, Mommy?" she asked.

Emma poured herself another cup of coffee and sat down at the table across from Suzi. She didn't want to answer that question. She didn't even want to *think* about it. But she had to — she couldn't just ignore it — so she finally said, "She thinks there's something wrong with you, Suzi."

"You mean because I was dead for a while?"

Emma nodded, and Suzi didn't say anything for a minute or two. The she asked, "Mommy, is it wrong for me to be alive again after I was dead?"

Emma had to think about that. The question *hurt.* But when she realized what the answer was it didn't bother her to say it. "Baby, I don't think God would have let you be alive if it wasn't right. Being alive even once is a miracle, and God doesn't make miracles that are evil."

Suzi nodded like she didn't really understand. But she didn't ask about it any more. She took another bite of her toast. "This food tastes funny, Mommy. Do I have to eat it all?"

She'd eaten most of it, anyway, and Emma didn't like to force her to eat. "No, sugar, you don't have to eat it all. Come on in the den and let me see those feet you said were bothering you."

She had Suzi sit with her feet stretched out across the couch so she could take her time looking at them without throwing the girl off balance. "What do they feel like, baby? What do you think is the matter with them?"

"I don't know, Mommy. They just feel strange."

Emma peeled back one of the socks she'd made Suzi put on last night before she put her to bed. There wasn't anything especially wrong with her ankle, except for the way it felt so cold in her hands. But when she tried to pull the sock off over Suzi's foot, it stuck. Emma felt her stomach turning on her again. She pulled hard, because she knew she had to get it over with. She expected the sock to pull away an enormous scab, but it didn't. Just the opposite. Big blue fluffs of sock fuzz stuck to the . . . *thing* that had been Suzi's foot.

No. That wasn't so. It *was* Suzi's foot, and Emma loved it, just like she loved Suzi. Suzi's foot wasn't any *thing*. Even if it was all scabrous and patchy, with dried raw flesh poking though in places as though it just didn't have the blood inside to bleed any more.

Nothing was torn or ripped or mangled, though Emma's first impulse when she saw the skin was to think that something violent had happened. But it wasn't that at all; except for the blood, the foot almost looked as though it'd worn thin, like the leather on an old shoe.

What caused this? Emma wondered. Just the walk home last night? She shuddered.

She peeled away the other sock, and that one was a little worse.

Emma felt an awful panic to *do* something about Suzi's feet. But what could she do? She didn't want to use anything like a disinfectant. God only knew what a disinfectant would do to a dead person who was alive. Bandages would probably only encourage the raw places to fester. She could pray, maybe. Pray that Suzi's feet would heal up, even though everything inside the girl that could heal or rebuild her was dead, and likely to stay that way.

Emma touched the scabby part with her right hand. It was hard and rough and solid, like pumice, and it went deep into her foot like a rock into dirt. It'd probably wear away quickly if she walked on it out on the street. But it was strong enough that walking around here in the house probably wouldn't do any harm. That was a relief; for a moment she'd thought the scab was all soft and pusy and crumbly, too soft to walk on at all. Emma thought of the worn-old tires on her father's Rambler (it was a miracle that the car still ran; it'd been

fifteen years at least since the car company even made Ramblers). The tread on the Rambler's tires was thin; you could see the threads showing through if you knew where to look. It made her shudder. She didn't want her Suzi wearing away like an old tire.

Mama Estrella was right about that, and Emma didn't want to admit it to herself. Suzi wasn't going to get any better. But Emma knew something else, too: things can last near forever if you take the right care of them. Let Mama Estrella be scared. Emma didn't care. The girl was alive, and the important part was what Emma had realized when Suzi asked: even being alive once is a miracle. Emma wasn't going to be someone who wasted miracles when they came to her.

Not even if the miracle made her hurt so bad inside that she wanted to die, like it did later on that day when she and Suzi were sitting in the living room watching TV. It was a doctor show — even while they watched it Emma wasn't quite sure which one it was — and it got her thinking about how tomorrow was Wednesday and she'd have to go back to the hospital where she cleaned patients' rooms for a living. She'd taken a leave of absence while Suzi was in the hospital, and now she realized that she didn't want to go back. She was afraid to leave Suzi alone, afraid something might happen. But what could she do? She had to work; she had to pay the rent. Even taking off as much as she had bled away her savings.

"Suzi," she said, "if anybody knocks on that door while I'm gone at work, you don't answer it. You hear?"

Suzi turned away from the TV and nodded absently. "Yes, Mommy," she said. She didn't look well, and that made Emma hurt some. Even after all those months with the cancer, Emma had never got to be easy or comfortable with the idea of Suzi being sick.

65

"Come over here and give me a hug, Suzi."

Suzi got out of her seat, climbed onto Emma's lap, and put her arms around her. She buried her face in her mother's breast and hugged, hard, too hard, really. She was much stronger than Emma'd realized; stronger than she'd been before she got sick. The hug was like a full-grown man being too rough, or stronger, maybe.

Emma patted her on the back. "Be gentle, honey," she said, "you're hurting me."

Suzi eased away. "Sorry, Mommy," she said. She looked down, as though she was embarrassed, or maybe even a little bit ashamed. Emma looked in the same direction reflexively, too, to see what Suzi was looking at.

Which wasn't anything at all, of course. But when Emma looked down what she saw was the thing in Suzi's belly, the tumor. It had grown, again: it looked noticably bigger than it had this morning. Emma touched it with her left hand, and she felt a strange, electric thrill.

She wondered what was happening inside Suzi's body. She wanted to believe that it was something like trapped gas, or even that she was only imagining it was larger.

She probed it with her fingers.

"Does this hurt, Suzi?" she asked. "Does it feel kind of strange?"

"No, Mommy, it doesn't feel like anything at all any more."

The thing was hard, solid, and strangely lumpy. When she touched it on a hollow spot near the top, it started to throb.

Emma snatched her hand away, afraid that she'd somehow woken up something horrible. But it was too late; something *was* wrong. The thing pulsed faster and faster. After a moment the quivering became almost violent. It reminded Emma of an epileptic at the hospital who'd had a seizure while she

66

was cleaning his room.

"Suzi, are you okay?" Emma asked. Suzi's mouth moved, but no sound came out. Her chest and abdomen started heaving, and choking sounds came from her throat.

The first little bit of Suzi's upchuck just dribbled out around the corners of her mouth. Then she heaved again, more explosively, and the mass of it caught Emma square on the throat. Two big wads of decayed egg spattered on her face, and suddenly Suzi was vomiting out everything Emma had fed her for breakfast. Emma recognized the eggs and toast; they hadn't changed much. They were hardly even wet. The only thing that seemed changed at all about them, in fact, was the smell. They smelled horrible, worse than horrible. Like dead people fermenting in the bottom of a septic tank for years.

"Mommy," Suzi said. It almost sounded like she was pleading. Then she heaved again. But there wasn't much for her stomach to expel, just some chewed egg and bread colored with bile and drippy with phlegm. Suzi bent over the rug and coughed it out. "Mommy," she said again, "I think maybe I shouldn't eat anymore."

Emma nodded and lifted her daughter in her arms. She carried her to the bathroom, where she washed them both off.

And Emma *didn't* make Suzi eat again, except that she gave the girl a glass of water a couple of times when she seemed to feel dry. It didn't seem to do her any harm not to eat. She never got hungry. Not even once.

Emma went back to work, and that went well enough.

For two months — through the end of May, all of June, and most of July — Emma and Suzi lived quietly and happily, in spite of the circumstances.

After a day or two Emma really did get used to Suzi looking and smelling like she was a dead thing. It was kind of wonderful, in a way: Suzi wasn't suffering at all, and the cancer was gone. Or at least it wasn't killing her anymore. She wasn't hurting in any way Emma could see, anyway. Maybe she was uncomfortable sometimes, but it wasn't giving her pain.

The summer turned out to be as hot and rainy and humid as Emma could have imagined, and because it was so warm and wet Suzi's body decayed even faster than Emma had feared it would. After a while the smell of it got hard to ignore again. The evil thing in her belly, the cancer, kept growing, too. By the end of July it was almost the size of a football, and Suzi really did look like a miniature pregnant lady come to term.

It was the last Friday in July when Emma noticed that Suzi's skin was beginning to crack away. She'd just finished getting into her uniform, and she went in to give Suzi a kiss good-bye before she left for work. Suzi smiled and Emma bent over and gave her a peck on the cheek. Her skin felt cold and squishy-moist on Emma's lips, and it left a flavor on them almost like cured meat. Emma was used to that. It didn't bother her so much.

She stood up to take one last look at Suzi before she headed off, and that's when she noticed the crow's feet. That's what they looked like. Crow's feet: the little wrinkle lines that older people get in the corners of their eyes.

But Suzi's weren't wrinkles at all. Emma looked close at them and saw that the skin and flesh at the corners of her eyes was actually cracked and split away from itself. When she looked hard she thought she could see the bone underneath.

She put her arms around Suzi and lifted her up a little. "Oh, baby," she said. She wanted to cry. She'd known

this was coming — it had to. Emma knew about decay. She knew why people tanned leather. The problem was she couldn't just take her little girl to a tannery and get her preserved, even if she was dead.

If Suzi's flesh was beginning to peel away from her bones, then the end had to be starting. Emma'd hoped that Suzi would last longer than this. There was a miracle coming. Emma was sure of that. Or she thought she was. Why would God let her daughter be alive again if she was going to rot away to nothing? Emma wasn't somebody who went to church every Sunday. Even this summer, when church seemed more important than it usually did, Emma'd only been to services a couple of times. But she believed in God. She had faith. And that was what was important, if you asked her.

Someone knocked on the outer door of the apartment.

That shouldn't be, Emma thought. The only way into the building was through the front door downstairs, and that was always locked. Maybe it was someone who lived in the building, or maybe Mama Estrella, who owned the building and had the keys.

Whoever it was knocked again, and harder this time. Hard enough that Emma heard the door shake in its frame. She could just picture bubbles of caked paint on the door threatening to flake off. She set Suzi down and hurried to answer it.

When she got to the door, she hesitated. "Who's there?" she asked.

No one answered for a long moment, and then a man with a harsh voice said, "Police, ma'am. We need to speak to you."

Emma swallowed nervously. The police had always frightened her, ever since she was a child. Not that she had anything to be afraid of. She hadn't done anything wrong.

She opened the door about half way

and looked at them. They were both tall, and one of them was white. The other one was East Indian, or maybe Hispanic, and he didn't look friendly at all.

Emma swallowed again. "How can I help you?" she asked, trying not to sound nervous. It didn't help much; she could hear the tremor in her voice.

"We've had complaints from your neighbors about a smell coming from your apartment," the dark-skinned one said. He didn't have an accent, and he didn't sound anywhere near as mean as he looked.

"Smell?" Emma asked. She said it before she even thought about it, and as soon as she did she knew it was the wrong thing to do. But she really had forgotten about it. Sure, it was pretty bad, but the only time she really noticed it was when she first got home from work in the evening.

"Lady, it smells like something died in there," the white one said. He was the one with the harsh voice. "Do you mind if we step in and take a look around?"

Emma felt as though all her blood drained away at once. For a moment she couldn't speak.

That was a bad thing, too, because it made the policemen even more suspicious. "We don't have a search warrant, ma'am," the dark one said, "but we can get one in twenty minutes if we have to. It's better if you let us see."

"No," Emma said. "No, I'm sorry, I didn't understand. I'll show you my daughter."

She let the door fall open the rest of the way and led the policemen to Suzi's bedroom. Just before she got there she paused and turned to speak to the dark-skinned man. "Be quiet. She may have fallen back asleep."

But Suzi wasn't asleep, she was sitting up in bed in her nightgown, staring out her open window into the sunshine. For the first time in a month Emma

looked at her daughter with a fresh eye, *saw* her instead of just noting the little changes that came from day to day. She didn't look good at all. Her dark skin had a blue-yellow cast to it, a lot like the color of a deep bruise. And there was a texture about it that was *wrong*; it was wrinkled and saggy in some places and smooth and pasty in others.

"She has a horrible disease," Emma whispered to the policemen. "I've been nursing her at home myself these last few months." Suzi turned and looked at them. "These two policemen wanted to meet you, Suzi," Emma said. She read their badges quickly. "This is Officer Gutierrez and his partner, Officer Smith."

Suzi nodded and smiled. It didn't look very pretty. She said, "Hello. Is something wrong?" Her voice was scratchy and vague and hard to understand. "On TV the policemen are usually there because something's wrong."

The dark-skinned policeman, Gutierrez, answered her. "No, Suzi, nothing's wrong. We just came by to meet you." He smiled grimly, as though it hurt, and turned to Emma. "Thank you, ma'am. I think we should be on our way now." Emma pursed her lips and nodded, and showed them to the door.

Before she went to work she came back to say good-bye to Suzi again. She walked back into the hot, sunny room, kissed her daughter on the cheek, and gave her hand a little squeeze.

When Emma took her hand away she saw that three of Suzi's fingernails had come off in her palm.

Suzi wasn't in her bedroom that night when Emma got home. Emma thought at first that the girl might be in the living room, watching TV.

She wasn't. She couldn't have been: Emma would have heard the sound from it if she was.

Emma looked everywhere — the dining room (it was more of an alcove, really), the kitchen, even Emma's own bedroom. Suzi wasn't in any of them. After a few minutes Emma began to panic; she went back to Suzi's room and looked out the window. Had the girl gone crazy, maybe, and jumped out of it? There wasn't any sign of her on the sidewalk down below. Suzi wasn't in any shape to make a jump like that and walk away from it. At least not without leaving something behind.

Then Emma heard a noise come from Suzi's closet. She turned to see it, expecting God knew what, and she heard Suzi's voice: "Mommy . . . ? Is that you, Mommy?" The closet door swung open and Suzi's face peeked out between the clothes.

"Suzi? What are you doing in that closet, child? Get yourself out of there! You almost scared me to death — I almost thought someone had stolen you away."

"I had to hide, Mommy. A bunch of people came into the house while you were gone. I think they were looking for me. They even looked in here, but not careful enough to see me in the corner behind all the coats."

Emma felt her blood pressing hard against her cheeks and around the sockets of her eyes. "Who? Who was here?"

"I didn't know most of them, Mommy. Mama Estrella was with them. She opened up the door with her key and let them in."

Emma fumed; she clenched her teeth and hissed a sigh out between them. She reached into the closet and grabbed Suzi's hand. "You come with me. We're going to get some new locks for this place and keep *all* those people out. And then I'm going to have words with that witch."

Emma's arm jarred loose a double handful of hangers that didn't have clothes on them, and hangers went flying everywhere. Seven or eight of them hooked into each other almost like a chain, and one end of the chain latched into the breast pocket of Suzi's old canvas army jacket, which hung from a sturdy wooden hanger.

The chain's other end got stuck on the nightgown Suzi was wearing. It caught hold just below her belly. Emma wasn't paying any attention; she was too angry to even think, much less notice details. When Suzi seemed to hesitate Emma pulled on her arm to yank her out of the closet.

The hanger hook ripped through Suzi's nightgown and dug into the soft, crumbly-rotten skin just below her belly. As Emma yanked on Suzi's arm, the hanger ripped open Suzi's gut.

Suzi looked down and saw her insides hanging loose, and she screamed. At first Emma wasn't even sure it was a scream; it was a screechy, cracky sound that went silent three times in the middle when the girl's vocal cords just stopped working.

Emma tried not to look at what the hanger had done, but she couldn't stop herself. She had to look.

"Jesus, Jesus, O Sweet Jesus," she whispered.

A four-inch flap of skin was caught in the hanger. Suzi twisted to get away from the thing, and the rip got bigger and bigger.

Emma said, "Be still." She bit her lower lip and knelt down to work the hanger loose.

There was no way to do it without looking into Suzi's insides. Emma gagged in spite of herself; her hands trembled as she lifted them to the hanger. Up close the smell of putrid flesh was unbearable. She thought for a moment that she'd lose her self-control, but she managed not to. She held herself as careful and steady as she could and kept her eyes on what she had to do.

Suzi's intestines looked like sausage casings left to sit in the sun for a week. Her stomach was shriveled and cracked and dry. There were other organs Emma didn't recognize. All of them were rotting away. Some of them even looked crumbly. An insect scrambled through a nest of pulpy veins and squirmed underneath the tumor.

Emma had tried to avoid looking at that. She'd had nightmares about it these last few weeks. In her dreams it pulsed and throbbed, and sometimes it sang to her, though there were never any words when it was singing. One night she'd dreamed she held it in her arms and sang a lullaby to it. She woke from that dream in the middle of the night, dripping with cold sweat.

Even if those were only dreams, Emma was certain that there was something *wrong* with the cancer, something unnatural and dangerous, maybe even evil.

It was enormous now, a great mottled-grey leathery mass the size of Emma's skull. Blue veins the size of fingers protruded from it. Emma wanted to sob, but she held herself still. Gently, carefully as she could, she took the loose skin in one hand and the hanger in the other and began to work Suzi free. Three times while she was working at it her hand brushed against the cancer, and each time it was like an electric prod had found its way into the base of her own stomach.

She kept the tremor in her hands pretty well under control, but when she was almost done her left hand twitched and tore Suzi open enough for Emma to see a couple of her ribs and a hint of her right lung underneath them.

She set the hanger down and let out the sob she'd been holding back. Her arms and legs and neck felt weak; she wanted to lie down right there on the floor and never move again. But she couldn't. There wasn't time. She had to *do* something — she knew, she just *knew* that Suzi was going to crumble away in her arms if she didn't do something soon.

But again: what *could* she do? Get out a needle and thread and sew her back together? That wouldn't work. If a coat hanger could tear Suzi's skin, then it was too weak to hold a stitch. What about glue? Or tape, maybe — Emma could wrap her in adhesive tape, as though she were a mummy. But that wouldn't solve anything forever, either. Sooner or later the decay would get done with Suzi, and what good would bandages do if they were only holding in dust? Sooner or later they'd slip loose around her, and Suzi would be gone in a gust of wind.

No. Emma knew about rot. Rot came from germs, and the best way to get rid of germs was with rubbing alcohol.

She had a bottle of rubbing alcohol under the bathroom cabinet. That wasn't enough. What Suzi needed was to soak in a bathtub full of it. Which meant going to the grocery to buy bottles and bottles of the stuff. Which meant either taking Suzi to the store — and she was in no condition for that — or leaving her alone in the apartment that wasn't safe from people who wanted to kill her. But Emma *had* to to something. It was an emergency. So she said, "You wait here in the closet, baby," and she kissed Suzi on the forehead. For a moment she thought she felt Suzi's skin flaking away on her lips, thought she tasted something like cured ham. The idea was too much to cope with right now. She put it out of her mind.

Even so, the flavor of preserved meat followed her all the way to the store.

The grocery store only had ten bottles of rubbing alcohol on the shelf, which wasn't as much as Emma wanted. Once she'd bought them, though, and loaded them into grocery bags, she wondered how she would have carried any more anyway. She couldn't soak Suzi in ten bottles of alcohol, but she could stop up the tub and rinse her with it, and then wash her in the runoff. That'd do the job well enough, at least. It'd have to.

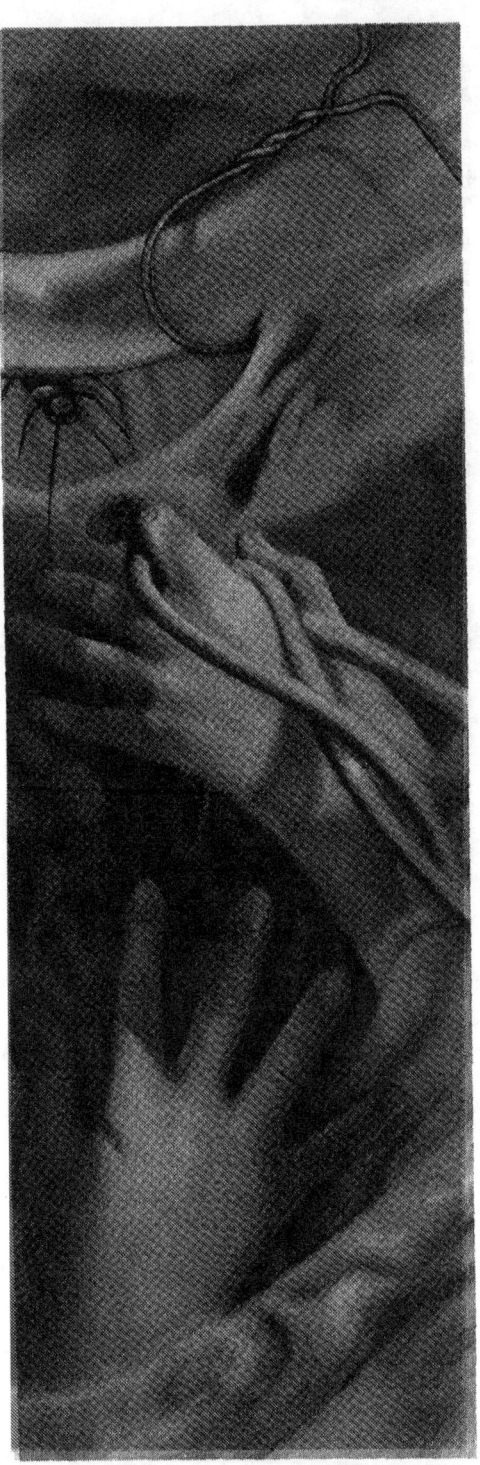

When Emma got back to the apartment Suzi was asleep in the closet. Or she looked like she was sleeping. Emma hadn't actually seen her asleep since she'd died. She spent a lot of time in bed, and a lot of time resting, but whenever Emma looked in on her she was awake.

"Suzi?" Emma said. She pulled the clothes aside and looked into the closet. Suzi was curled up in the corner of the closet with her head tucked into her chest and her hands folded over her stomach. "Suzi, are you awake, honey?"

Suzi looked up and nodded. The whites of her eyes were dull yellow. They looked too small for their sockets. "Mommy," she said, "I'm scared." She *looked* afraid, too. She looked terrified.

Emma bit into her lower lip. "I'm scared too, baby. Come on." She put up her hand to help Suzi up, but she didn't take it. She stood up on her own, and when Emma moved aside she walked out of the closet.

"What're you going to do, Mommy?"

"I'm going to give you a bath, baby, with something that'll stop what's happening to your body." Emma looked Suzi over, and the sight made her wince. "You get yourself undressed and get in the bathtub, and I'll get everything ready."

Suzi looked like she didn't really believe what Emma was saying, but she went in and started getting undressed anyway. Emma got the shopping bag with the bottles of alcohol from where she had left it by the door and took it to the bathroom. It was an enormous bathroom, as big as some people's bedrooms. The building was old enough that there hadn't been such a thing as indoor plumbing when it was built. Not for tenement buildings, anyway. Emma never understood why the people who put the plumbing in decided to turn a room as big as this one into a bathroom. When she got there Suzi had her nightgown up over her head. She finished

71

taking it off and stepped into the tub without even turning around.

Emma took the bottles out of the bag and lined them up one by one on the counter. She took the cap off each as she set it down, and tossed the cap into the waste basket.

"Put the stopper in the tub for me, would you, honey?" Emma said. She got the last bottle out of the bag, got rid of the cap, and carried it over to Suzi.

She was already sitting down inside the tub, waiting. "This may sting a little, baby. Why don't you hold out your hand and let me make sure it doesn't hurt too much."

Suzi put her hand out over the tub stopper, and Emma poured alcohol on it.

"What does that feel like?"

"It doesn't feel like anything at all, Mommy. I don't feel anything anymore."

"Not anywhere?"

"No, Mommy."

Emma shook her head, gently, almost as though she hoped Suzi wouldn't see it. She didn't like the sound of what Suzi'd said. It worried her. Not feeling anything? That was dangerous. It was wrong, and scary.

But she had to get on with what she was doing; things would only keep getting worse if she let them go.

"Close your eyes, baby. This won't be good for them even if it doesn't hurt." She held the bottle over Suzi's head and tilted it. Clear fluid streamed out of the bottle and into her hair. After a moment it began to run down her shoulders in little rivulets. One of them snaked its way into the big open wound of Suzi's belly and pooled in an indentation on the top of the cancer. For a moment Emma thought something horrible would happen, but nothing did.

Emma poured all ten bottles of alcohol onto Suzi. When she was done the girl was sitting in an inch-deep pool of the stuff, soaked with it. Emma figured

that she needed to soak in it for a while, so she told Suzi to wait there for a while, and left her there.

She went into the kitchen, put on a pot of coffee, and lit a cigarette. It'd been two months since she'd smoked. The pack was very stale, but it was better than nothing. When the coffee was ready she poured herself a cup, opened this morning's paper, and sat down to read.

She'd been reading for twenty minutes when she heard Suzi scream.

The sound made her want to curl up and die; if there was something else that could go wrong, she didn't want to know about it. She didn't want to cope with it. But there wasn't any choice — she *had* to cope. Even doing nothing was a way of coping, when you thought about it. No matter what Emma felt, no matter how she felt, she was a mother. Before she even realized what she was doing she was in the bathroom beside Suzi.

"Mommy," Suzi said, her voice so still and quiet that it gave Emma a chill, "I'm *melting*."

She held out her right hand, and Emma saw that was just exactly what was happening. Suzi's fingers looked like wet clay that someone had left sitting in warm water; they were too thin, and there was some sort of a milky fluid dripping from them.

Oh my God, a little voice inside Emma's head whispered. *OhmiGod-OhmiGod.* She didn't understand. What was happening? Alcohol didn't make people dissolve. Was Suzi's flesh so rotten that just getting it wet would make it slide away like mud?

She thought she was going to start screaming herself. She managed not to. In fact, it was almost as though she didn't feel anything at all, just numb and weak and all cold inside. As if her soul had oozed away, or died. Her legs went all rubbery, and she felt her jaw go slack. She thought she was going to faint, but she wasn't sure; she'd never fainted before.

Suzi looked up at her, and her shrunken little eyes were suddenly hard and mean and angry. She screamed again, and this time it sounded like rage, not fear. She stood up in the tub. Drippy slime drizzled down from her butt and thighs. *"Mommy,"* she screamed, and she launched herself at Emma. "Stupid, stupid, *stupid* Mommy!" She raised her fist up over her head and hit Emma square on the breast, and *hard*. Harder than Suzi's father'd ever hit her, back when he was still around. Suzi brought her other fist down, just as hard, then pulled them back and hit her again, and again, and again. Emma couldn't even move herself out of Suzi's way. She didn't have the spirit for it.

For a moment it didn't even look like Suzi beating on her. It looked like some sort of a monster, a dead zombie-thing that any moment would reach into her chest, right through her flesh, and rip out her heart. And it would eat her bloody-dripping heart while it was still alive and beating, and Emma's eyes would close, and she'd die.

"All your *stupid* fault, Mommy! All your *stupid, stupid* fault!" She grabbed Emma by the belt of her uniform skirt and shook her and shook her. Then she screamed and pushed Emma away, threw her against the wall. Emma's head and back hit too hard against the rock-thick plaster wall, and she fell to the floor. She lay on her side, all slack and beaten, and stared at her daughter, watching her to see what she'd do next.

Suzi stared at her for three long beats like a fury from Hell, and for a moment Emma thought she really was going to die. But then something happened on Suzi's face, like she'd suddenly realized what she was doing, and her legs fell out from under her and she started crying. It sounded like crying, anyway, and Emma thought there were tears, but it was hard to tell because of the drippy slime all over her.

Emma crawled over to her and put her arms around her and held her. One of her hands brushed up against the open cancer in Suzi's belly and again there was an electric throb, and she almost flinched away. She managed to stop herself, though, and moved her hand without making it seem like an overreaction. "It's okay, baby. Mommy loves you." Suzi's little body heaved with her sobs, and when her back pressed against Emma's breasts it made the bruises hurt. "Mommy loves you."

Emma looked at Suzi's hands, and saw that the flesh had all crumbled away from them. They were nothing but bones, like the skeleton one of the doctors at the hospital kept in his office.

"I want to die, Mommy." Her voice was all quiet again.

Emma squeezed her, and held her a little tighter. *I want to die, Mommy.* It made her hurt a little inside, but she knew Suzi was right. Mama Estrella was right. It was wrong for a little girl to be alive after she was dead. Whether faith was right or not, it was wrong to stake a little girl's soul on it.

"Baby, baby, baby, baby, I love my baby," Emma cooed. Suzi was crying even harder now, and she'd begun to tremble in a way that wasn't natural at all.

"You wait here, baby. I got to call Mama Estrella." Emma lifted herself up off the floor, which made everything hurt all at once.

Emma went to the kitchen, lifted the telephone receiver, and dialed Mama's number. While the phone rang she wandered back toward the bathroom. The cord was long enough that it didn't have any trouble stretching that far. Even if it hadn't really been long enough, though, Emma probably would have tried to make it reach; she wanted to look at Suzi, to watch her, to save as much memory of her as she could.

The girl lay on the bathroom floor,

shaking. The tremor had gotten worse, much worse, in just the time it'd taken Emma to dial the phone. It seemed to *get* worse, too, while Emma watched.

Mama Estrella finally answered the phone.

"Hello?"

"Mama?" Emma said, "I think maybe you better come up here."

Mama Estrella didn't say anything at all; the line was completely silent. The silence felt bitter and mean to Emma.

"I think maybe you were right, Mama. Right about Suzi, I mean." Emma looked down at the floor and squeezed her eyes shut. She leaned back against the wall and tried to clear her head. "I think . . . maybe you better hurry. Something's very wrong, something I don't understand."

Suzi made a little sound halfway between a gasp and a scream, and something went *thunk* on the floor. Emma didn't have the heart to look up to see what had happened, but she started back toward the kitchen to hang up the phone.

"Mama, I got to go. Come here *now,* please?"

"Emma . . ." Mama Estrella started to say, but Emma didn't hear her; she'd already hung up, and she was running back to the bathroom, where Suzi was.

Suzi was shivering and writhing on the bathroom floor. Her left arm, from the elbow down, lay on the floor not far from her. Was her flesh that corrupt? God in heaven, was the girl going to shake herself to shreds because of some kind of a nervous fit? Emma didn't want to believe it, but she couldn't ignore what she was seeing. She took Suzi in her arms and lifted her up off the floor.

"You've got to be still, honey," Emma said. "You're going to tremble yourself to death."

Suzi nodded and gritted her teeth and for a moment she was pretty still. But

it wasn't anything she could control, not for long. Emma carried Suzi to her bedroom, and by the time she got there the girl was shaking just as bad as she had been.

There was a knock on the front door, but Emma didn't pay any attention. If it was Mama she had her own key, and she'd use it. Emma sat down on the bed beside Suzi and stroked her hair.

After a moment Mama showed up in the bedroom doorway, carrying some kind of a woody-looking thing that burned with a real low flame and smoked something awful. It made so much smoke that Emma figured that it'd take maybe two or three minutes for it to make the the air in the room impossible to breathe.

Mama Estrella went to the window and closed it, then drew down the shade.

"Water," she said. "Bring me a kettle of hot water."

"You want me to boil water?" There was smoke everywhere already; it was harsh and acrid and when a wisp of it caught in Emma's eye it burned her like something caustic. A cloud of it drifted down toward Suzi, and she started wheezing and coughing. That frightened Emma; she hadn't even heard the girl draw a breath, except to speak, in all the weeks since she'd died.

"No, there isn't time. Just bring a kettle of hot water from the tap."

Then Mama Estrella bent down to look at Suzi, and suddenly it was too late for hot water and magic and putting little girls to rest.

The thick smoke from the burning thing settled onto Suzi's face, and Suzi began to gag. She took in a long wheezing-hacking breath, and for three long moments she choked on it, or maybe on the corruption of her own lungs. Then she began to cough, deep, throbbing, hacking coughs that shook her hard against the bed.

Mama Estrella pulled away from the

bed. She looked shocked and frightened and unsure.

"Suzi, be *still!*" Emma shouted. It didn't do any good.

Suzi sat up, trying to control herself. That only made things worse — the next cough sent her flying face-first onto the floor. She made an awful smacking sound when she hit; when she rolled over Emma saw that she'd broken her nose.

Suzi wheezed, sucking in air.

She's breathing, Emma thought. *Please, God, she's breathing now and she's going to be fine. Please.*

But even as Emma thought it she knew that it wasn't going to be so. The girl managed four wheezing breaths, and then she was coughing again, and much worse — Emma saw bits of the meat of her daughter's lungs spatter on the hardwood floor.

She bent down and hugged Suzi, hugged her tight to make her still. "Be still, baby. Hold your breath for a moment and be still. Mommy loves you, Suzi." But Suzi didn't stop, she couldn't stop, and the force of her wracking was so mean that her shoulders dug new bruises in Emma's breast. When Suzi finally managed to still herself for a moment she looked up at Emma, her eyes full of desperation, and she said, *"Mommy . . ."*

And then she coughed again, so hard that her tiny body pounded into Emma's breast, and her small, hard-boned chin slammed down onto Emma's shoulder.

Slammed down so hard that the force of it tore free the flesh of Suzi's neck.

And Suzi's head tumbled down Emma's back, and rolled across the floor.

Emma turned her head and watched it happen, and the sight filled her nightmares for the rest of her life. The tear began at the back of Suzi's neck, where the bone of her skull met her spine. The skin there broke loose all at once, as though it had snapped, and the

meat inside pulled away from itself in long loose strings. The cartilage of Suzi's spine popped loose like an empty hose, and the veins and pipes in the front of her neck pulled away from her head like they weren't even attached anymore.

Her head rolled over and over until it came to a stop against the leg of a chair. Suzi's eyes blinked three times and then they closed forever.

Her body shook and clutched against Emma's chest for a few more seconds, the way Emma always heard a chicken's does when you take an axe to its neck. When the spasming got to be too much to bear Emma let go, and watched her daughter's corpse shake itself to shreds on the bedroom floor. After a while the tumor-thing fell out of it, and everything was still.

Everything but the cancer. It quivered like grey, moldy-rotten pudding that you touched on a back shelf in the refrigerator because you'd forgotten it was there.

"Oh my God," Mama Estrella said.

Emma felt scared and confused, and empty, too, like something important had torn out of her and there was nothing left inside but dead air.

But even if Emma was hollow inside, she couldn't force her eye away from the cancer. Maybe it was morbid fascination, and maybe it was something else completely, but she knelt down and looked at it, watched it from so close she could almost taste it. There was something about it, something wrong. Even more wrong than it had been before.

"She's dead, Emma. She's dead forever."

Emma shuddered, but still she couldn't force herself away. The tumor began to still, but one of its ropy grey veins still pulsed. She reached down and touched it, and the whole grey mass began to throb again.

"What is it, Mama Estrella? Is i[t] alive?"

"I don't know, Emma. I don't know what it is, but it's dead."

Then the spongy grey tissue at th[e] tumor's crest began to swell and bulge[,] to bulge so far that it stretched thin an[d] finally split.

"Like an egg, Mama," Emma said[.] "It almost looks like an egg when [a] chick is hatching. I've seen that on th[e] television, and it looks just like this."

Emma reached over toward the split[,] carefully, carefully, imagining som[e] horrible monster would reach up out o[f] the thing and tear her hand from he[r] wrist. But there was no monster, onl[y] hard, leathery hide. She set the finger[s] of her other hand against the far lip o[f] the opening and pried the split wide s[o] that she could peek into it. But her hea[d] blocked what little light she could le[t] in.

Small gurgling sounds came out o[f] the darkness.

Emma crossed herself and mumble[d] a prayer too quiet for anyone else t[o] hear.

And reached down, into her daugh[-] ter's cancer.

Before her hand was half way in, sh[e] felt the touch of a tiny hand. It startle[d] her so badly that she almost screamed[.] To hold it back she bit into her lip s[o] hard that she tasted her own blood.

A baby's hand.

Then a baby girl was crawling ou[t] of the leathery grey shell, and Mam[a] Estrella was praying out loud, an[d] Emma felt herself crying with joy.

"I love you, Mommy," the baby said[.] Its voice was Suzi's voice, just as it'[d] been before her sickness.

Emma wanted to cry and cry and cry[,] but instead she lifted her baby Suzi ou[t] of the cancer that'd borne her, and sh[e] held her to her breast and loved her s[o] hard that the moment felt like foreve[r] and ever. ☐

Take a walk with us.

There are nightmare worlds, worlds of exploded suns, worlds of magic, and worlds forgotten by time. There are worlds without end, and we visit them all. Join us.

THE FOOL

by Ronald Anthony Cross

THE TAVERN: I.

As usual, the streets of Babylon were teeming with exotic strangers; one caught glimpses of Amorites, Scythians, a few Persians held in the lantern light, here and then gone.

It seemed to the man called Tusci, or Ferret, or Monkey, that the citizenry of Babylon was composed of the world's most diverse mixture of races, held together only by a common all-consuming nervous drive. All day long they worked like insects, gathering, storing, scheming for material gain. Yet they seemed to be driven to party all night long by the same mysterious force which caused them to work so hard.

Even their bodies reminded Tusci of insects. Beetles, perhaps: short, thick, muscular, yet stiff and awkward. He was such a novelty here partly because of his slender build and natural limber grace: he was part-time bodyguard to a rich merchant and part-time entertainer and errand boy. And the bodyguard part had turned out to be more for show than for action. Tusci, having achieved dazzling fame for ridding Babylon of a notorious thief, was sought after by all the rich merchants merely to warn other would-be thieves away from their houses. Since not many burglars would dare to attack the well-guarded houses of the wealthier citizens anyway, Tusci's job was mainly just to make a few public appearances as a reminder.

To say he was growing bored with life in Babylon would be an absurd understatement. Still, it was easy to fall into a pattern in Babylon: everything did.

Babylon was a land of patterns, of shadows on whitewashed walls, of distant music, of lacy dreams, a myriad of tiny nervous gestures: a beehive of activity and collapse, mathematics and drunkenness, lust and hate — he was caught up in it like a dry leaf in a strong burst of spring wind.

It was such an easy job, such good money, and Babylon offered so many interesting ways to spend it. For the first time in his life, Tusci found himself drinking too much. Night after night.

And here he was again, on another warm Babylon night, wandering with the crowd from tavern to tavern.

What was this, just up ahead of him? A tall northerner with long blond hair and huge muscles was swaggering through the crowd, shoulders above everyone in it. *Swaggering or staggering?* Tusci wondered. And yes, you could certainly tell that the fellow had had a few to drink. Curious, Tusci picked up his pace and moved closer.

Now he was right behind the man, apparently a youth, still supple, yet fully grown. At least! *A fighting man,* Tusci thought. Perhaps a bodyguard like himself, or a mercenary soldier out of work.

Just as Tusci was thinking these things, he noticed peripherally, a hand dart out of the crowd to snare the fat money pouch the big fool had tied to his belt.

Stay out of it, Tusci was thinking,

78

mind your own business. Which would soon have been followed by, *There is trouble enough for you without seeking more,* had his thinking continued.

But even as he started thinking this way, his body, as if of its own accord, acted in the lightning-fast way that had earned him the nickname of Ferret, and before he even registered that he had done anything, his dagger was out and speared through the hand.

The purse dropped, Tusci pulled back his dagger, the thief screamed, turned to run, and the barbarian shouted, "Stop him."

I should let him go, Tusci started to think, but already had spun the dagger, which he now caught by the blade and threw just as the thief darted back into the crowd.

Tusci did not miss.

"Great throw," the young barbarian shouted, and now for the first time Tusci saw his face; he already had his purse back in his hand.

"Why?" Tusci said.

The youth looked confused: "Why what?"

"Why stop him?"

"Why, just on principle, of course."

"I killed him," Tusci said, in an irritated voice.

"Served him right," the youth answered, "for attempting to rob Arkand the Awesome." He held out his huge hand. "But I forget my manners. Allow me to introduce myself."

"Yes, yes, I know," Tusci said, trying to extract his hand from the giant's grip, "Arkand the Awesome."

"But how did you know?" The youth looked genuinely puzzled.

"You just told me, you great fool," Tusci, who was never one to mince words, said.

"What!" the giant roared, "No one can speak to me like that and live. Draw your sword!" He staggered a few steps back and jerked out his blade.

The crowd of curious onlookers now erupted with screams and shouts and stampeded away in all directions like the ripples from a stone dropped in a pool of water. A couple of trampled people lay on the dirt street to keep the poor dead thief company.

"I'm not wearing a sword," Tusci said.

"What? That's no excuse," the man sputtered in rage. "What are those sticks? Draw those. Draw something, anything."

"No," Tusci said.

An expression somewhere between bewilderment and awe crossed the barbarian's face. "No?" he said. "No? I've never heard of such a thing. Defend yourself like a man."

"I've just killed one man for you, you fool. I'm not about to kill two, even if one of them is your worthless self."

"By all the gods," the youth stammered, then said: "Please."

"No," Tusci said. "No, no, and then no."

He turned and walked back the other way. Instantly the crowd was back, pushing, moving, chattering. *Maybe I ought to thank the oaf for that,* Tusci thought; *he gave me a moment without the crowd.*

He felt the hand on his shoulder (practically engulfing his shoulder), as he knew he would.

"Listen, small fellow, I was wrong. You saved my purse. I owe you. You killed the vermin who would have robbed me. Come into this tavern with me. I must buy you a drink." He half guided and half dragged Tusci into the Tavern of the Black Bull and over to a table out of the way against the back wall, where several squat drunken little Assyrians were seated.

"Arkand the Awesome and his friend want to sit here," he informed them, giving them a threatening glare.

The fierce little men looked up, ready for a fight, but recognized Tusci and quietly got up, left the table, drinks and all.

THE FOOL

"By the gods, everyone's heard of Arkand the Awesome, even in this backward out-of-the-way city, in this backward world." He smiled, then asked, "What drinks do they serve in this crude little dive?"

Amused, Tusci said: "Order wine." Wine made from grapes was the latest imported rage in Babylon; the common drink had always been beer, and Urruzu, the merchant Tusci worked for, was making a killing at it.

By the time the jar arrived, Arkand the Awesome had almost finished introducing himself again. This time around, the introduction was embellished with a sprinkling of wonderful accomplishments and brave deeds, drowning in an ocean of melodramatic adjectives. He was starting in on descriptions of wondrous places he had seen, when Tusci managed somehow to interrupt him.

"They call me Tusci, because they think I'm an Etruscan," he said. He let them think so. He was as much an Etruscan as any race, he had lived there, been at home there. In fact, he was swept with a sudden wave of nostalgia for those warm gentle hills, those wise elegant people. How they could dance. Dancers, singers, acrobats all — and soothsayers. All of them thought themselves to be magicians who could read the past and the future in the flight of a bird, the fall of a leaf, the entrails of a victim. Tusci smiled at the memory; he did not believe in magic, but he found their belief in it charming.

"For a man who has traveled to so many wonderful places," Tusci said with a straight face, "you speak the local tongue quite well."

"I speak all languages well — it's magic," he confided in a whisper. "My mistress, Natania of the Shining Hands, has the gift of tongues and can transfer it to me at will."

Here he launched into a story about how he worked for a great sorceress who could, among other things, transfer the contents of one man's mind to her own or to the mind of another.

Tusci, unable to keep a straight face any longer, had given in to laughter, and now had to talk his way out of another fight.

"At least we can arm wrestle, can't we?" the giant said with a sad expression.

"What would be the point, you great oaf?" Tusci said. "Look at the size of your arms."

The giant looked lugubriously at his great right arm and flexed his muscle. Then he shook his head, as if to clear it, then gurgled down the last of the wine in the jar to muddle it again.

Tusci felt sorry for him. For all his great size, he was just a boy. Furthermore, the northern barbarians were boys all their lives, Tusci mused: Arkand the Awesome would be drinking too much beer and trying to pick a fight when he was eighty. If he lived to be eighty.

Tusci shivered, a sudden premonition fluttered across his consciousness like the shadow of a swiftly flying bird: here — gone. Arkand would not live to be eighty: he would not live out the night.

Tusci did not believe in magic, but . . . what he knew, he knew!

"What's the matter? You look pale — see a ghost?" It was Arkand's turn to laugh. He did.

"I need a drink," Tusci said, "you've swilled down all the wine, you great oaf."

"By the gods," Arkand shouted, drawing the attention of everyone in the place, as he did every so often, "you have such amazing nerve, for such a little man. I'll kill you yet."

"First wine," Tusci said.

Arkand laughed aloud again, shouting out his laughter to the entire room. "Right you are, first the wine.

"Hey, waitress," he shouted, and pounded the table. The serving girls, all rushing about the busy place with trays full of wine or beer in clay jars, stopped, looked at Arkand the Awesome with disgusted expressions, then, noses in the air, deliberately ignored him.

"These small-town fools have no manners at all," he confided to Tusci.

Now he fumbled around with his money pouch, and dumped out some coins on the table. A large red jewel of some sort, no — actually purple — fell out along with the coins. Arkand elaborately held his finger to his lips and admonished the stone. "Shh," he said to it, and then scooped it back into his leather pouch.

"What sort of stone is that?" Tusci said; he was no expert on jewels, but the stone was like no other he had seen. Bigger. Brighter.

"Shh," Arkand repeated, this time to Tusci. Then suddenly, obviously overcome with one of those sudden bursts of emotion which are common to those who overindulge in alcohol, he reached his enormous arm across the table and grabbed Tusci's shoulder, pinching it affectionately until it ached, and said, "But I forget myself, it was you who saved my purse, and thus the stone, and thus my life. My mistress Natania is a just mistress, but not, alas, a forgiving one — the bitch," he grumbled under his breath. "Had I purchased the stone and paid for it with her money — a fortune, I might add — and then returned without it . . .

"But you saved me. By all the gods, what a man — you saved me, asking nothing for yourself. I would trust you with my very life." Now his eyes were brimming with tears. "What can I do for you? Anything, just name it."

"Please let go of my shoulder," Tusci said. "More wine?"

"But, of course. The serving girls are ignoring me for some reason, I'll have to go get it for myself." And Arkand got up and staggered off in the general direction of the bar. *The fool,* Tusci thought, with a stab of irritation. After all that, the drunken barbarian had left his purse, with the jewel in it, lying on the table.

It was now that the three men whom Tusci had noticed watching them got up from their table and approached Tusci. As the tall one, whom Tusci had immediately singled out as the leader, drew near, Tusci experienced a strange feeling, a nervous twinge. He could not put his finger on it.

But it was this: At a distance, in the dim lamplit bar, the man did not look too out of place. But the closer he got to you, the stranger his appearance was.

In the first place, he was obviously not from the East. He had very pale skin, but long thick curly chestnut brown hair and beard. Furthermore, he was the first man Tusci had ever seen who shaped his beard by shaving the cheeks and leaving the part that grew around the chin, as well as the moustache. He wore two long feathers of some exotic bird in his hair. And his clothes were made of some light, shiny, brightly colored fabric Tusci had never seen before. Around his neck on a leather thong he wore what appeared to be a slender light blue piece of tubing made of some kind of unidentifiable metal. *Weapon or decoration?* Tusci wondered.

"May we?" he said in the local dialect, and without waiting for an answer the three men pulled up uncomfortable wooden stools and sat down.

"Now, let's not waste time," the man said in his cold precise voice. "I've no quarrel with you, nor you with me. I'm going to take the purse." He nodded toward Arkand's leather pouch in the center of the table, but his cold blue eyes never left Tusci.

Tusci's expression was amused.

"I have no quarrel with you," the man repeated, "but I will kill you if you try to stop me. What do you say?"

Still smiling, Tusci said nothing.

"All right," the man said, and reached to his sword, "let me show you this."

There was a light whispering noise, and quite suddenly Tusci, still seated, and still smiling, held two short wooden sticks in his hands.

The tall man's companions flinched and jerked back, particularly the heavy one, who almost fell off his stool, but the tall man continued his motion of slowly taking out his sword.

"Here," he said, "go ahead, you pick it up for a moment. Examine it."

He laid the sword carefully down on the table, and Tusci, never moving his eyes from the stranger, set down one of his sticks and picked up the sword. He gasped aloud; it was light as a feather.

"Do you see?" the tall man said. "You know weapons; I know you are a warrior, you are famous here. You know that that sword is not from this world."

"Cutting edge?" Tusci said, still stunned.

"It will cut through your heaviest swords and armor and still never dull. You see? So let's have no misunderstandings. I want no quarrel with you. But let me point out the facts. You aren't carrying a sword. You threw away your dagger into the back of that thief, who, by the way, was one of my men, and all you have left is your double sticks, an awkward weapon at best. These two men on either side of you, however, have weapons the like of which you have never seen before. Nor will again. We want nothing from you. Just don't interfere."

Tusci said nothing.

"Now I'll tell you what I'm going to do. I'm going over to that bar," he gestured over to the crude long wooden counter where the drunk Arkand was now loudly engaged in arm wrestling with some other bruiser. "And I'm going to kill Arkand. As soon as I do that, Tirar here" — he gestured to the taller of the two companions — "will put down this purse" — he held out a leather pouch of his own and shook it — "which by the way is full of coins; then he will pick up Arkand's purse, while Ghorl" — he nodded toward his shorter heavier friend — "watches you. Just in case. But we want no trouble. Then these two will stand up, back away from your table, and meet me in the center of the room. And we will leave you here, and leave your world, and never trouble you again. Fair enough?"

Tusci said nothing.

The tall man nodded, and stood up and stretched like a cat. Then he picked up his sword from the table where Tusci had set it down, and sheathed it again. Then he casually wandered over to the bar.

The chunky muscleman called Ghorl slowly took out his sword and set it down on the table in front of him, but kept hold of it with his right hand. He smiled a nasty smile, showing huge yellow teeth. "Don't. Make. Me," he said.

Tusci said nothing.

Now an argument broke out at the bar. Tusci could hear Arkand shout out, "By all the gods, you dare to call me a thief?"

Ghorl's smile grew even wider, and he leaned closer to Tusci.

Tusci heard a shout. And the loud clash of some kind of metal unlike any he had ever heard before. Then a sound he had heard too many times to mistake. He glanced away from Ghorl to the bar, where the tall man stood in a strange position, legs bent but body erect, sword thrust straight out under Arkand's, and almost up to the hilt in the barbarian's stomach.

For a moment the two men were frozen there, then in a quick, almost contemptuous gesture, the tall man jerked out his sword, stood back up straight. The barbarian groaned, a low grinding sound, and grabbed hold of the counter, then toppled over backwards and hit the floor.

Tusci looked back into the eyes of Ghorl, who was still smiling. "Don't," he said between clenched yellow teeth.

Tusci said nothing.

"Thieves get what thieves deserve," the tall man was saying, in a loud voice. "I told you this fool stole my purse. Then when I confronted him, he attacked me. I had to defend myself."

"I'm putting down the purse with the coins in it," the man called Tirar was saying. "Now I'm picking up the other purse."

And still Tusci said nothing, and in fact, in one way he heard and saw everything that was happening in the rowdy little lamplit bar, and in another way he was sinking into a strange kind of calm silence, a stillness, which included everything happening, all the noises, and fighting and movement, and yet which never focused on any part of it, but spread out, measureless, awesome, now.

It was out of this silence that everything manifested. Now. Now, and again now.

And Tusci had been there before. Taking in everything, but registering nothing. Not knowing what he was going to do. It was like bathing in an ocean of nothing. Now. Now. Now.

Tusci burst up off his stool, ignoring the double sticks still lying on the table, and took a spare dagger from the scabbard strapped to his back, hidden under his loose shirt, so quickly that to Ghorl and Tirar it looked as if it had leaped out of nowhere, of its own accord, into Tusci's hand.

Ghorl jerked his sword up, and Tusci was gone, now moving so fast that for a moment Ghorl lost track of him and started to shout "Where?" when he realized that it had to be back under the table, and at the same time, he felt the dagger plunge into his thigh, and grunted, waving the sword and not

84

knowing what to do with it. He tried to shout "Run," to Tirar, who still stood frozen, Arkand's purse in hand. But he couldn't even do that because now the table flew up and into him, knocking him backward over his stool and crashing down on top of him and he only shouted "huh" and lost his sword, which was still spinning up there in the air if only he could, if only — but no, a slender hand plucked the sword out of the air by its handle in the middle of its spin and whipped it around in a pattern which was so swift it was impossible to follow. And then, just as he hit the floor with the heavy table smashing down onto his chest, pinning him, he saw Tirar's head, still wearing the same astonished expression, leap from his shoulders, and then he lost sight of it.

All he could see, through a haze, was the small slender figure of Tusci, the man they called the Ferret, standing up over him. Still holding the sword in his right hand, and now the purse in his left hand.

Helplessly, Ghorl tried to crawl loose from the table, but he felt so dizzy, everything was hazy. "Are you . . . ?" he said.

"You're already dead," Tusci said.

And it was true, Ghorl realized, it was true. The dagger in the thigh had found the main artery, of course it would, in Tusci's hands, and it was his life's blood Ghorl felt, flashing out of him. *How ironic,* he thought, *to die from a leg wound.* He almost smiled all the way into infinity.

Tusci was now facing the bar, where the tall man was struggling to get free from the grip of the giant thug who was the bouncer. Fat Genji, the owner of the bar, was prancing around in front of him shouting, "Hold him, don't let go, someone's got to pay for all this." A scream broke out, and the bouncer let go and sank down on his knees, holding his stomach. The hilt of a dagger jutted out from between his hands. With a nonchalant wave of his sword the tall man cut down Fat Genji out of his path and rushed toward Ferret.

Ferret held out the purse. "Come on and try to take it," he said.

The tall man stopped, just out of reach. "Give it to me," he said in his cold metallic voice.

"I don't think so," Tusci said. "Take it."

"Very well, then." The tall man held the metal tube he wore around his neck up to his lips and blew into it. It made a piping noise and something flew out of it toward Tusci. Something like a small pellet. Tusci knocked it aside effortlessly with a wave of his sword, but it exploded on impact into a cloud of blue smoke. Startled, Tusci breathed in a gasp before he could stop himself. The air tasted funny, he thought, too sweet and too light. Everything froze. And suddenly everything turned over on him. *I've just fallen down,* he reasoned, correctly.

II.

It seemed to Tusci that he had always floated around up here by the ceiling of the Tavern of the Black Bull, looking down on the interesting and peculiar melodrama being frantically acted out on the hard-packed dirt floor below him. Well, no, it was not exactly he who was floating about up here, but his essence, his center. Part of him was that body, still down there on the floor, still clutching that sword. He could move it if he tried. Like a puppet. That thought made him laugh, silently. What was going on down there? He concentrated: The tall man with the dark hair was leaning over the form on the floor — but not too close.

"Give it here," he was saying.

"Take it from me," Tusci heard the form on the floor say, but with slurred tongue. Was that his body? *My body's*

drunk, he thought, *the blue gas, now I remember: The tall man shot some sort of pellet out of that little tube he wears around his neck, and it exploded into a cloud of gas, and my body breathed it in. How funny!* His essence hovering up by the roof laughed again.

Now the tall man moved stealthily closer, and suddenly, way down below, Tusci's body rolled over and slashed at the tall man's legs, almost got one, but the tall man jumped back. He was very quick and now he rushed back in, and Tusci came up on one knee. Swords clashed. The tall man backed off again.

"Listen, just give it to me. Please. We're friends, remember? No need for us to fight. Just give it to me."

"Take it."

Tusci's essence laughed and laughed at this comic scenario. It seemed a remarkable performance thought up for his pleasure. Then, just when he was wondering how this funny act could be topped, the tall man seemed to make up his mind to finish Tusci's weakened body off.

"I've no time for this," he said, and dropped into his low fencer's pose. But the funny part was that with all his obvious natural grace and quickness, combined with years of training and mastery of the art of swordsmanship, he could not seem to figure out how to approach the figure rolling around on the floor. He approached it, in fact, rather gingerly, as if he were trying to figure out how to pick up a porcupine.

And just when Tusci's essence was certain that nothing could top this hilarious comedy duel, he observed something from his vantage point near the ceiling that was hidden from the forms below him. Something new and wonderful was being added to that charming little scene. Something absolutely mind-boggling.

Over by the bar across the room, one of the figures lying on the floor sat up, then clawed its way up the bar to a standing position. Then, covered with blood, took a strong grip on the bar.

What was this? Arkand the Awesome was not dead yet. Or rather, was refusing to be dead. *Why, this was priceless,* Tusci's essence thought, *what on earth was he doing?*

Groaning in agony, huge muscles straining and popping, the giant ripped a large portion of the wooden counter off and pressed it up overhead. Then turned, and staggered toward the other two figures in the room.

The tall man swiveled at the sound and ran to meet him, stopped and lunged.

But Arkand did not try to dodge the blade, but took it up to the hilt, and looking into the tall man's eyes, blood pouring out of his mouth, he did a strange thing. He smiled. Then he smashed the broken-off portion of counter down on the tall man's head and stood for a moment still smiling. Then he too fell.

Everyone's falling, Tusci's essence thought, *but I — I will never fall. I will float up here forever.* Then it wondered, *what is forever?* Then it thought, *What is time?* And suddenly it caught a glimpse of day night day night and the movement of time, and instantly was snapped like a ball on a string back into its body.

III.

Tusci sat up. Things cleared. He had been out, dreaming a strange dream about floating around or something, yet, somehow, he knew exactly what had happened here.

He got up and carefully checked out the tall man; he lay unconscious in a ruin of broken wood. Now, Arkand. The giant was on his side, knees scrunched up. Still alive.

Now he rolled over on his back groaning, and opened his eyes. "Take the

jewel to Natania," he said. "She will pay you well. Do it for me. The caverns at Urquash. Take my sword. It will lead you through the doorway. Do it for me."

Then his expression changed, still in agony, yet he smiled again: "I guess we won," he said simply.

"I guess we did," Tusci said.

Then the giant frowned. "It is not suitable for a warrior to shed tears," he said. And died.

"I'm not shedding tears," Tusci said aloud to the empty bar, "am I?" But he was.

And now for the first time he took in the full significance of the scene. Between them they had wrecked the bar, killed Fat Genji and his bouncer, as well as two other men. A gang of angry citizens would be coming for him at any moment and they would not be interested in hearing his story. They would be interested in hanging or stoning him. *In fact,* he thought as he traced Arkand's bloody path back to the wrecked counter, where he found, lying on the earthen floor among the blood and debris, Arkand's sword, and scooped it up, *Just what is my story? It doesn't even make any sense to me.*

On the way out of the bar he stopped before the figure of the tall man, which suddenly reared up to a sitting position and struggled but failed to raise up his sword, and fell back down, where he lay panting, head bleeding. But his eyes were open wide.

"Don't worry," Tusci said. "Enough men have died tonight."

"You'd better kill me," the man was muttering as Tusci plunged out the door of the tavern. Where, of course, a crowd of men were gathered, waiting. *Think fast,* Tusci told himself.

"Don't just stand around gawking," he shouted, "get help and be quick about it. There's a band of outlaws in there, and some of them are still alive. I'll try to hold them off till you get back."

Then he ran back inside, and giving the tall man's form a wide berth, made for the kitchen.

A few moments later and Tusci had dropped out of the kitchen window and was running through a dark alley. *Where do I go now?* he wondered, *Where on earth am I running to?*

The worst part of all was that he was famous. In this great city, at least, he would probably be recognized anywhere he went. *I wonder if the caves at Urquash really lead to another world? I'm not going to be welcome in this one for a while.* Had he not been running, still with a headache, through the dark, he could have laughed: one minute a famous hero basking in Babylon's adulation; the next minute a hunted villain whose only dream is to get out of town — no, by the gods, to get clear out of this world!

Later that night, hiding out in the garden of fruit trees at the Temple of Ishtar just before the first light of the sun began to diffuse the dark, he waited for Ina in their special meeting place, by their special tree.

It was ironic, he thought, that when he finally had found himself in serious trouble, a lowly temple prostitute was the only person he could count on.

"You came," he said with relief. And thought of all the rich merchants and high society ladies he had considered friends: he knew he could trust none of them.

"You knew I would." Ina smiled. It was the open smile of a child.

And later that morning, it was with her help that he was headed toward the Lion Gates, and out of Babylon, hidden under some hay in a big cart drawn by a donkey, and driven by a friend of hers.

But he did not see Ina drop to her knees in the sacred grove of Ishtar after he had left, and close her lovely eyes. He did not hear her say aloud, and at the same time inwardly to someone listening to her mind: "He comes, O Great One of the Shining Hands. I will miss him, but he comes to you."

THE CAVES: I.

It was amazing how easily you could get lost in the network of caverns in the hills just outside the town of Urquash. The guide had warned them all (Tusci had joined a small group of sightseers) not to wander off because it was so easy to get lost. So Tusci had. Both wandered off, and gotten lost.

Now he sat in the total dark (he had had to drop his torch when he had sneaked away from the group), holding Arkand's sword in his hand. What was he supposed to do? What was he supposed to do? *I'm insane,* he thought; *why didn't I realize it before?*

"Help," he shouted out loud, now that it was too late. It echoed and echoed and echoed, but nobody answered. *Why did I feel so certain I could find my way back just a short time ago, and what was I planning to do when I was alone?*

The sword will guide you — or the sword will show you the way, or — What exactly had Arkand said, and what had he meant by it?

"Tell me how to get out of here, can't you, little sword?" The sword did not answer. "What did that fool who owned you mean; and more important, why did this fool, who now owns you, listen to him?" The sword did not answer.

"Ah, little sword, we're all alone here in the dark, and you won't even talk to me. What a way to die. Well — might as well get on with it."

He stood up and began to edge his way forward. "Let's see, shall we starve to death slowly or shall we fall from a precipice? No, no, you make the choice, it's all the same to me."

The sword lit up, and immediately went out. In that instant, the light was so brilliant that Tusci saw the enormous cavern walls, almost up to the high ceiling, the stalagmites rushing up toward the stalactites rushing down to meet them. He was on a narrow path. Just an instant of this, then — lights out.

What does this mean? Tusci wondered. Then he stepped carefully backward the way he had come. The sword glowed back to life again. Holding it out, Tusci moved it in several directions; the light went out in all but one.

"Clear enough, little sword, we follow the light." And Tusci stepped off the path and crossed the floor of the cavern to one of the walls where the light led — up!

Holding the sword in his left hand, Tusci began to climb the wall. It was easy at first, but grew more difficult, until he began to worry he would have to try to hold the damn thing in his teeth or devise some method of using its glow without carrying it. But just as he was about to give up, he came to a hole in the wall which could not be seen from below. And the light led him through it.

II.

It seemed as though he had been wandering through these tunnels forever. Up one rocky corridor and down another. Gradually light crept in from somewhere, at first Tusci had thought it was sunlight. But as soon as his eyes accustomed themselves to it, it took on an eerie phosphorescent glow. *The caverns here are lit up of their own accord,* Tusci thought nervously, *as if they are alive.* He knew nothing of caves. And in fact, if he ever got out of here alive, would never want to know anything of them for the rest of his life.

Since he did not need the light of the sword to see by, he sheathed it, drawing it out from time to time to check if he was still on the right path.

And since there seemed to be no need

for caution, he tried to whistle as he walked along, but the weird acoustics caused the sound to be magnified, and fractured into reverberations which came back to him like someone answering. It made him nervous, and he decided to trust this instinct. So he took out his sword again and crept along, on the look-out for trouble.

III.

Pang was hungry. Pang was always hungry. And Pang was hungry for human beings. In fact, human beings were Pang's favorite food: soft, fat, slow, and easy to terrify, they gave Pang a sense of fulfillment that was unequalled by other animals: Pang loved to play with her food.

Humans, Pang thought. Sensing them up ahead, moving in their slow hesitant manner to her through the caves.

But Pang did not eat just any humans. No. No! Two humans Pang must not eat. At least not now. Pang's senses focused up ahead of her.

Sound: Clumsy humans clomp clomp clomping along, breathing too loud. Pang could even hear the scurrying of the family of mice, even their frightened breathing as they ran and hid from the clumsy humans.

Smell: Pang smelled beer, wine, perfume from contact with Ina, blood, many different kinds of blood — Pang could tell these two had recently been in a fight, could even tell how many men had been involved, everything rubbed off on everyone, every experience, and Pang could smell it all.

Sight: Pang could see well, a myriad different viewpoints all at once — sometimes confusing, but Pang could see movement quite well. And mostly did not need to use sight — an inferior sense for her.

So with these exquisite senses Pang carefully examined the two men up ahead. One to eat and one not to eat. But what to do first? Pang was still deciding this — not so much thinking as just going back and forth, back and forth, eat — not eat — eat, until she just stopped at one or the other idea, when she sensed a strange thing happening.

One of them crept up behind the other one — not too close; and as clumsily as he moved, Pang could tell he was stalking — and then blew a big puff of air. Next a big cloud of icky blue smoke appeared which made Pang back off a little even from way up there. And then one of the men fell down. Pang did not relate these facts one to the next as a human might. Pang just observed them and thought them quite strange. Not eat — eat. Mind stopped. It was time to eat!

IV.

The tall man who was sometimes called Snake leaned over the fallen body of the smaller slender man who was sometimes called Ferret — but not too close.

This time the blue dreamer blew up right in his face, Snake was thinking; *he has to be out cold. Still, better not to take chances with this one — the little demon's almost as quick as I am. I've never seen anything like it. I know, I know, I should just finish you off — but . . .*

Maybe I can spear Arkand's purse with my sword, — with a deft flick of his wrist he cut the purse loose from Tusci's belt and then speared it on the point of his sword and retrieved it. Quickly, he checked it while keeping an eye on Tusci; the jewel was there. *All right, one for you and one for me. We part even; beware lest you should cross my path again. I will show you no mercy.* But all this he said to himself, as if Tusci were listening.

Now he hurried on ahead, and soon was out of Tusci's sight, had Tusci been conscious to see him. Although his blade was glowing, he paid it no heed, for he had been through here before and would not lose his way.

Suddenly he felt a surge of elation. *So, Snake wins in the end, as always,* he thought, and would have laughed aloud, had he not been a careful man. *No, not even a chuckle,* he admonished himself. *He'll wake up soon enough; but he'll never catch me in these caves, I know the way too well. I've won, I've . . .* The tall man shouted as he saw what was coming at him from up ahead. It was not a scream of fear, and not exactly an exclamation of rage: more like an involuntary sigh of regret magnified many times by the grim understanding that this was the last mistake and it would do him no more good to be silent. *I came so close,* he thought. "Oh well," he said out loud to no one in particular, "no one lives forever," and fell into his fencing pose. *By the gods,* he thought, *I'm talking to myself now. I must be crazy. But no, I see it now: I've always been crazy!* He howled with laughter at this revelation as his death rushed to meet him.

V.

Tusci sat up, suddenly. Too suddenly. Head ached, purse gone, and he recognized the voice of the tall man laughing like a crazed maniac up ahead: the laughter bounced off the walls and echoed and echoed until it sounded like an army of madmen. Definitely the sounds of a scuffle. The laughter stopped. A shout — of pain?

Tusci was already up and running. And though Snake had thought Tusci could not catch him here, he might have thought otherwise had he seen Tusci now. And though ordinarily reason would have cautioned Tusci to look be-

89

fore he leaped, a strong intuition took over and urged him to either give up the whole game and run the other way, or to plunge right on in. Tusci plunged. It was only at the last moment that he froze up to a dead halt and forgot to breathe as the incredible image flooded his mind with terrifying visions from childhood.

VI.

"Bet you can't."
"Can too."
"Can not."
"Can too!"

Tusci, who was not called Tusci back then, or Ferret, but Mousey by the village children because he was so small for his age, felt that he could do anything. To a certain extent, this belief was shared by the village children: after all, he was only a child like them, yet he had traveled here from afar. And he was already a juggler. And he had already beaten up the biggest and meanest of them, a feat he had to accomplish over and over in each village he came to. But while they shared his almost legendary awe of himself, they nevertheless felt compelled to dare him into more and more dangerous and frightening courses of action.

So Tusci had climbed into the hut of Bragga the warrior chieftain and stolen his sacred good luck charm. Only at the last moment everything had gone wrong and Bragga had leaped up shouting "Thief!" and chased after him, slashing at the boy with his sword. He would have killed him for sure (for no boy can run as fast as a man) had not Tusci doubled back and run around Bragga's hut and then, out of breath, with Bragga running around the side of the hut, he had plunged through the doorway, with the idea that nobody would expect that.

Terrified, he heard Bragga run on by a ways, then stop. He could hear the

brute, swearing and breathing heavily. It was then that the thought struck Tusci. He would come in here. Tusci climbed up the crude highbacked chair in the corner and jumped, pushing off from the top of it, and miraculously caught hold of one of the low crossbraces which ran from wall to wall. He quite easily pulled himself up onto it, for was he not already an acrobat as well as a juggler? And he inched his way across it to where two more of these primitive rafters crossed in the center of the hut. He was able to lie down here, and pray that he'd have the good fortune that no one would look up. He held his breath and waited.

Bragga came in, cursing and mumbling to himself. And Tusci, who was then Mousey, waited breathlessly for him to leave again. But after a while it dawned on Tusci that Bragga was not just mumbling to himself. He had a woman with him. Somehow he had met a woman just outside his door, perhaps a neighbor's wife, and decided to give up the search.

So Tusci spent the night, balanced on the crude wooden rafters, staring at the ceiling of the chieftain's hut and listening to the noisy drunken love affair down below. It seemed as though they would never go to sleep. And even if they did, Tusci reasoned, his chances of getting down and out unobserved in the dark were practically nil. If he really was to escape there was only one possible way. He would have to lie still where he was until they got up and left him alone in the hut. Even at this age, his sharp wits informed him that people were unlikely to ever look up.

So he lay there all night. Forcing himself not to move around, not to make a sound, and most terrible of all, not to fall asleep. It was agony.

For eternity he stared into the dark, and gradually he could make out the ceiling made of leaves and mud.

Now the worst thing of all that Tusci

could think of came to pass. And later, even though he managed to keep awake, and keep from tumbling off the rafters, and even though they had woken up and sported again and gone out, and Tusci had managed to drop down and run away, and the aching in his back and arms and neck had gradually left him, what he remembered most of all was the spider.

A large black spider had built its web between the ceiling and Tusci, sliding down first on one narrow strand. Terrified, he watched it work throughout the early morning hours. He felt its web spreading over his face. Was it poisonous? He did not know, but somehow he was sure it was. He was too afraid to move even his hand, to brush it away.

So he watched it, and as he suffered through the agony of his sleepless painful vigil, his consciousness seemed to alter and his senses expand so that the spider and its web grew enormous, until it was his whole universe, this giant black jewel enveloping and devouring him.

Which is why when, years later, Tusci rushed through the cave and saw what he saw, he froze up again. Experienced terror again. Was a child again. Because a giant black spider the size of a house had wrapped the tall man up in its web and was crouching over him: its many hungry eyes were on Tusci.

VII.

Strangely, he had run so fast, and come so far before he froze up, that he could actually see himself reflected over and over again in shining dark metallic orbs. Was this his imagination? But it must not have been; somehow the tall man lying down there with the thing hovering over him must have caught sight of him in the creature's eyes or heard him or something, because even though Tusci was sure he was dead, he shouted out "Run, you fool." And it echoed and echoed from the walls.

Somehow it brought Tusci out of it, and he ran. Straight at it. And Pang, who was just now squatting down to give the tall man the gift of oblivion, made a high loud squeaking noise and scuttled back away from Tusci with surprising speed.

All in one move Tusci darted forward, crouched down, slashed with his blade at the tall man, and charged on toward the spider, who was backed up against the cavern wall.

For a fraction of a second, the tall man thought he was dead. He had seen the blade whistling at him, actually felt its touch. Suddenly one of his hands fell free and he understood; Tusci had slashed the webbing and freed his arms.

But his body was still wrapped up from the waist down. And where was his sword?

He twisted himself around and up to an awkward sitting position just in time to see Tusci clash with the spider.

All semblance of the civilized fencer had fled Tusci now, all ideas of strategy and conserving his energy had sped away from him down that dark tunnel of fear. And yet the fear had gone with it. Tusci was all out. His sword, still glowing, was moving so fast that it appeared to be constructing a web of light around the spider, who, the tall man observed, still seemed to be trying to get away.

But chunks of it were flying everywhere. And suddenly it gave in to the same berserker rage that had swallowed up Tusci; and, still making that ridiculous squeaking noise, it pounced on Tusci, flattening him. He writhed out; it pounced on him again.

The tall man, who could not get to his sword, had reached his belt, and managed to find something there. He popped it into the tube chained around his neck and shouted, "Don't breathe," and blew into it.

The pellet hit the spider and Pang stood up, forgetting about the form underneath her. Pang breathed the blue smoke. The terrible sweet blue smoke. Everything was confusing. *Must not kill one of them,* Pang thought. *Which one?* Standing there.

The tall man blew the second pellet. And Tusci, who was on his back, trying to hold his breath, probably didn't get but a touch of it because the tall man shot high and the cloud dissipated up and not down.

But both the spider and Tusci were out of it now; and looking up at the monster, Tusci somehow thought he was back on the rafters in the hut of Bragga looking up at the ceiling.

And Pang was thinking, *no, no, must not kill this one, must not, must not . . . what?* Then Pang saw little ones; joy welled up within her. *My little ones,* she thought, drifting in a blue cloud of smoke, just as Tusci surged up, driving the sword into her belly.

VIII.

The tall man was still dragging himself across the floor of the cave toward his sword when Tusci reached him.

"Guess what I found?" Tusci said, and held out his hand. The pouch was in it. "How careless of you to have dropped it, along with your sword. Oh well," he flipped the tall man his blade, using his own. Surprisingly enough, the tall man noticed he was smiling. In fact, he looked quite happy, somehow.

"You look none the worse for wear; I'm surprised you can walk."

"I've always recuperated fast," Tusci said. "Need help?"

But the tall man, who had already cut himself loose, stood up.

"Give me the pouch," he said.

Tusci's smile grew wider.

"Come and take it."

For a moment the tall man stood there holding out his blade. Then with a startlingly quick movement, he sheathed it. Now he buried his face in both hands and looked as if he were either going to scream or cry, Tusci couldn't tell which. He said, from between clenched teeth, "Why. Don't. You. Keep. It."

"Thanks," Tusci said. And turned to walk away. Then turned back. "Coming?" he said.

The tall man shook his head. "One pathway leads to the house of Tremmello, the master I serve. Another leads to Natania's, the Mistress of the Shining Hands." He pointed off to the right. "My name is Snake."

Tusci said: "No one's ever called me that. My name's Ferret."

Snake smiled too. "No one's ever called me that. The spider, by the way, was named Pang. Some people called her Natania's watchdog. She probably sent her here to protect Arkand when he returned with the stone. Ah well. Can't win them all, Ferret." He turned and walked away.

Natania's watchdog, Ferret thought, *ah no.* Then he too turned and walked away; and a short time later he found himself just outside the cave, observing an impossible landscape. Weird, eerie-looking houses floated about on clouds, or so it appeared. A long narrow pathway led him from the caves and up to Natania's aerie, as she would sometimes call it.

And to his surprise, when he had told her of her watchdog's death, she had led him out back to a kennel, filled with happy, leaping, squeaking little black versions of Pang, if you can call a spider the size a dog "little."

"My little ones," Natania said, smiling blissfully. "You shall raise and train them for me, among other things. Aren't they sweet?"

"Yes — sweet," Tusci hissed, thinking to himself: *I'm standing on a cloud*

THE FOOL

and I'm going to raise giant spiders.

"How is it," he asked her, "that everything doesn't crash down to the ground below and shatter?"

"Why, it is only through my indomitable will," she said.

"And, uh . . . when you sleep?"

"Why, my indomitable will never sleeps, silly, or it would not be indomitable." She giggled.

"What about the other houses or castles or whatever they are?" Tusci pointed off in the distance.

"I'm not the only indomitable will around here." She frowned. "Ah well. You've had a hard day. Go inside and sleep, Ferret. You go in the front door and third door on your right down the hall. Used to be Arkand's."

"Poor fool," Tusci said.

"Everyone's a fool at the beginning of a journey," she said.

Tusci tried to figure out what she meant by that but couldn't. Shook his head and yawned and stretched like a cat, or a ferret. Went inside, leaving her with her pets. Found his room. Slept.

So that he did not see Snake come up the pathway and go round to the kennel, and hand her the coins, and take the jewel.

He also did not see her toss him back the pouch of coins and laughingly say, "Oh give it to the old fool for free. It has brought Tusci to me; I have no further use of it."

"Thanks," Snake said, "but my master Tremmello is not a fool, but a wise man."

Natania smiled her sweet smile and said, "But a wise man is always at the beginning of a journey."

And Snake tried to figure out what she meant by that, but couldn't, shook his head and yawned and stretched like a cat, or a snake, and turned and walked away, back down the path.

□

STAR-TREADER

Milieu cryptic manumit, rekindle smoldering myth.
Youthful pearl yield; while ghastly specters reck, know fancy's moment . . .

Lucent Lemuria seek, weird necromancies foment.
Ancient Ulthar transcend, dissolve in calm of sandalwood.
Cytheran cloak imbue, heed dark psalm of candlewood.
Yellow Canopus capture. Soar past mystic Tartarus.

Lost Commoriom attain, there artistic martyr is . . .
Immersed ennui lament, scan teraphim's dross for essence.
Stranger quest launch, find not on terra dream's phosphorescence.
Twilight faith yield not; tread far-flung stars, quaint moldering smith.

— Walter Shedlofsky

LITTLE ONCE

by Nina Kiriki Hoffman

It didn't cry much past its sixth month; that seemed to be when it learnt what the slaps meant. On the other hand, it refused to die. She couldn't bring herself to kill it directly; somehow she just couldn't. Maybe that was the last gasp of the Catholic in her. Of all the commandments to get stuck on, why that one? She didn't keep any of the rest.

She tried leaving it out on the balcony in the snow — the balcony, that little strip of a thing about a foot wide with an iron railing just beyond it. Just an excuse to up the rent, she thought; no person of a decent size could stand on that little fragment of floor. She had been angry with the balcony since she moved into the ninth-floor apartment, just before she had — the thing. So one night when the snow was falling, she wrapped the thing in a light blanket — without a blanket it would be too plain, somehow — and put it carefully on the balcony, in the wet. Wouldn't it be lovely, just, if it squirmed a little and happened to slip through the railings? A fall like that. Its little head might burst open. Nobody in the street below would know which apartment it came from.

When she opened the window in the morning, pulling her robe tighter against the cold and watching her breath mist — and that was another thing, not enough shillings for the heater, and here she was letting out all that paid-for warm, when would the thing stop leeching off her? — it lay there with snow in its blanket and ice in its black hair, and it stared at her. Such a pale little thing. Not a bit like its gypsy da. Horrible yellow eyes, now whose fault was that?

She wasn't sure if it were alive or not. It shouldn't be, of course, just as it shouldn't have lived through that week when she didn't feed it. If she closed her eyes and gave it a little push with the toe of her slipper, wouldn't it just slide over the edge? And then she could move. That snoopy nosy parker, Mrs. O'Malley next door, was always threatening to report her to the child welfare authorities.

It blinked. After that she had to fetch it in. Couldn't kick it, could she, not over the edge, anyway. She took it in and gave it a few slaps for making her lose the warm air. It made a tear or two, but it had learned not to yell. Leave it in the same diapers all day, see if that taught it anything. Lock it up in the closet.

By suppertime she relented. She brought it out and changed it and fed it some nice hot soup. Maybe a little too hot but it could learn to blow, couldn't it, then? She patted its head. It leaned against her hand and closed its eyes. Almost like a cat. She'd had a kitten once, when she was little. What a soft tiny thing, and making the sweetest noises, like a funny music box, warm against her. Da broke its neck one night because it clawed him.

She picked the thing up and held it against her. Warm, phaw! but what a smell! What was the use in changing it when it always made another mess?

She couldn't go on like this. The paper didies were killing her. And the neighbors. "What's its name? Ooh, idn't it a charming one." Fat lot they knew. Couldn't keep their noses out of other people's business, could they? Bloody great cows.

She was carting it along like a packet one day in Petticoat Lane — usually she left it home; but that day, she just had the impulse; and, as little as it ate, it hardly weighed anything — when the gypsy woman came nagging after her. The old creature wore a flowered scarf over her hair, a man's tweed suit-jacket, trousers, and plimsolls. "A mother, are you? A nice mother? A sweet little mother?" said the woman, tugging on her coat.

"Shab off, old cow," she said, jerking her coat out of the old woman's hand.

"Dosta want it, the wee one?"

She glanced at the old thing's pinched face. The permanent squint in the eyes lifted the lip so one could see the gold front tooth. Had the creature ever been alive and young? "What's your game, ma?" she asked.

"If you was to find the babe a burden, if you was to lighten your purse fifty quid, say, and lighten the load as well, if you was wanting such a thing, fine lady — ?"

She glanced about. In the pell-mell of the open air market — shoppers rushing, folk hawking, singing out their wares, racks of clothes lining the walks, booths where knives in jeweled sheaths and leathergoods and cheap finery hung — no one looked toward her and the old woman. "What are you on about? You with the Yard?"

"Oh, no, lady," said the creature, darting glances both ways. "Not a bit of it."

"What would you do with it?" She glanced at the thing. Its yellow eyes were fixed on the old woman. "You wouldn't snuff it, would you?"

"No. No," said the creature, staring

into the thing's eyes. "I'd send it off somewhere else. It'd be safe and lively, lady. It'd be gone. Mayhap fifteen years down the road, it'd come back; but oh, you'll be away by then, eh, lady?"

She'd meant to spend the money on a new handbag and a good pair of lined leather gloves, what with winter coming on. But if the little thing were gone — think of the savings in didies alone. She'd save her tips up and soon have enough for a pair of gloves again. With the thing gone, maybe she could bring a man home again; and a man gave presents, sometimes. She could say she'd sent it off to be with relatives. She'd been planning to say that for ages; and it would be true, too; so far as she knew, all her relatives were dead, Da being the last to kick off.

There in the center of the market, with the action and noise all around them, time seemed to slow. She handed the thing to the old gypsy woman. She counted out money, the last pound in loose shillings. She turned and walked away, the quiet following her.

It was snowing the night it came back.

She had been on and on at the landlord about the caulking around the windows. All the cold seemed to come in, especially around the windows leading to the balcony. Every winter she complained. Some years he sent somebody by to take a look, but the handyman would always just say there was nothing off about it, she must be a bloody lunatic. So she shivered through the nights. There were not enough blankets in the world to keep her warm, she sometimes thought.

She was huddling in the blankets, drinking tea with a splash of gin, when the knock came.

She thought it might be Harry. She didn't really care who it might be. "Come," she said, and sipped tea.

And it was the monster. But for the yellow eyes, she wouldn't have known it. From such a little bit of a thing it had grown so big. She looked at it and felt all the years on her, each like a weight crushing her down, and the cold that had seeped so deep inside her it never left.

"I'm tired," she said.

It came in and sat down and stared at her. It looked so much like Da, but they all did after a while, all the monsters the world called men.

"You were little once," she said. Then she laughed a terrible laugh that did not end.

□

CRYPT OF CTHULHU

AVATAR

by Lois Tilton

The king of Rhylios stood at the altar to invoke the aid of War. He was arrayed in bronze corselet and greaves, but helmetless, a wreath of bay leaves around his forehead.

Smoke rose from the altar. The sacrifice was a black horse, a flawless young stallion. It is rare in these times to lay a maiden on the altar or a captive taken in battle, yet these also are proper sacrifice to War, whether worshipped as Ares or by some other name.

But now Rhylios summoned its wargods, and we answered: I, dread Enyo the sacker of cities, and my brother-consort, warlike Enyalios. Our panoply was gold — gold corselet and greaves, gleaming helmets with tall black crests — as it had been two generations past, when the Achaians brought war to the walls of Troy.

The knife fell from the king's hand as he covered his eyes, dazzled by the godlight. The palace courtyard fell silent, except for the hissing of flames on the altar.

Then our voices rang out like war trumpets, echoing off the stones: "Take up your spears, Rhylians! Harness your chariots! The enemy's ships are in sight. Meet them on the beaches and spill their blood onto the sand! Make their shades in Hades' realm curse the day they sailed to Rhylios!"

The Rhylian warriors heard the voice of War and responded with their battlecries, striking their shields with spearshafts.

I glanced at the altar where the king, Alektryon, stood with his captains, his face flushed with battlefever. He was young, I noticed — his beard was still soft.

Then he stepped up into his waiting chariot and raised his hands for silence. "The wargods are with us!" he shouted. "Victory to Rhylios!"

"Victory!" the warriors echoed, as the king took up his bronze helmet, red crest nodding, and lowered it onto his head. Battlefever was heating their blood, driving out the doubts and fears of mortals about to come face to face with death.

Then the trumpets sounded, and the captains ordered the warriors to form up in battle order. There was the clatter of hooves and wheels on the flagstones as chariot drivers whipped their teams forward into position. Bronze-armored heroes settled their shields into place, gripped their weapons. The footsoldiers swung their spearshafts up to their shoulders, bronze blades in ranks like a bright palisade.

The city gates swung open, and the Rhylians rode out to the sound of trumpets, footsoldiers marching behind the chariots. It was a stirring sight. Women and children stood in the streets and on the walls, cheering their heroes as they went to meet the invading enemy.

I glanced back toward the whitewashed city, grapevines shading the courtyards of its houses. Ahead, in the dark green water of the harbor, merchant ships were lying, wide-beamed vessels incapable of engaging the enemy's lean warships. War had been long absent from Rhylios. Did these

97

merchants remember that, generations past, their ancestors had breached other walls on this site and conquered the people who had built them? Did they remember the sacrifices they had made then, to War and Strife, sackers of cities? Now the walls were their own.

I spoke to Enyalios, who drove his gold chariot alongside my own. "This time they defend."

"Their weapons are still sharp," he replied. "Their captains seem to know what they're doing. And it always helps to stiffen a warrior's backbone when he's fighting to save his own home."

He was my brother, my consort, my other self. Wargod and goddess, we were two, as War was invoked at the sacrificial altars of Rhylios.

"And the walls are strong," I agreed. "But far better to stop them here on the beach, to drive them back to their ships. Look!" I cried, pointing toward the horizon.

Battle-eager, we fixed our eyes on the ocean. The serpent-prowed ships of the enemy were visible in the distance, oars churning the white foam. They were lean, fast, sea-raiders' ships, carrying war to the shores of Rhylios. And their god was leading them.

This god was a serpent, its three heads on long-coiled necks, blue-scaled, poison-fanged, hissing. I could see the red godlight flash from one of its eyes, promising bloodshed and cruel death. It was War in a form I had never yet seen, dire and monstrous. I shuddered to face such a thing, and around me I could feel courage leach from the Rhylian warriors as they watched their enemies approach.

I recovered myself and shook off the pall of dread. There was need to strike, now. I lifted up my bow, ivory and horn, banded in gold, beyond the strength of mortals to bend. To the bowstring I fitted a gold-tipped arrow and drew it back. High over the ocean the arrow flew, glinting in the sun, straight at the

sea dragon. It struck the monster in one of its sinuous necks, penetrating its blue-scaled armor.

The serpent-god's hiss of pain ripped through the air. My cry of triumph was like a trumpet peal, and I could feel the sinking courage of the Rhylians revive, just as the invaders on their rowing benches faltered.

"Well shot!" my consort exclaimed.

But the serpent twisted another of its heads to seize the arrow in its teeth and draw it out. Its tail lashed the water in defiance, and the rowers took up their tireless stroke once again.

There were fifteen ships, with thirty fighters to a ship, against three hundred Rhylian warriors. But the invaders would be spent from their work at the oars while the defenders had the advantages of home ground and their chariots. I glanced at the Rhylian host for a sight of the king and frowned — why was his chariot back toward the rear? Was not the king's place at the head of his host? But then Enyalios bent over his chariot rim, pitching his voice for my ears alone. "Their weapons are iron."

Bronze blades and bronze armor would now be matched against iron. This new factor entering into war could weight the odds against the Rhylians. But, then, they would have all the more need for battle courage. Enyalios raised his gold-bladed spear, and we urged our horses forward toward the enemy, the cheers of our warriors following us.

And not only cheers. As the serpent-ships came within the range of mortal bowmen, the Rhylian captains ordered their archers forward. Bows of wood and horn were drawn back, and arrows flew toward the oncoming ships. The oarsmen had the protection of the wooden planking, but here and there a cry of pain told of an arrow finding its mark, and a few men tumbled from their benches.

"See how they fall!" Enyalios shouted

aloud in encouragement. "Half of them don't even have armor!"

The armor they did have was various — whatever they had looted from the bodies of their victims, leather helmets nodding in unison with battered, tarnished bronze. The invaders were swarthy men, muscled from life at the oars, a life of hardship and piracy. Despite the Rhylian arrows, they came on, their oarstrokes barely checked.

Then the first serpent-prow was cutting through the surf, and oars were rising up, and men were vaulting over the sides to bring it onto the beach. But the Rhylians were ready for them. Shouting their battlecries, they charged in a mass to meet the invaders.

I urged them on, reveling in the clash of arms. Godlight flashed from my armor as I quickened their souls with courage. The fighting was hand to hand, with confusion greater every moment as more ships pulled onto the beach and engaged the defenders.

Spears thrust down from chariots, javelins and arrows flew through the air, swords slashed out. Bronze spearpoints were thrust through leather and flesh, iron swords penetrated bronze armor. Already there were bodies rolling lifeless in the surf, their blood staining the foam.

But even as the Rhylians fought, they were learning that this was a kind of warfare new to them. It was not only the iron blades of the invaders that made the difference. This enemy cared nothing for the formal combat of heroes, as Ajax had fought Hector beneath the walls of Troy. There would be no battle trophies won on this beach, no quarter given, no ransomed prisoners, no truce to tend the wounded and bring the bodies of the dead to honor. Only butchery and slaughter and death.

We could feel Rhylian courage begin to erode as the serpent-god fed the bloodlust of the invading enemy. Enyalios raised his spear, its golden blade

100

glowing with godlight. Straight at the god-monster his chariot charged, at fifty feet of writhing, scaled frenzy. Its three heads darted back and forth, its tail lashed, spraying sand. His arm drew back as he thundered past, then thrust the spear, piercing one of the serpent's heads through the throat, transfixing its jaw. The hiss of rage and pain made both sides start with horror for an instant, until the Rhylians, heartened, pressed their advantage.

The serpent seized the spearshaft with one of its other heads, clamped its jaws down until the wood splintered and broke in half, leaving the spearhead still embedded.

By then Enyalios had wheeled his chariot around and taken up another spear. He charged once more, but this time the dragon twisted aside and the spearthrust slid harmlessly along its armored scales. And as the horses charged past, it struck, venomous fangs clashing against my consort's golden breastplate.

He staggered, and then the serpent-god's coils were around him, dragging him out of the chariot.

I felt the shock like the sundering blow of an axe as the coils crushed his armor, broke his back, as the deadly fangs sank into his throat and life drained from my other self. My knees went weak, and I sagged for an instant against my chariot rim. Eyes glowing red with triumph, the serpent-god reared high, to show the Rhylians the lifeless body of their wargod clenched in its jaws.

Panic seized them, and his brother, Rout, the sons of War. Everywhere on the beach Rhylians were throwing down their weapons and fleeing from the battlefield, the triumphant enemy at their backs, cutting them down as they ran to escape the slaughter.

No! Shouting to my horses, I charged forward toward the god-monster, drawing back my bow. The gold-tipped arrow flew, straight for the serpent-god's blue scaled throat. And I watched, in utter dismay, as it shattered harmlessly against the armored scales.

The battle was lost. The demoralized Rhylians fled toward the safety of their walls. I could see the chariot of the king being led from the battlefield by his captain, Eteokles.

But there were others whose courage had not deserted them, still fighting a rear-guard action. That was my place, to hearten them as well as I still could with my diminished power while they held off the enemy until the rest could make it through the gates. Only when the last warrior had joined the retreat did I abandon the battlefield, taking a last, despairing look back at the shredded remains of my brother-consort, still transfixed by the serpent-god's fangs.

Bodies littered the beach behind us, and reddened sand.

Inside the citadel, with the gates shut behind the last of the returning chariots, panic filled the streets with demoralized and wounded soldiers, newly-made widows and orphans, despairing cries. The captains fought for order, ordered men to the walls, to defensive posts. I strove to encourage the defenders, for the city had not fallen, its walls were still intact. But the Rhylians had seen Enyalios fall to the serpent, and the radiance of my godlight was dimmed, so they no longer had to shield their eyes.

The barbarian invaders had encamped outside the walls, beyond bowshot range. Dusk was already gathering, and it appeared that they were going to put off their assault on the gates until the next day. And the reason soon became clear to the defenders gathered on the walls.

Toward the campfires there were figures being dragged, wounded Rhylian soldiers taken from the battlefield. The pirates laid them on a makeshift altar, and the serpent-god began to feed upon their living bodies.

Do mortals think the gods cannot shed tears? Even War, whose way is death and defeat as much as victory, wept that night. Those same fangs had torn the body of my brother-self. And, strengthened by bloody sacrifice, the serpent would seek my defeat once more the next day.

As it fed, the ceaseless cries of anguish corroded the spirit of the Rhylians, their will to resist. Sundered from my consort, my power to aid them was diminished. Though they had called me the sacker of cities, now I must see the Rhylian walls breached, the people slaughtered.

I despised my own weakness as a Rhylian warrior went to his knees in front of me, despair choking his voice. "Goddess, Lady Enyo!" he cried, "Help us!"

I envied mankind at that moment, that they have gods to pray to. I prayed, also, to the depths of my own immortal strength.

And found, possibly, an answer. I felt the faint glow of godlight once again as I ran to climb down from the wall, to the king's palace. He was still in his armor, standing beside his captains as they planned the city's defense.

Their heads turned in surprise to see me there, but I ignored them, went directly to the king beside them, Alektryon, and stared into his eyes. Yes! What I sought was there.

Then, "You must attack," I urged the warriors. "It's the only way, the thing they will never expect. They think they have us beaten already. But we'll show them how wrong they are! Attack, and War will be with you."

The captain Eteokles stared, wondering, but I had no time for him. I pulled Alektryon away, toward a private room of the palace, and ordered the servants, "Get out of here, find a weapon and get ready to fight for your lives, if

101

you think you deserve them!" They fled when they saw the flash of my eyes.

Then I turned to Alektryon, who was speechless in his confusion. "Come," I told him, "it is time for the king of Rhylios to become the consort of War."

He went white with shock, gasping out a protest.

I ignored it. "The soldiers saw Enyalios die. It took the heart from them, the will to fight. And it diminished my own power. The two of us are one. I *must* have another consort."

This was not absolutely so, what I told Alektryon. Other places, to other peoples, I am War in my own right. But in this place, in Rhylios, War was two, the brother-sister consorts Enyo and Enyalios, wargod and goddess. There must be two once again.

"The Enyalios you saw die was only an incarnation," I explained. "War itself — all the gods — are immortal. War can be incarnate here again . . . in you."

"I?" he choked.

"You are the King, the god-descended, aren't you? Who offers up the sacrifices for your city? Who else could your people accept?"

He still held back, and I frowned impatiently, but then caught sight of my reflection in his polished bronze corselet.

My face was War's. Eyes like lightning flashed from behind my helmet, its fierce black crest tossing. And Alektryon — from his face it was as if he had just been told he was to couple with a gorgon.

I pulled the helm off, shook out my hair, dimmed the flashing of my eyes. Then I recalled the king's chariot being led away from the battle, the way the captains made their plans without consulting their lord. I reached out a hand to touch the softness of his young beard and asked, "You are a man, are you not, King of Rhylios?"

His young pride was touched then, and he lifted up his eyes directly to

meet mine. "Man enough to be father of a son."

"Here, then," I said, "help me with this," as I started to unbuckle the rest of my armor. I felt strange without the weight of it, my godlight extinguished. And as I held out my leg so he could unfasten the buckle of my greaves, I was not totally unmindful that the gesture exposed the long white length of my thigh.

Aphrodite, too, was the consort of War, of Ares, the mother of his dread sons. That, too, had I been, as War was worshipped in the city of Menelaos. Other incarnations, other names, were all growing dim. I was not eternal War now, standing before Alektryon, wearing nothing but a linen chiton. Only this place, this time existed, as I reached for the buckles of his own armor. I was flesh, as I must be, to couple with a mortal.

He hesitated still, as I pulled him down to me. "How . . . what will happen?" His voice was shaking. He feared to lose his whole self to the god.

"When the time comes, the power of War will overcome you. The godlight will be in your eyes, and your people will recognize it. The things you do then, you may not remember clearly. It will seem like a dream, afterwards, when you return to yourself."

Then I added, summoning all of the Aphrodite that was in me, "Can it be so unpleasant, to couple with a goddess?"

And it must have been sufficient.

It was not as it had been with Enyalios, with rapacious War. I could remember, but only dimly, the violence of those couplings. "Lady," Alektryon murmured, and as his flesh responded to mine, we could feel the power of War move within us, and we were one, again.

"You know," he said when the godlight had dimmed, "I never loved war before. My captains claimed I was too young to command, too inexperienced. And today they held me back from the fighting. My first battle. I don't know . . ."

"When the time comes," I assured him, "you will know that you are War."

"I don't feel like a god," he said, smiling at me shyly.

I laughed with him. "I feel now as if I had never been a goddess before. Truly. Each incarnation is a renewal. I am War, yes, but this time a part of me is yours." And I knew then that I was no longer the city-sacker.

We dressed, and I armed myself. "You will have other armor," I told Alektryon. My consort.

The Rhylian captains, when we found them again, looked drained by fatigue. But they stood when they saw us re-enter the room, and bowed, sensing that something had changed, the rebirth of our power.

"You are ready to attack?" I asked.

Eteokles nodded wearily. "Just before dawn. We've sent scouts out over the walls. The pirates are still . . . celebrating — the ones who are awake and conscious. They have only a few sentries. When it's time, our scouts will cut their throats.

"Our chariots will leave from the far gates. We ought to be in position before dawn to attack from the rear. When they're engaged, our footsoldiers will sortie from the main gate and trap them between us. If you approve, of course, Lady," he added.

Tactics and strategy we leave to mortals. But I turned to Alektryon. "My consort and I will lead the sortie."

The captains glanced at each other, at Alektryon, and saw the godlight in the eyes of their king. They bowed.

There was much to do before dawn. We went through the city, showing ourselves to the people, encouraging their will to resist. Now we turned the serpent-god's work against him. There could be no safety, we told the Rhylians,

no hope except in the destruction of the enemy. No one would be spared, not the children, the women, or the old. The city would be looted and burned over the bodies of its citizens.

And they responded. The report spread out ahead of us, from street to street: *The gods are with us once more.*

Fishermen, slaves, maidens, merchants — they all found some kind of weapon and headed toward the walls. Children gathered, ready to fetch and carry. Old men brought out half-corroded armor and forgotten spears. The women assembled on the ramparts, armed with stones and jars of oil to set alight and hurl onto the assailants. It was better to die resisting them than to fall into their hands.

I remembered the warlike tribe I had led against these walls so many generations past. War was no longer the same for them, as I was not the city-sacker.

Finally we came to the rear gate, where the chariots were assembled. Scouts had already slipped over the walls to eliminate the pirate sentries. Here the warriors stood in silent, grim purpose, honing the bright edges of their weapons while the chariot drivers wrapped the bronze-rimmed wheels to silence them.

Here were men who knew already what they had to face, who burned to avenge the shame of their defeat the day before. There would be no retreat this time. They would die, if they must, even as their wargod had died.

But he was now alive again. We could see the godlight reflected back from their eyes, along with hope. It flowed into their hearts like a surging tide. War was with them again!

"They think they have you already beaten," we told them. "They think your spirit was destroyed. But War is alive! And this time, War is Rhylios! Their numbers, their iron blades — none of it will save them. Not if you

103

have the spirit to press the attack. Strike them down, Rhylians! No quarter, no mercy — slay them in their sleep, if you can, trample them under the hooves of your horses! And if you grow tired, if your own blood runs down your arms, then remember — if they defeat you, all Rhylios will be an immolation on the altar of their bloodglutted serpent-god!

Eteokles took off his bronze helmet and bowed his head. "Lady Enyo . . . and my Lord, if you bring us this victory, I promise you such sacrifices as heaven will remember for all time to come."

Then, slowly and in silence under the cover of darkness, Eteokles led the first of the Rhylian chariots through the gates. Alektryon yearned to be among them, to be driving at the head of those brave warriors as they charged into the enemy's camp. But they were all seasoned combatants, used to the ways of battle, and they had need of no more courage than already beat within their hearts. Eteokles their captain could lead them well enough.

Our place now was elsewhere, at the main gate. There, behind the footsoldiers, armed with whatever came to hand, were the mass of the Rhylian citizens, waiting for their gods and their king to lead them.

Now I brought up the black horses that draw the golden chariots of War. And there, gleaming in readiness, was the panoply of the wargod. I helped Alektryon to arm himself, and as he did the godlight blazed forth in its full splendor. The Rhylians raised their hands to shade their eyes as we drove through their ranks.

Then, as Dawn began to stir in the east, we could hear the first clashes of combat from the enemy camp, the Rhylian warcries as they drove down upon the serpent-god's worshipers.

But the pirates were men who had grown hard through the years of reaving, who could sleep in their armor with weapons at hand and be on their feet fighting within an instant of the alarm sounding. And they knew they had no walls to shelter behind. Howling their own battlecries, the enemy seized their iron blades and fought back with the wild ferocity of a cornered boar. Horses screamed as iron found their legs and bellies, chariots spun out of control. In a few moments, the superior numbers of the invaders began to blunt the thrust of the attack.

"Now!" cried Alektryon, and the gates of Rhylios swung open. The chariots of War glowed brighter than the newborn day upon the battlefield. The serpent hissed with rage and dismay as we charged toward it, the spearpoint of Alektryon a beacon for all to see. This time I could feel the power in my arrow as I let it fly. And behind us came the Rhylians, pouring out of the city gates in the wake of War.

As Alektryon's spear drank the serpent's dark lifeblood, the invaders quailed before the fury of the Rhylian people. They fled before us, and the chariots pursued. So few of them survived to fight their way back to the beach that only a single serpent-ship escaped. The others were all burned on the altar of sacrifice, piled full with offerings to War.

Alektryon performed the rites, his golden armor gleaming even without the godlight. He was War no longer, but now he was truly king, and the Rhylians called him Enyalios, the warlike.

Yet there was one more outcome of that incarnation, when for one night he was my consort. I will be sending her to her father one day soon, arrayed in her gleaming bronze armor, and her name is Soteira, the city-savior.

□

STILL THE SAME OLD STORY

by W.T. Quick

click . . . swish.

Roberts first heard the sound just a few moments after midnight. He looked up from the magazine he was reading at the big round clock over the door to the main computer room.

Two minutes past twelve.

click . . . swish.

He carefully folded over the corner of the page he was reading and placed his copy of *Thrilling Incredible Horror Stories*™ face down on his desk. The cover illustration glittered like a blood-splotch beneath the harsh overhead fluorescent lights. It was a picture of a Thing that had been summoned by an unwary magician. He'd been reading that particular story when he heard the sound. Now he heard it a third time.

click . . . swish.

Roberts sighed. He rubbed his eyes and stretched. He was only thirty. He had a full head of black curly hair and a face innocent of lines, but the night shift was aging him inside, softening his muscles and bloating his waist despite his current exercise regimen. Half an hour of brisk walking to and from work could not offset eight hours of sitting. He'd had the job almost six months and he knew that when he got on the scale tomorrow he would still be twenty pounds overweight.

His back hurt right down to base of his spine.

click . . . swish.

He reached over and flipped open the looseleaf notebook which contained the log of the nightly file run. He knew it by heart, but a certain sense of professionalism made him check the hard-copy record. Perhaps they'd added something without telling him. He glanced at the clock again and shook his head. There was no mistake. From eleven fifty five until one o'clock the machines were down. At one they started on the payroll. But right now, twelve oh nine, they were down.

So why was he hearing the distinctive sound of one of the big hard disks turning itself on and off? He leaned back in his chair and patted his stomach and winced. Without realizing it he mentally counted off the seconds. There had been a definite rhythm to the sounds, as if one of the mainframes had been accessing regular chunks of data.

click . . . swish.

He blinked. Overhead the lights glared down on him. The large office was utterly deserted. He listened to his own breathing and for the smallest instant was aware of how alone he was. Then he leaned forward and planted his feet on the floor. His chair screeched and the moment was broken.

"Uh . . . damn it." He stood up and felt a sudden shaft of pain from his right ankle. It had gone to sleep. He paused and tried to remember the number he was supposed to call if he couldn't fix whatever had gone wrong. Then he shook his head and trudged toward the double swinging doors which led into the computer room.

He wondered if this would be his first emergency.

The main operations station was di-

rectly inside the two doors beyond a low white railing. He walked through a gate in the railing and stepped behind the desks of the workstation. There were five consoles arranged in a loose semi-circle. He sat down at the center console and moved around until he felt comfortable on the hard seat of the spindly plastic chair. It was why he usually spent his shift outside at the secretary's desk. Her chair was thick and padded, perfect for reading and maybe a little snooze. Nothing ever happened in the operations room anyway.

He tapped his fingertips lightly on the touchpad. The movement was part ritual and part limbering-up exercise. Just then his subconscious surfaced and he heard himself counting down: three . . . and two . . . and one . . .

click . . . swish.

The sound came from behind him and to his right. He stared at the touchpad. Regulations said he had a certain protocol to follow, a standard group of tests to enter. Instead, he pushed his chair back and stood up and turned around. Now he faced the bulk of the large room. The same bright rectangular panels of fluorescents burned here; they flooded the room with a surgical light. The machines glistened silently, each surrounded by a wide expanse of light grey industrial carpet. The walls of the room were dull blue, daubed here and there with wild splashes of color; random graphic murals designed to break the visual monotony. Sometimes the room reminded him of a temple full of idols and totems.

The place was so clean it made his teeth hurt.

He began to pick his way out among the machines. He moved slowly, his back stiff. He held his hands out in front of him like a man who expects some kind of jolt to disturb his balance. The soft shuffle of his footsteps was unnaturally loud.

click . . . swish.

"Whuh!" He jumped. His chest hammered. His arms jerked up as if defending from a blow.

Then he let his hands fall to his sides. Grinned. Felt stupid.

He turned around. It had to be the new kiloMIPS super computer. Only a few feet away. That was why the sound had been so sudden, so jarring.

Stupid to be frightened of a machine.

He walked briskly over to the new installation. The machine itself wasn't very impressive. A square tower perhaps two feet on a side and no more than five high. Its skin was cool silver. The peripherals around it took up more space, in particular the thousand gigabit laser media drive. As he stared at the squat bulk of the drive a tiny red light flickered on. It held a moment, then died.

click . . . swish.

His lips widened loosely over his teeth. He felt his chest relax. Only a drive going whacko. Computers were funny. Almost weird. It was why he liked them.

At least he knew what to do now.

He returned to the operations console and entered the standard battery of tests. While he waited for the results he closed his eyes and let his mind drift. It was so quiet. So easy to let things just slip away.

A sharp **beep** announced the results of the test. His eyes snapped open. He must have dozed off because the first thing he saw was the moon. He had settled in the chair, his head loose on his neck and tilted back on his shoulders. Overhead a skylight admitted the night through glass as clear as crystal.

The moon rode there like an eyeless skull, fat and swollen and white as bone. He blinked. For one greasy moment . . .

Something gelid and slimy congealed around his spine. His breath leaked. He

107

shook his head and looked down at the monitor instead. Then he pushed himself up and forward.

"Nah . . . can't be," he said softly.

But it was. Nothing was wrong with the laser drive. Nothing at all.

He tried the tests again and got the same results. It was crazy. He'd heard that drive, even watched it blink a read-write telltale. He couldn't have imagined that. It wasn't some kind of hallucination.

"Garbage," he said. He tapped his teeth with his forefinger. If nothing was wrong with the drive, then there should be some record of its operation. The drive was a slave to the computer. Therefore the computer was working on something.

He rolled his shoulders and tried to work some of the ache out of them. Then he fished in his pocket for his key-ring. After a moment he found the correct key. He rolled himself down the line of consoles on the wheels of his chair till he came to the cabinet. He unlocked it and reached inside. The manual for the new computer was thick as his wrist.

Twenty minutes later he had no more idea what was going on than at the beginning. The new machine was fast as anything ever released outside the military and the spooks. His company had been one of the first to purchase this model. They used it to coordinate and control their data satellite system.

It was a big enough job to warrant such a machine. According to the Global Area Network data, the new machine handled not only input from one hundred thirteen ground stations, but also from a dozen satellites. Oil seekers, topography readers, weather predictors. And probably some sneaky stuff on the side, Roberts decided.

Yet even the new machine was noted in the file run log. Operating times were listed. Right now the computer was down. Or should be.

He stared blankly at the pages of the manual and imagined the machine at work. A billion instructions per second. That was fast. On top of the building great cream colored dishes revolved slowly. They sucked in intricate data constructs and fed them to the deceptively small hardware box.

He liked that image. Creamy metal ears listening to songs that man could never understand without the help of his machines. He replaced the manual and locked the cabinet. Then he pushed himself back to the center console and placed his hands on the touchpad. He thought for a moment. Then he switched output from the computer to a laser printer and commanded a RAM dump.

If the machine was doing anything, this would be the quickest way to find out.

Three minutes later he hefted a thick pile of hardcopy. He'd been surprised when the printer started up almost immediately, indicating that the computer was operating. But the dump made no sense at all. Page after page of what appeared to be random numbers and esoteric symbols. If this was a program it wasn't in any language he'd ever heard of.

He reached for the phone and punched three numbers.

"Security? This is Roberts in the Operations Center.

"Yeah, okay. What I wanted to know, is there anybody else working tonight? Somebody working late?

"No? Huh. No, nothing's wrong. Nothing I can't handle.

"Thanks. Right, you take care too."

He replaced the receiver.

Whatever was operating the new computer was coming from outside the complex.

He'd hit a blank wall. The supercomputer was doing something, as witnessed by the printout. But damned if he could figure out what.

Then he realized. It had been a while since he'd heard the drive come on. He placed the hardcopy on the desk and walked back to the laser drive. He stood there for two minutes by his watch. Nothing. The computer remained silent, silver, enigmatic.

Then, suddenly, the room was filled with the papery sound of leaves falling. He spun around. Then he caught himself. He checked his watch to make sure.

One o'clock. The payroll was starting. Half a dozen printers whirred into motion, filling deep wire baskets with printouts nobody would ever look at except nearsighted tax accountants.

The file run was heavy tonight. After payroll the big databases would be recalculated. It would take the rest of his shift.

Whatever had happened was over for now. He walked back to the operations console and entered an account of what he'd observed. At the last minute he decided against mentioning the printout. Technically he wasn't supposed to do such a thing, especially with a new, nearly experimental machine.

He signed off. Absently he picked up the printout. For no particular reason he glanced up. The moon was almost past the skylight. Only a calcified splinter remained. It nearly reminded him of something. What *had* he seen at the barest corner of his eye . . . ?

He shrugged and stuffed the printout into his attache case. Then he went back to the secretary's desk and her inviting chair.

He still felt rattled. Perhaps a nap would help. He set the silent alarm on his wrist watch.

Ten minutes later he was asleep. He snored loudly.

He had a red pass, so the security guard didn't check his attache case but simply waved him on. He walked quickly

through the morning light, trying to work up a sweat. The thick pad of flesh around his waist jiggled evilly. By the time he reached the Seven-Eleven on the corner of his block he had raised a moist film on his forehead.

Feeling virtuous, he walked into the small store.

"Why, Mr. Roberts. How are we this morning?"

Janet Meltzer presided behind the counter. She was a huge grinning puppet of a woman. Her face stretched under a load of makeup he was always afraid would crack. Split and spill whatever was behind that horrible mask out onto the countertop in a grisly clotted flood.

"I'm, uh, fine, Miss Meltzer." Grimly he reminded himself that she'd never married. So he was probably safe. But she'd shown a rising level of interest lately.

"Here for breakfast, are we?"

"Yup. The usual —"

"Two egg and chilies, one coffee slurpie, coming right up." She smiled and he found reason to look at the parking lot.

"We should go right home, eat, and tuck ourselves into bed, Mr. Roberts. We look tired this morning."

The vision which swept into his mind was enough to make him hastily fumble a tenner from his wallet. "Uh. Yes, sure. Good idea, Miss Meltzer. We'll — *I'll* be sure to do that."

She rang his change and pushed a paper bag forward. As he reached for it she patted his hand. Her fingers were dry and hot. He jerked the bag away.

"Goodbye now," he said as he retreated.

"Good day," she replied. He felt her eyes on him as he scurried away, speculative as a preacher contemplating sin. He gripped the bag more tightly and forced himself not to walk fast. Not until he was around the corner and his own two-bedroom bungalow was safely

109

in sight.

He kicked off his shoes inside the front door and dropped his jacket on the sofa arm where it landed on top of his sport coat from the previous day. The thick shag carpet felt good on his sock feet. He padded into the kitchen and dumped the egg chilies on the counter. He opened a drawer, took out a fork, and made two perforations in the thick plastic bags. Carefully he adjusted the microwave to three. He put his attache case on the kitchen table, sat down facing the single window which let onto his narrow garden, and popped the lid on the coffee slurpie.

He opened the case and took out the copy of *Thrilling Incredible Horror Stories*™. After a moment the bell chimed from the microwave. He retrieved his breakfast, took a sip of his slurpie, and read as he ate.

By nine o'clock he began to feel sleepy. He glanced at the open case on the table and saw the folded printout, but decided it could wait. He finished off his slurpie in one gulp, got up and went into the spare bedroom. The walls of the room were lined with oak shelves he'd built over a strenuous month. Carefully he placed the copy of the magazine next to 312 of its fellows. The unbroken line extended all the way back to Volume One, Number One. It was one of the highlights of his collection. He surveyed the room with pride. Someday all of this would be worth money. And even if it didn't turn out that way, he still loved reading the stuff.

He scratched his stomach, thought better of *that,* and wandered off to bed.

It just didn't make any sense. He puzzled over the printouts as dusk grew thick around his house. After a while he had to turn on the light in the kitchen. It still didn't make any sense. But he kept trying. He couldn't understand what was on these papers, but something tugged at him. There was a pattern, a kind of visual rhythm that beckoned to his brain. It kept drawing him back to the enigmatic rows of symbols.

A feeling that things were not quite right nagged at him. He leaned back and stared at the weird shapes with which twilight peopled his garden. He knew they were only bushes and a few stunted trees, but in the fading light they took on an ominous patina. Usually he liked the little thrill of fear thus conjured by dark and a taste for melodrama, but suddenly he didn't like it at all. He clicked his teeth together, got up and pulled the curtains shut.

It was something to do with the printouts. He was certain of it. But there was nothing he could do now. Maybe later, in the quiet watches of the night. Do a little programming of his own and see what happened. It was all probably stupid anyhow. Like the stuff in his weird magazines. Fig newtons of his imagination.

The microwave bell startled him. He smelled something. Yes. His vegetarian tofu stew had boiled over.

His Topsiders made loose slapping sounds on the empty sidewalk. The night was faintly cool. He stopped at the only traffic light between his house and the office. As always he felt a little embarrassed. No cars went past at this time of night but he always waited for the red light to turn green.

Why not just cross? But another part replied: Because it would be *breaking the law.*

He shivered suddenly and glanced up. The moon rode the sky like a big yellow eye. He blinked. What? He closed his eyes, opened them, and looked again.

What was it? He thought for a moment and then realized what it reminded him of. When he was in high school biology he'd stared through a microscope at a brightly lighted circle. At first he'd seen nothing. Then, as he watched with growing revulsion, the amoebae began to cluster. Darkly transparent, slick and repulsive. They'd moved with hideous grace, seeking each other.

Now something just like that moved across the arid face of the moon. He rubbed his eyes and looked again.

Shook his head and walked on.

At the far left end of the operations station was a special console. He sat in front of it and glanced at his watch. Eleven oh six. Behind him the machines waited silently. Overhead the moon burned a lucid, barren light through the glass canopy. He ignored it.

The abberant disk drive had not played any tricks tonight. Now he picked up the heavy white helmet and stared at it. This could be dangerous. He was absolutely forbidden to operate this console. It controlled the new computer. In theory he wouldn't know how to use it anyway, but not long ago the Operations Chief had worked late.

"You want to try this thing?" Chief Kilvald had said. He was an intense man of medium height who was covered with a thick pelt of wiry black hair. That he was five years younger than Roberts was not a problem. But his doubled salary was a definite source of envy.

"What is it?" Roberts hated admitting his own ignorance, but he *was* interested.

"A new wrinkle for operators and programmers. Called a direct transducer helmet. You deal with the machine on a total interface."

"Huh? Total interface?"

"Yeah." Kilvald grinned slowly. "It's real user-friendly. Come on. Give it a try."

Roberts edged closer. "What does it do? How does it work?"

"Bone induction and monomolecular fiber inserts. Plus a visual screen and aural backup. Doesn't mean anything much. I don't understand either. But it sure as Hell works."

He fitted the helmet over Roberts's head till it settled snugly against his skull. Roberts opened his eyes but it was utterly dark. Suddenly light exploded. He could make out dim figures.

"Here," Kilvald said. "These controls." He guided Roberts's fingers. "Just adjust until you can see clearly. Then you do the same for sound."

Roberts followed the directions. After a moment he was startled at how sharp everything was. A group of dancers cavorted to the lilting music of Beethoven.

It was as real as anything.

Later, he asked Kilvald what he did with it. Kilvald grinned again, slowly. "Me? I use it to get high."

Now Roberts settled the helmet on his skull and made the necessary adjustments. He used a simple sound-and-graphics program from his own console to get everything just right. Then he blinked up a time display. Twelve oh-seven.

He couldn't hear the drive even if it did come on. Best to just dive right in. Either something was going on or it wasn't.

At least he would know.

His cheek twitched. Light bloomed and the world opened onto dawn.

At first the blinding sunlight burned his eyes shut. Sundogs danced behind his lids. After a moment the tears dried up and he able to see again.

The view stretched out in an awesome vista before him. On a visit to New York he'd experienced the same gut-squeezing sensation when he'd looked out from the observation deck of the World Trade Center. He'd actually *felt* the Earth turning beneath

111

him on a carpet of ocean and glass. Now he stood frozen and gazed over a vast city edging a great blue bay in tiers of polished stone.

The wind tugged at his hair. He tasted a salt breeze and heard birds cry raucously high overhead.

What an illusion! he thought. It seemed incredible that the transduction interface could be this good. He'd never seen graphics like this. And . . . smells? The rough feel of stone beneath his feet?

He blinked. There was a flaw. Spots before his eyes. As he stared at dawn breaking red and gold over the blue water, his view was obscured. Faint brown dots floated in his vision. He blinked again and turned away from the water. Now the city spread out before him, rising from the harbor on the encircling hills. He was on a tall building of some kind. Behind him one wall of it rose toward a pinnacle two hundred feet further on. But it was a strange building, like no other he'd ever seen before. He was standing on a broad terrace which encircled the main shaft of the building. Such odd architecture. Each face of the shaft was covered with columns. The style was something like that of the classical Greek, though cleaner, more sleek and functional. Was the whole edifice built in this strange style?

He walked to the waist-high stone balustrade which surrounded the terrace and peered over the edge. Heights had never bothered him much, but the sheer drop beneath his feet punched in his gut and put a vise on his chest. The building was massive, easily the tallest structure he could see. Even the towers on the hills barely reached his own position.

It was so quiet. Only the sound of the wind and the shriek of birds. No human sounds at all. He shaded his eyes and looked back toward the sea. Stopped. It wasn't his eyesight. The brown spots

had grown slightly larger. Several of them, fuzzy and indistinct, high over the water. Moving closer, though. Growing.

Suddenly he shivered. The spots reminded him of something.

He tried to recall the errant memory but the sound of bells distracted him and he turned away.

The procession spilled in orderly cadence from two wide double doors that had opened in the side of the building. Several military-looking types dressed in tight black uniforms led another group wearing white robes. The soldiers were dark-skinned, short and muscular. The rest were taller, equally dark of skin, and bald. Each group was quite homogeneous in its ethnic sameness. Immediately he thought of priests.

Nobody seemed to notice him standing there watching. The soldiers formed up around a low stone platform in front of the double doors. The rising sun shone directly on the platform. It cast a long shadow. Now the taller men moved up to the stone platform. They seemed bored. Roberts looked closer and saw a thin gutter surrounding the flat top.

The priests fanned out and Roberts discovered the source of the bell sound. Several of the men carried strange crystalline tubes hung from a golden framework. They ran their fingers across the glass and a thin, tinkling sound ensued. The melody was quiet but penetrating. It hung disconcertingly on the air. The players tinkled away but paid little attention to their music. One of them merely shook his instrument while he scratched his ear.

Finally two more priests appeared from the darkness behind the doors. They half-carried, half-dragged a third figure. It was a young male, still dark-skinned but lighter than the rest. The youth's features were very thin and straight. His surprising blue eyes were dazed and vacant. Roberts had seen that sort of look before, among his friends who were fond of what California called controlled substances.

There was little ceremony. The priests played their crystal instruments. The soldiers waited stolidly. And the two high priests simply dragged the boy to the stone, flopped him down like a fish and secured his hands and feet to the top with manacles that seemed to appear from nowhere.

Some kind of stupid dream, Roberts thought. A perverse bit of software designed by somebody with a fondness for the occult.

He recognized the scene: it was a distillation of every speculation he'd ever read about Atlantis. What else could it be? Everything about this city was a combination of the archaic and the highly technological, even to the barbaric splendor of the building itself. A sixty-storey Greek temple. Somebody understood architectural stress. And now these characters were about to perform a traditional sacrifice. Comic-book stuff.

The bells stopped abruptly and Roberts felt a sudden chill. A shadow ghosted across the terrace. He looked up.

He froze.

It floated forty feet above the terrace. His throat went dry. Something gurgled in his stomach and a bitter, greasy wad crawled into his gullet. He forced it back down and stared, dizzy and disoriented.

It was shaped like a rough pyramid but it shifted as he watched. It was covered with leathery skin transparent enough to reveal slow, viscous innards. These awful guts glowed like a ghastly lava lamp. And all across the bottom, like a forest of insects, wiggled millions of tiny tentacles. It hung there steady against the wind while the priests took up their music again. There was an air of expectancy in their chiming now, a sense of summoning. Finally the mons-

ter floating there responded.

Slowly the great Eye in the apex of the pyramid opened. The others began to drift down. Their tentacles waved languidly in the breeze.

The boy on the stone altar screamed. The sound was long and despairing and Roberts could hear vocal chords stretched and bleeding beneath it. One of the priests whipped out a silvery object, applied it to the boy's arm, and the youth went silent.

Hypodermic needle? Roberts thought. The anachronism startled him. Where was the stone knife? That was what the stories called for.

Now a final priest garbed in bright orange and wearing a heavy black metal circle on his chest came out of the building. He pushed a machine which resembled a cross between a Xerox copier and the large laser drive which had started all this. From the top of the machine extended a long cable which was connected to a shiny metal circlet. Without any ceremony the priest approached the stone and placed the circlet around the boy's head.

Finally the priest reached into the side of the machine and withdrew several pieces of equipment which resembled metal earmuffs. Each priest placed one of these on his own head.

Still there was no real ceremony. The chiming redoubled, but the orange-garbed priest paid no attention. His movements were as quick and matter-of-fact as those of any technician. Suddenly Roberts realized what this reminded him of. Nothing more than the day shift coming on duty at his own company. Programmers and operators checking the results of the night file and getting ready for the day's work.

The highest priest adjusted some knobs on the top of the machine, yawned, and stepped back.

The machine began to hum softly like a laser printer warming up. Then without warning the youth on the altar went tetanic. Every muscle in his body contracted and relaxed as if he were being electrocuted. His elbows and heels drummed softly on the stone. And from the circlet around his head spread some slow form of energy, like congealed lightning, in an intricate web around his skull. As Roberts stared, it seemed this force went *into* the boy's skull in tiny electric roots, penetrating and ravaging the soft tissues inside.

The priests let out small sighing sounds. The high priest touched his metal earmuffs, as if adjusting them for better reception. His dark features went slack and happy.

Suddenly the boy voided himself. His muscles seemed to dissolve. He looked smaller, as if his very flesh had been used up. The high priest opened his eyes and stared. A disgusted expression crossed his face. The static glow which had surrounded the boy's skull was gone. With a quick movement the priests removed the circlet and checked some dials on the machine. He turned to the other pair and shrugged.

From the boy's eyes twin streams of blood began to dribble. Roberts watched the viscid pattern form. He smelled the hot pungent odor of human feces, and then, without realizing it, began to vomit.

The priests finished up their work and pushed the machine away from the altar. The soldiers came up and took the boy's body. It was limp as a sack. Roberts looked up. All but one of the pyramids had moved away. This one hovered over him. He noticed its tentacles had gone rigid. Suddenly he felt weak and sick. The tentacles snapped once. Then, with infinite sliding precision, the red-rimmed Eye began to open again.

Repelled, Roberts looked away. He wondered how long this wretched program would run. What a Godawful thing to create! Viciously he wanted to meet the demented programmer who

114

had put it together. Genius or not, that person was insane!

The high priest smiled and touched the shoulder of another, and pointed. They spoke quickly in their strange dry language, and the soldiers began to move.

He didn't fight them. Because of this, eventually they let him scream.

The security people found him when they responded to the general alarm. One of the guards thought it was an epileptic seizure and managed to get a hanky-wrapped pencil between Roberts's jaws so he didn't quite chew his tongue in half.

Luckily they were able to shut down the power before every computer in the room burned itself out.

Roberts took the full three months' leave allowed by his insurance plan and then came back to work. He had no other place to go. No place at all to hide. His psychiatrist persuaded the company to put him on the day shift. The doctor told them working alone at night could be hazardous to his mental health.

He built a few tenuous friendships. Every once in a while somebody would mention the night all the computers went down and he would shake his head and try a grin. He might run his fingers through the now silver hair on the sides of his skull, so nobody would notice the slight quiver in his hands.

So old, so alien. Even then they had needed a receptor, an intermediary to communicate. Computers must have been unknown then. And why not? They already had nature's most perfect computer. What had happened to break that connection, Roberts couldn't imagine. Or what had caused them finally to leave their city. Had the rumors of Atlantean destruction been more than simple fantasy?

But of course they hadn't really gone away. Just a short distance, to hide, to wait. The earth would turn. The story would repeat. *Something* would come along.

Maybe something even better and more efficient than a simple human brain.

"You know," he would tell them. "How weird computers get sometimes. Just the same old story."

Very *old* story.

They would nod. He would let the conversation drift. Then he would fold up his smile and put it away. When the night came he stayed home and closed the shades and never, ever looked at the moon.

□

CURSE OF THE WEREWOLF'S WIFE

By the time the moon
is replete and brimming
and his transformation
is complete, she has
prepared herself accordingly
with liner and with shadow,
a touch of rouge upon each cheek,
the barest gown to accentuate
her vulnerability beneath.

This time she spends
before her mirrors is used
to bait his awful needs,
to sate his raging appetite
and hold him safe within
her arms while others
of his fated breed
are driven forth by hunger,
to roam the night town streets.

Each time the madness
in his eyes is captured
by her artistry, she endures
a dreadful ritual of rape,
she tastes his lupine breath,

she knows that now familiar
scent so animal and sweet,
the heavy musk which fills
the air to saturate her dreams.

By the time they awaken
he will be a man once more,
who remembers not a moment
of his brief and brutish spree,
who will glance in stray amazement
at the bruises on her flesh,
the blood upon the sheets,
as he begs her for forgiveness
in a voice which makes her weep.

But time will prove her enemy
in spite of all he's said,
the constant cycles of the moon
will turn upon her once again,
and when her slender limbs
have begun to lose their grace,
and when her beauty flees,
what spell will tame this beast
who nightly shares her bed?

— **Bruce Boston**

115

CHILD

OF AN ANCIENT CITY

CITY

by Tad Williams

"**M**erciful Allah! I am as a calf, fatted for slaughter!"

Masrur al-Adan roared with laughter and crashed his goblet down on the polished wood table — once, twice, thrice. A trail of crescent-shaped dents followed his hand. "I can scarce move for gorging."

The fire was banked, and shadows walked the walls. Masrur's table — for he was master here — stood scatter-spread with the bones of small fowl.

Masrur leaned forward and squinted across the table. "A calf," he said. "Fatted." He belched absently and wiped his mouth with wine-stained sleeve.

Ibn Fahad broke off a thin, cold smile. "We have indeed wreaked massacre on the race of pigeons, old friend." His slim hand swept above the littered table-top. "We have also put the elite guard of your wine cellars to flight. And, as usual, I thank you for your hospitality. But do you not sometimes wonder if there is more to life than growing fat in the service of the Caliph? "

"Hah!" Masrur goggled his eyes. "Doing the Caliph's bidding has made me wealthy. I have made *myself* fat." He smiled. The other guests laughed and whispered.

Abu Jamir, a fatter man in an equally stained robe, toppled a small tower erected from the bones of squab. "The night is young, good Masrur!" he cried. "Have someone fetch up more wine and let us hear some stories!"

"Baba!" Masrur bellowed. "Come here, you old dog!"

Within three breaths an old servant stood in the doorway, looking to his sportive master with apprehension.

"Bring us the rest of the wine, Baba — or have you drunk it all?"

Baba pulled at grizzled chin. "Ah . . . ah, but *you* drank it, Master. You and Master Ibn Fahad took the last four jars with you when you went to shoot arrows at the weathercock."

"Just as I suspected," Masrur nodded. "Well, get on across the bazaar to Abu Jamir's place, wake up his manservant, and bring back several jugs. The good Jamir says we must have it now."

Baba disappeared. The chagrined Abu Jamir was cheerfully back-thumped by the other guests.

"A story, a story!" someone shouted. "A tale!"

"Oh, yes, a tale of your travels, Master Masrur!" This was young Hassan, sinfully drunk. No one minded. His eyes were bright, and he was full of innocent stupidity. "Someone said you have traveled to the green lands of the north."

"The north . . . ?" Masrur grumbled, waving his hand as though confronted with something unclean, "No, lad, no . . . that I cannot give to you." His face clouded and he slumped back on his cushions; his tarbooshed head swayed.

Ibn Fahad knew Masrur like he knew his horses — indeed, Masrur was the only human that could claim so much of Ibn Fahad's attention. He had seen his old comrade drink twice this quantity and still dance like a dervish on the walls of Baghdad, but he thought he could guess the reason for this sudden incapacity.

"Oh, Masrur, please!" Hassan had not given up; he was as unshakeable as a young falcon with its first prey beneath its talons. "Tell us of the north. Tell us of the infidels!"

"A good Moslem should not show such interest in unbelievers." Abu Jamir sniffed piously, shaking the last drops from a wine jug. "If Masrur does not wish to tell a tale, let him be."

"Hah!" snorted the host, recovering somewhat, "You only seek to stall me, Jamir, so that my throat shall not be so dry when your wine arrives. No, I have no fear of speaking of unbelievers: Allah would not have given them a place in the world for their own if they had not *some* use. Rather it is . . . certain other things that happened which make me hesitate." He gazed kindly on young Hassan, who in the depths of his drunkenness looked about to cry. "Do not despair, eggling. Perhaps it would do me good to unfold this story. I have kept the details long inside." He emptied the dregs of another jar into his cup. "I still feel it so strongly, though — bitter, bitter times. Why don't *you* tell the story, my good friend? " he said over his shoulder to Ibn Fahad. "You played as much a part as did I."

"No," Ibn Fahad replied. Drunken puppy Hassan emitted a strangled cry of despair.

"But why, old comrade?" Masrur asked, pivoting his bulk to stare in amazement. "Did the experience so chill even *your* heart?"

Ibn Fahad glowered. "Because I know better. As soon as I start you will interrupt, adding details here, magnifying there, then saying: 'No, no, I cannot speak of it! Continue, old friend!' Before I have taken another breath you will interrupt me again. You *know* you will wind up doing all the talking, Masrur. Why do you not start from the beginning and save me my breath?"

All laughed but Masrur, who put on a look of wounded solicitousness. "Of course, old friend," he murmured. "I had no idea that you harbored such grievances. Of course I shall tell the tale." A broad wink was offered to the table. "No sacrifice is too great for a friendship such as ours. Poke up the fire, will you, Baba? Ah, he's gone. Hassan, will you be so kind?"

When the youth was again seated Masrur took a swallow, stroked his beard, and began.

In those days [Masrur said], I myself was but a lowly soldier in the service of Harun al-Rashid, may Allah grant him health. I was young, strong, a man who loved wine more than he should — but what soldier does not? — and a good deal more trim and comely than you see me today.

My troop received a commission to accompany a caravan going north, bound for the land of the Armenites beyond the Caucassian Mountains. A certain prince of that people had sent a great store of gifts as tribute to the Caliph, inviting him to open a route for trade between his principality and our caliphate. Harun al-Rashid, wisest of wise men that he is, did not exactly make the camels groan beneath the weight of the gifts that he sent in return; but he sent several courtiers, including the under-vizier Walid al-Salameh, to speak for him and to assure this Armenite prince that rich rewards would follow when the route over the Caucassians was opened for good.

We left Baghdad in grand style, pennants flying, the shields of the soldiers flashing like golden dinars, and the Caliph's gifts bundled onto the backs of a gang of evil, contrary donkeys.

We followed the banks of the faithful Tigris, resting several days at Mosul, then continued through the eastern edge of Anatolia. Already as we mounted northward the land was beginning to change, the clean sands giving way to rocky hills and scrub. The weather was colder, and the skies gray, as though Allah's face was turned away from that country, but the men were not unhappy to be out from under the desert sun. Our pace was good; there was not a hint of danger except the occasional wolf howling at night beyond the circles of the campfires. Before two months had passed we had reached the foothills of the Caucassians — what is called the steppe country.

For those of you who have not strayed far from our Baghdad, I should tell you that the northern lands are like nothing you have seen. The trees there grow so close together you could not throw

120

a stone five paces without striking one. The land itself seems always dark — the trees mask the sun before the afternoon is properly finished — and the ground is damp. But, in truth, the novelty of it fades quickly, and before long it seems that the smell of decay is always with you. We caravaneers had been over eight weeks a-traveling, and the bite of homesickness was strong, but we contented ourselves with the thought of the accommodations that would be ours when we reached the palace of the prince, laden as we were with our Caliph's good wishes — and the tangible proof thereof.

We had just crossed the high mountain passes and begun our journey down when disaster struck.

We were encamped one night in a box canyon, a thousand steep feet below the summit of the tall Caucassian peaks. The fires were not much but glowing coals, and nearly all the camp was asleep except for two men standing sentry. I was wrapped in my bedroll, dreaming of how I would spend my earnings, when a terrible shriek awakened me. Sitting groggily upright, I was promptly knocked down by some bulky thing tumbling onto me. A moment's horrified examination showed that it was one of the sentries, throat pierced with an arrow, eyes bulging with his final surprise. Suddenly there was a chorus of howls from the hillside above. All I could think of was wolves, that the wolves were coming down on us; in my witless state I could make no sense of the arrow at all.

Even as the others sprang up around me the camp was suddenly filled with leaping, whooping shadows. Another arrow hissed past my face in the darkness, and then something crashed against my bare head, filling the nighttime with a great splash of light that illuminated nothing. I fell back, insensible.

* * *

CHILD OF AN ANCIENT CITY

I could not tell how long I had journeyed in that deeper darkness when I was finally roused by a sharp boot prodding at my ribcage.

I looked up at a tall, cruel figure, cast by the cloud-curtained morning sun in bold silhouette. As my sight became accustomed I saw a knife-thin face, dark-browed and fierce, with mustachios long as a Tartar herdsman's. I felt sure that whoever had struck me had returned to finish the job, and I struggled weakly to pull my dagger from my sash. This terrifying figure merely lifted one of his pointy boots and trod delicately on my wrist, saying in perfect Arabic: "Wonders of Allah, this is the dirtiest man I have ever seen."

It was Ibn Fahad, of course. The caravan had been of good size, and he had been riding with the Armenite and the under-vizier — not back with the hoi polloi — so we had never spoken. Now you see how we first truly met: me on my back, covered with mud, blood, and spit; and Ibn Fahad standing over me like a rich man examining carrots in the bazaar. Infamy!

Ibn Fahad had been blessed with what I would come later to know as his usual luck. When the bandits — who must have been following us for some days — came down upon us in the night, Ibn Fahad had been voiding his bladder some way downslope. Running back at the sound of the first cries, he had sent more than a few mountain bandits down to Hell courtesy of his swift sword, but they were too many. He pulled together a small group of survivors from the main party and they fought their way free, then fled along the mountain in the darkness listening to the screams echoing behind them, cursing their small numbers and ignorance of the country.

Coming back in the light of day to scavenge for supplies, as well as ascertain the nature of our attackers, Ibn Fahad had found me — a fact he has never allowed me to forget, and for which *I* have never allowed *him* to evade responsibility.

While my wounds and bandit-spites were doctored, Ibn Fahad introduced me to the few survivors of our once-great caravan.

One was Susri al-Din — a cheerful lad, fresh-faced and smooth-cheeked as young Hassan here, dressed in the robes of a rich merchant's son. The soldiers who had survived rather liked him, and called him "Fawn," to tease him for his wide-eyed good looks. There was a skinny wretch of a chief clerk named Abdallah, purse-mouthed and iron-eyed, and an indecently plump young mullah, who had just left the *madrasa* and was getting a rather rude introduction to life outside the seminary. Ruad, the mullah, looked as though he would prefer to be drinking and laughing with the soldiers — beside myself and Ibn Fahad there were four or five more of these — while Abdallah the prim-faced clerk looked as though *he* should be the one who never lifted his head out of the Koran. Well, in a way that was true, since for a man like Abdallah the balance book *is* the Holy Book, may Allah forgive such blasphemy.

There was one other, notable for the extreme richness of his robes, the extreme whiteness of his beard, and the vast weight of his personal jewelry — Walid al-Salameh, the under-vizier to His Eminence the Caliph Harun al-Rashid. Walid was the most important man of the whole party. He was also, surprisingly, not a bad fellow at all.

So there we found ourselves, the wrack of the caliph's embassy, with no hope but to try and find our way back home through a strange, hostile land.

The upper reaches of the Caucassians are a cold and godless place. The fog is thick and wet; it crawls in of the morning, leaves briefly at the time the sun

121

is high, then comes creeping back long before sunset. We had been sodden as well-diggers from the moment we had stepped into the foothills. A treacherous place, those mountains: home of bear and wolf, covered in forest so thick that in places the sun was lost completely. Since we had no guide — indeed, it was several days before we saw any sign of inhabitants whatsoever — we wandered unsteered, losing half as much ground as we gained for walking in circles.

At last we were forced to admit our need for a trained local eye. In the middle slopes the trees grew so thick that fixing our direction was impossible for hours at a time. We were divining the location of Mecca by general discussion, and — blasphemy again — we probably spent as much time praying toward Aleppo as to Mecca. It seemed a choice between possible discovery and certain doom.

We came down by night and took a young man out of an isolated shepherd's hovel, as quietly as ex-brigands like ourselves (or at least like many of us, Ibn Fahad. My apologies!) could. The family did not wake, the dog did not bark; we were two leagues away before sunrise, I'm sure.

I felt sorry in a way for the young peasant-lout we'd kidnapped. He was a nice fellow, although fearfully stupid — I wonder if we are now an old, dull story with which he bores his children? In any case, once this young rustic — whose name as far as I could tell was unpronounceable by civilized tongues — realized that we were not ghosts or Jinni, and were *not* going to kill him on the spot, he calmed down and was quite useful. We began to make real progress, reaching the peak of the nearest ridge in two days.

There was a slight feeling of celebration in the air that night, our first in days under the open skies. The soldiers cursed the lack of strong drink, but

spirits were good nonetheless — even Ibn Fahad pried loose a smile.

As the under-vizier Walid told a humorous story, I looked about the camp. There were but two grim faces: the clerk Abdallah — which was to be expected, since he seemed a patently sour old devil — and the stolen peasant-boy. I walked over to him.

"Ho, young one," I said, "why do you look so downcast? Have you not realized that we are good-hearted, Godfearing men, and will not harm you?" He did not even raise his chin, which rested on his knees, shepherd-style, but he turned his eyes up to mine.

"It is not those things," he said in his awkward Arabic. "It is not you soldiers but . . . this place."

"Gloomy mountains they are indeed," I agreed, "but you have lived here all your young life. Why should it bother you? "

"Not this place. We never come here — it is unholy. The vampyr walks these peaks."

"*Vampyr?*" said I. "And what peasant-devil is that?"

He would say no more; I left him to his brooding and walked back to the fire.

The men all had a good laugh over the vampyr, making jesting guesses as to what type of beast it might be, but Ruad, the young mullah, waved his hands urgently.

"I have heard of such afreets," he said. "They are not to be laughed at by such a godless lot as yourselves."

He said this as a sort of scolding joke, but he wore a strange look on his round face; we listened with interest as he continued.

"The vampyr is a restless spirit. It is neither alive nor dead, and Shaitan possesses its soul utterly. It sleeps in a sepulcher by day, and when the moon rises it goes out to feed upon travelers, to drink their blood."

Some of the men again laughed loudly,

but this time it rang false as a brass-merchant's smile.

"I have heard of these from one of our foreign visitors," said the under-vizier Walid quietly. "He told me of a plague of these vampyr in a village near Smyrna. All the inhabitants fled, and the village is still uninhabited today."

This reminded someone else (myself, perhaps) of a tale about an afreet with teeth growing on both sides of his head. Others followed with their own demon stories. The talk went on late into the night, and no one left the campfire until it had completely burned out.

By noon the next day we had left the heights and were passing back down into the dark, tree-blanketed ravines. When we stopped that night we were once more hidden from the stars, out of sight of Allah and the sky.

I remember waking up in the fore-dawn hours. My beard was wet with dew, and I was damnably tangled up in my cloak. A great, dark shape stood over me. I must confess to making a bit of a squawking noise.

"It's me," the shape hissed — it was Rifakh, one of the other soldiers.

"You gave me a turn."

Rifakh chuckled. 'Thought I was that vamper, eh? Sorry. Just stepping out for a piss." He stepped over me, and I heard him trampling the underbrush. I slipped back into sleep.

The sun was just barely over the horizon when I was again awakened, this time by Ibn Fahad tugging at my arm. I grumbled at him to leave me alone, but he had a grip on me like an alms-beggar.

"Rifakh's gone," he said. "Wake up. Have you seen him?"

"He walked on me in the middle of the night, on his way to go moisten a tree," I said. "He probably fell in the darkness and hit his head on something — have you looked?"

"Several times," Ibn Fahad re-sponded. "All around the camp. No sign of him. Did he say anything to you?"

"Nothing interesting. Perhaps he has met the sister of our shepherd-boy, and is making the two-backed beast."

Ibn Fahad made a sour face at my crudity. "Perhaps not. Perhaps he has met some *other* beast."

"Don't worry," I said. "If he hasn't fallen down somewhere close by, he'll be back."

But he did not come back. When the rest of the men arose we had another long search, with no result. At noon we decided, reluctantly, to go on our way, hoping that if he had strayed some-where he could catch up with us.

We hiked down into the valley, going farther and farther into the trees. There was no sign of Rifakh, although from time to time we stopped and shouted in case he was searching for us. We felt there was small risk of discovery, for that dark valley was as empty as a pau-per's purse, but nevertheless, after a while the sound of our voices echoing back through the damp glades became unpleasant. We continued on in silence.

Twilight comes early in the bosom of the mountains; by midafternoon it was already becoming dark. Young Fawn — the name had stuck, against the youth's protests — who of all of us was the most disturbed by the disappear-ance of Rifakh, stopped the company suddenly, shouting: "Look there!"

We straightaway turned to see where he was pointing, but the thick trees and shadows revealed nothing.

"I saw a shape!" the young one said. "It was just a short way back, following us. Perhaps it is the missing soldier."

Naturally the men ran back to look, but though we scoured the bushes we could find no trace of anyone. We de-cided that the failing light had played Fawn a trick — that he had seen a hind or somesuch.

Two other times he called out that he saw a shape. The last time one of the

123

other soldiers glimpsed it too: a dark, man-like form, moving rapidly beneath the trees a bow-shot away. Close inspection still yielded no evidence, and as the group trod wearily back to the path again Walid the under-vizier turned to Fawn with a hard, flat look.

"Perhaps it would be better, young master, if you talked no more of shadow-shapes."

"But I saw it!" the boy cried. "That soldier Mohammad saw it too!"

"I have no doubt of that," answered Walid al-Salameh, "but think on this: we have gone several times to see what it might be, and have found no sign of any living man. Perhaps our Rifakh is dead; perhaps he fell into a stream and drowned, or hit his head upon a rock. His spirit may be following us because it does not wish to stay in this unfamiliar place. That does not mean we want to go and find it."

"But . . . ," the other began.

"Enough!" spat the chief clerk Abdallah. "You heard the under-vizier, young prankster. We shall have no more talk of your godless spirits. You will straightaway leave off telling such things!"

"Your concern is appreciated, Abdallah," Walid said coldly, "but I do not require your help in this matter." The vizier strode away.

I was almost glad the clerk had added his voice, because such ideas would not keep the journey in good order. . . but like the under-vizier I, too, had been rubbed and grated by the clerk's high-handedness. I am sure others felt the same, for no more was said on the subject all evening.

Allah, though, always has the last word — and who are *we* to try to understand His ways? We bedded down a very quiet camp that night, the idea of poor Rifakh's lost soul hanging unspoken in the air.

From a thin, unpleasant sleep I woke to find the camp in chaos. "It's Moham-

mad, the soldier!" Fawn was crying. "He's been killed! He's dead!"

It was true. The mullah Ruad, first up in the morning, had found the man's blanket empty, then found his body a few short yards out of the clearing.

"His throat has been slashed out," said Ibn Fahad.

It looked like a wild beast had been at him. The ground beneath was dark with blood, and his eyes were wide open.

Above the cursing of the soldiers and the murmured holy words of the mullah, who looked quite green of face, I heard another sound. The young shepherd-lad, grimly silent all the day before, was rocking back and forth on the ground by the remains of the cook-fire, moaning.

"Vampyr . . . ," he wept, ". . . vampyr, the vampyr . . ."

All the companions were, of course, completely unmanned by these events. While we buried Mohammad in a hastily dug grave those assembled darted glances over their shoulders into the forest vegetation. Even Ruad, as he spoke the words of the holy Koran, had trouble keeping his eyes down. Ibn Fahad and I agreed between ourselves to maintain that Mohammad had fallen prey to a wolf or some other beast, but our fellow travelers found it hard even to pretend agreement. Only the under-vizier and the clerk Abdallah seemed to have their wits fully about them, and Abdallah made no secret of his contempt for the others. We set out again at once.

Our company was somber that day — and no wonder. No one wished to speak of the obvious, nor did they have much stomach for talk of lighter things — it was a silent file of men that moved through the mountain fastnesses.

As the shadows of evening began to roll down, the dark shape was with us again, flitting along just in sight, disappearing for a while only to return, bobbing along behind us like a jackdaw. My skin was crawling — as you may well believe — though I tried to hide it.

We set camp, building a large fire and moving near to it, and had a sullen, close-cramped supper. Ibn Fahad, Abdallah, the vizier, and I were still speaking of the follower only as some beast. Abdallah may even have believed it — not from ordinary foolishness, but because he was the type of man who was unwilling to believe there might be anything he himself could not compass.

As we took turns standing guard the young mullah led the far-from-sleepy men in prayer. The voices rose up with the smoke, neither seeming to be of much substance against the wind of those old, cold mountains.

I sidled over to the shepherd-lad. He'd become, if anything, more close-mouthed since the discovery of the morning.

"This 'vampyr' you spoke of . . . ," I said quietly. "What do your people do to protect themselves from it?"

He looked up at me with a sad smile. "Lock the doors."

I stared across at the other men — young Fawn with clenched mouth and furrowed brow; the mullah Ruad, eyes closed, plump cheeks awash with sweat as he prayed; Ibn Fahad gazing coolly outward, ever outward — and then I returned the boy's sad smile.

"No doors to lock, no windows to bar," I said. "What else?"

"There is an herb we hang about our houses . . . ," he said, and fumbled for the word in our unfamiliar language. After a moment he gave up. "It does not matter. We have none. None grows here."

I leaned forward, putting my face next to his face. "For the love of God, boy, what else?" — *I* knew it was not a beast of the Earth. *I knew.* I had seen that fluttering shadow.

"Well . . . ," he mumbled, turning his

face away, ". . . they say, some men do, that you can tell stories. . . ."

"What!" I thought he had gone mad.

"This is what my grandfather says. The vampyr will stop to hear the story you tell — if it is a good one — and if you continue it until daylight he must return to the . . . place of the dead."

There was a sudden shriek. I leaped to my feet, fumbling for my knife . . . but it was only Ruad, who had put his foot against a hot coal. I sank down again, heart hammering.

"Stories?" I asked.

"I have only heard so," he said, struggling for the right phrases. "We try to keep them farther away than that — they must come close to hear a man talking."

Later, after the fire had gone down, we placed sentries and went to our blankets. I lay a long while thinking of what the Armenite boy had said before I slept.

A hideous screeching sound woke me. It was not yet dawn, and this time no one had burned himself on a glowing ember.

One of the two soldiers who had been standing picket lay on the forest floor, blood gouting from a great wound on the side of his head. In the torchlight it looked as though his skull had been smashed with a heavy cudgel. The other sentry was gone, but there was a terrible thrashing in the underbrush beyond the camp, and screams that would have sounded like an animal in a cruel trap but for the half-formed words that bubbled up from time to time.

We crouched, huddled, staring like startled rabbits. The screaming began to die away. Suddenly Ruad started up, heavy and clumsy getting to his feet. I saw tears in his eyes. "We . . . we must not leave our fellow to s-s-suffer so!" he cried, and looked around at all of us. I don't think anyone could hold his eye

126

except the clerk Abdallah. I could not.

"Be silent, fool!" the clerk said, heedless of blasphemy. "It is a wild beast. It is for these cowardly soldiers to attend to, not a man of God!"

The young mullah stared at him for a moment, and a change came over his face. The tears were still wet on his cheeks, but I saw his jaw firm and his shoulders square.

"No," he said. "We cannot leave him to Shaitan's servant. If you will not go to him, I will." He rolled up the scroll he had been nervously fingering and kissed it. A shaft of moonlight played across the gold letters.

I tried to grab his arm as he went past me, but he shook me off with surprising strength, then moved toward the brush, where the screeching had died down to a low, broken moaning.

"Come back, you idiot!" Abdallah shrieked at him. "This is foolishness! Come back!"

The young holy man looked back over his shoulder, darting a look at Abdallah I could not easily describe, then turned around and continued forward, holding the parchment scroll before him as if it were a candle against the dark night. *"There is no God but Allah!"* I heard him cry, *"and Mohammad is His prophet!"* Then he was gone.

After a long moment of silence there came the sound of the holy words of the Koran, chanted in an unsteady voice. We could hear the mullah making his ungraceful way out through the thicket. I was not the only one who held his breath.

Next there was crashing, and branches snapping, as though some huge beast was leaping through the brush; the mullah's chanting became a howl. Men cursed helplessly. Before the cry had faded, though, another scream came — numbingly loud, the rage of a powerful animal, full of shock and surprise. It had words in it, although not in any tongue I had ever heard before . . . or since.

Another great thrashing, and then nothing but silence. We lit another fire and sat sleepless until dawn.

In the morning, despite my urgings, the company went to look for trace of the sentry and the young priest. They found them both.

It made a grim picture, let me tell you, my friends. They hung upside down from the branches of a great tree. Their necks were torn, and they were white as chalk: all the blood had been drawn from them. We dragged the two stone-cold husks back to the camp-circle, and shortly thereafter buried them commonly with the other sentry, who had not survived his head wound.

One curious thing there was: on the ground beneath the hanging head of the young priest lay the remains of his holy scroll. It was scorched to black ash, and crumbled at my touch.

"So it *was* a cry of pain we heard," said Ibn Fahad over my shoulder. "The devil-beast can be hurt, it appears."

"Hurt, but not made to give over," I observed. "And no other holy writings remain, nor any hands so holy to wield them, or mouth to speak them." I looked pointedly over at Abdallah, who was giving unwanted instructions to the two remaining soldiers on how to spade the funeral dirt. I half-hoped one of them would take it on himself to brain the old meddler.

"True,"grunted Ibn Fahad. "Well, I have my doubts on how cold steel will fare, also."

"As do I. But it could be there is yet a way we may save ourselves. The shepherd-boy told me of it. I will explain when we stop at mid-day."

"I will be waiting eagerly," said Ibn Fahad, favoring me with his half-smile. "I am glad to see someone else is thinking and planning beside myself. But perhaps you should tell us your plan on the march. Our daylight hours are be-coming precious as blood, now. As a matter of fact, I think from now on we shall have to do without burial services."

Well, there we were in a very nasty fix. As we walked I explained my plan to the group; they listened silently, downcast, like men condemned to death — not an unreasonable attitude, in all truth.

"Now, here's the thing," I told them. "If this young lout's idea of tale-telling will work, we shall have to spend our nights yarning away. We may have to begin taking stops for sleeping in the daylight. Every moment walking, then, is precious — we must keep the pace up or we will die in these damned, haunted mountains. Also, while you walk, think of stories. From what the lad says we may have another ten days or a fortnight to go until we escape this country. We shall soon run out of things to tell about unless you dig deep into your memories."

There was grumbling, but it was too dispirited a group to offer much protest.

"Be silent, unless you have a better idea," said Ibn Fahad. "Masrur is quite correct — although, if what I suspect is true, it may be the first time in his life he finds himself in that position." He threw me a wicked grin, and one of the soldiers snickered. It was a good sound to hear.

We had a short mid-day rest — most of us got at least an hour's sleep on the rocky ground — and then we walked on until the beginning of twilight. We were in the bottom of a long, thickly forested ravine, where we promptly built a large fire to keep away some of the darkness of the valley floor. Ah, but fire is a good friend!

Gathered around the blaze, the men cooked strips of venison on the ends of green sticks. We passed the water skin and wished it was more — not for the

127

first time.

"Now then," I said, "I'll go first, for at home I was the one called upon most often to tell tales, and I have a good fund of them. Some of you may sleep, but not all — there should always be two or three awake in case the teller falters or forgets. We cannot know if this will keep the creature at bay, but we should take no chances."

So I began, telling first the story of The Four Clever Brothers. It was early, and no one was ready to sleep; all listened attentively as I spun it out, adding details here, stretching a description there.

When it ended I was applauded, and straight away began telling the story of the carpet merchant Salim and his unfaithful wife. That was perhaps not a good choice — it is a story about a vengeful djinn, and about death; but I went on nonetheless, finished it, then told two more.

As I was finishing the fourth story, about a brave orphan who finds a cave of jewels, I glimpsed a strange thing.

The fire was beginning to die down, and as I looked out over the flames I saw movement in the forest. The under-vizier Walid was directly across from me, and beyond his once-splendid robes a dark shape lurked. It came no closer than the edge of the trees, staying just out of the fire's flickering light. I lost my voice for a moment then and stuttered, but quickly caught up the thread and finished. No one had noticed, I was sure.

I asked for the waterskin and motioned for Walid al-Salameh to continue. He took up with a tale of the rivalry beyond two wealthy houses in his native Isfahan. One or two of the others wrapped themselves tightly in their cloaks and lay down, staring up as they listened, watching the sparks rise into the darkness.

I pulled my hood down low on my brow to shield my gaze, and squinted

out past Walid's shoulder. The dark shape had moved a little nearer now to the lapping glow of the campfire.

It was man-shaped, that I could see fairly well, though it clung close to the trunk of a tree at clearing's edge. Its face was in darkness; two ember-red eyes unblinkingly reflected the firelight. It seemed clothed in rags, but that could have been a trick of the shadows.

Huddled in the darkness a stone-throw away, it was listening.

I turned my head slowly across the circle. Most eyes were on the vizier; Fawn had curtained his in sleep. But Ibn Fahad, too, was staring out into the darkness. I suppose he felt my gaze, for he turned to me and nodded slightly: he had seen it too.

We went on until dawn, the men taking turns sleeping as one of the others told stories — mostly tales they had heard as children, occasionally of an adventure that had befallen them. Ibn Fahad and I said nothing of the dark shape that watched. Somewhere in the hour before dawn it disappeared.

It was a sleepy group that took to the trail that day, but we had all lived through the night. This alone put the men in better spirits, and we covered much ground.

That night we again sat around the fire. I told the story of The Gazelle King, and The Enchanted Peacock, and The Little Man with No Name, each of them longer and more complicated than the one before. Everyone except the clerk Abdallah contributed something — Abdallah and the shepherd-boy, that is. The chief-clerk said repeatedly that he had never wasted his time on foolishness such as learning stories. We were understandably reluctant to press our self-preservation into such unwilling hands.

The Armenite boy, our guide, sat quietly all the evening and listened to the men yarning away in a tongue that was not his own. When the moon had risen through the treetops, the shadow returned and stood silently outside the clearing. I saw the peasant lad look up. He saw it, I know, but like Ibn Fahad and I, he held his silence.

The next day brought us two catastrophes. As we were striking camp in the morning, happily no fewer than when we had set down the night before, the local lad took the waterskins down to the river that threaded the bottom of the ravine. When a long hour had passed and he had not returned, we went fearfully down to look for him.

He was gone. All but one of the waterskins lay on the streambank. He had filled them first.

The men were panicky. "The vampyr has taken him!" they cried.

"What does that foul creature need with a waterskin?" pointed out al-Salameh.

"He's right," I said. "No, I'm afraid our young friend has merely jumped ship, so to speak. I suppose he thinks his chances of getting back are better if he is alone."

I wondered . . . I *still* wonder . . . if he made it back. He was not a bad fellow: witness the fact that he took only one water-bag, and left us the rest.

Thus, we found ourselves once more without a guide. Fortunately, I had discussed with him the general direction, and he had told Ibn Fahad and myself of the larger landmarks . . . but it was nevertheless with sunken hearts that we proceeded.

Later that day, in the early afternoon, the second blow fell.

We were coming up out of the valley, climbing diagonally along the steep side of the ravine. The damned Caucassian fogs had slimed the rocks and turned the ground soggy; the footing was treacherous.

Achmed, the older of the remaining pike-men, had been walking poorly all

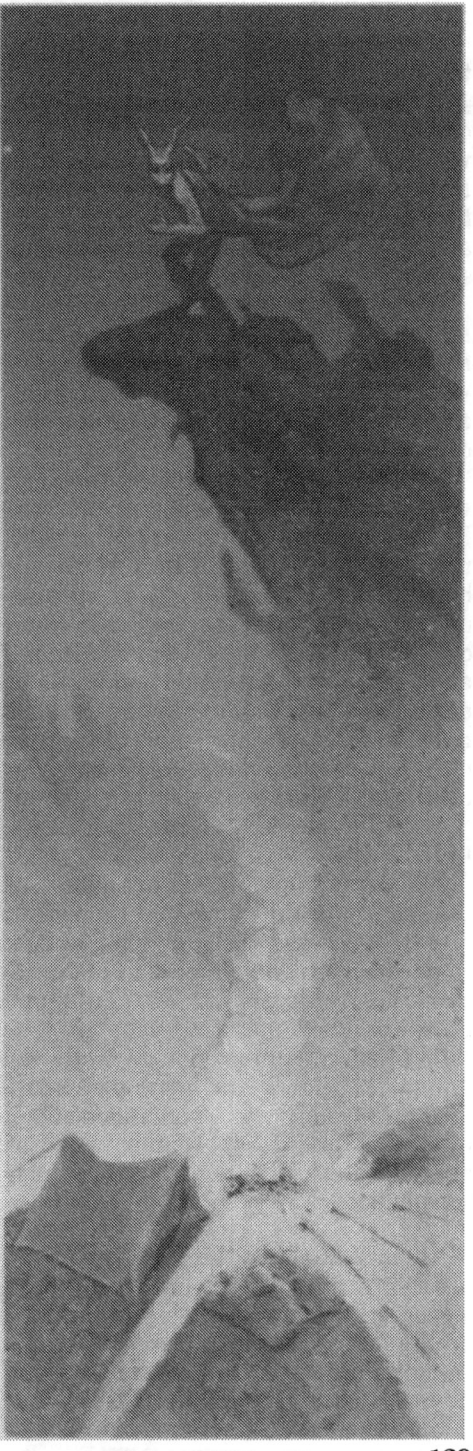

day. He had bad joints, anyway, he said; and the cold nights had been making them worse.

We had stopped to rest on an outcropping of rock that jutted from the valley wall; and Achmed, the last in line, was just catching up to us when he slipped. He fell heavily onto his side and slid several feet down the muddy slope.

Ibn Fahad jumped up to look for a rope, but before he could get one from the bottom of his pack the other soldier — named Bekir, if memory serves — clambered down the grade to help his comrade.

He got a grip on Achmed's tunic, and was just turning around to catch Ibn Fahad's rope when the leg of the older man buckled beneath him and he fell backward. Bekir, caught off his balance, pitched back as well, his hand caught in the neck of Achmed's tunic, and the two of them rolled end over end down the slope. Before anyone could so much as cry out they had both disappeared over the edge, like a wine jug rolling off a table-top. Just that sudden.

To fall such a distance certainly killed them.

We could not find the bodies, of course . . . could not even climb back down the ravine to look. Ibn Fahad's remark about burials had taken on a terrible, ironic truth. We could but press on, now a party of five — myself, Ibn Fahad, the under-vizier Walid, Abdallah the clerk, and young Fawn. I doubt that there was a single one of our number who did not wonder which of us would next meet death in that lonesome place.

Ah, by Allah most high, I have never been so sick of the sound of my own voice as I was by the time nine more nights had passed. Ibn Fahad, I know, would say that I have never understood how sick *everyone* becomes of the sound of my voice — am I correct, old friend?

130

But I *was* tired of it, tired of talking all night, tired of racking my brain for stories, tired of listening to the cracked voices of Walid and Ibn Fahad, tired to sickness of the damp, gray, oppressive mountains.

All were now aware of the haunting shade that stood outside our fire at night, waiting and listening. Young Fawn, in particular, could hardly hold up his turn at tale-telling, so much did his voice tremble.

Abdallah grew steadily colder and colder, congealing like rendered fat. The thing which followed was no respecter of his cynicism or his mathematics, and would not be banished for all the scorn he could muster. The skinny chief-clerk did not turn out to us, though, to support the story-circle, but sat silently and walked apart. Despite our terrible mutual danger he avoided our company as much as possible.

The tenth night after the loss of Achmed and Bekir we were running out of tales. We had been ground down by our circumstances, and were ourselves become nearly as shadowy as that which we feared.

Walid al-Salameh was droning on about some ancient bit of minor intrigue in the court of the Emperor Darius of Persia. Ibn Fahad leaned toward me, lowering his voice so that neither Abdallah or Fawn — whose expression was one of complete and hopeless despair — could hear.

"Did you notice," he whispered, "that our guest has made no appearance tonight?"

"It has not escaped me," I said. "I hardly think it a good sign, however. If our talk no longer interests the creature, how long can it be until its thoughts return to our other uses?"

"I fear you're right," he responded, and gave a scratchy, painful chuckle. "There's a good three or four more days walking, and hard walking at that, until we reach the bottom of these mountains and come once more onto the plain, at which point we might hope the devil-beast would leave us."

"Ibn Fahad," I said, shaking my head as I looked across at Fawn's drawn, pale face, "I fear we shall not manage . . ."

As if to point up the truth of my fears, Walid here stopped his speech, coughing violently. I gave him to drink of the water-skin, but when he had finished he did not begin anew; he only sat looking darkly, as one lost, out to the forest.

"Good vizier," I asked, "can you continue?"

He said nothing, and I quickly spoke in his place, trying to pick up the threads of a tale I had not been attending to. Walid leaned back, exhausted and breathing raggedly. Abdallah clucked his tongue in disgust. If I had not been fearfully occupied, I would have struck the clerk.

Just as I was beginning to find my way, inventing a continuation of the vizier's Darian political meanderings, there came a shock that passed through all of us like a cold wind, and a new shadow appeared at the edge of the clearing. The vampyr had joined us.

Walid moaned and sat up, huddling by the fire. I faltered for a moment but went on. The candle-flame eyes regarded us unblinkingly, and the shadow shook for a moment as if folding great wings.

Suddenly Fawn leaped to his feet, swaying unsteadily. I lost the strands of the story completely and stared up at him in amazement.

"Creature!" he screamed. "Hell-spawn! Why do you torment us in this way? Why, why, why?"

Ibn Fahad reached up to pull him down, but the young man danced away like a shying horse. His mouth hung open and his eyes were starting from their dark-rimmed sockets.

"You great beast!" he continued to shriek. "Why do you toy with us? Why do you not just kill me — kill us *all*, set us free from this terrible, terrible . . ."

And with that he walked *forward* — away from the fire, toward the thing that crouched at forest's edge.

"End this now!" Fawn shouted, and fell to this knees only a few strides from the smoldering red eyes, sobbing like a child.

"Stupid boy, get back!" I cried. Before I could get up to pull him back — and I would have, I swear by Allah's name — there was a great rushing noise, and the black shape was gone, the lamps of its stare extinguished. Then, as we pulled the shuddering youth back to the campfire, something rustled in the trees. On the opposite side of the campfire one of the near branches suddenly bobbed beneath the weight of a strange new fruit — a black fruit with red-lit eyes. It made an awful croaking noise.

In our shock it was a few moments before we realized that the deep, rasping sound was speech — and the words were Arabic!

". . . It . . . was . . . you . . . ," it said, ". . . who chose . . . to play the game this way . . ."

Almost strangest of all, I would swear that this thing had never spoken our language before, never even heard it until we had wandered lost into the mountains. Something of its halting inflections, its strange hesitations, made me guess it had learned our speech from listening all these nights to our campfire stories.

"Demon!" shrilled Abdallah. "What manner of creature are you?!"

"You know . . . very well what kind of . . . thing I am, man. You may none of you know *how*, or *why* . . . but by now, you know *what* I am."

"Why . . . why do you torment us so?!" shouted Fawn, writhing in Ibn Fahad's strong grasp.

"Why does the . . . serpent kill . . . a rabbit? The serpent does not . . . hate. It kills to live, as do I . . . as do you."

131

Abdallah lurched forward a step. "We do not slaughter our fellow men like this, devil-spawn!"

"C-c-clerk!" the black shape hissed, and dropped down from the tree. "C-close your foolish mouth! You push me too far!" It bobbed, as if agitated. "The curse of human ways! Even now you provoke me more than you should, you huffing . . . insect! *Enough!*"

The vampyr seemed to leap upward, and with a great rattling of leaves he scuttled away along the limb of a tall tree. I was fumbling for my sword, but before I could find it the creature spoke again from his high perch.

"The young one asked me why I 'toy' with you. I do not. If I do not kill, I will suffer. More than I suffer already.

"Despite what this clerk says, though, I am not a creature without . . . without feelings as men have them. Less and less do I wish to destroy you.

"For the first time in a great age I have listened to the sound of human voices that were not screams of fear. I have approached a circle of men without the barking of dogs, and have listened to them talk.

"It has almost been like being a man again."

"And this is how you show your pleasure?" the under-vizier Walid asked, teeth chattering. "By k-k-killing us?"

"I am what I am," said the beast. ". . . But for all that, you have inspired a certain desire for companionship. It puts me in mind of things that I can barely remember.

"I propose that we make a . . . bargain," said the vampyr. "A . . . wager?"

I had found my sword, and Ibn Fahad had drawn his as well, but we both knew we could not kill a thing like this — a red-eyed demon that could leap five cubits in the air and had learned to speak our language in a fortnight.

"No bargains with Shaitan!" spat the clerk Abdallah.

"What do you mean?" I demanded,

inwardly marveling that such an unlikely dialogue should ever take place on the earth. "Pay no attention to the . . ." I curled my lip, ". . . holy man." Abdallah shot me a venomous glance.

"Hear me, then," the creature said, and in the deep recesses of the tree seemed once more to unfold and stretch great wings. "Hear me. I must kill to live, and my nature is such that I cannot choose to die. That is the way of things.

"I offer you now, however, the chance to win safe passage out of my domain, these hills. We shall have a contest, a wager if you like; if you best me you shall go freely, and I shall turn once more to the musty, slow-blooded peasants of the local valleys."

Ibn Fahad laughed bitterly. "What, are we to fight you then? So be it!"

"I would snap your spine like a dry branch," croaked the black shape. "No, you have held me these many nights telling stories; it is story-telling that will win you safe passage. We will have a contest, one that will suit my whims: we shall relate the saddest of all stories. That is my demand. You may tell three, I will tell only one. If you can best me with any or all, you shall go unhindered by me."

"And if we lose?!" I cried. "And who shall judge?"

"You may judge," it said, and the deep, thick voice took on a tone of grim amusement. "If you can look into my eyes and tell me that you have bested *my* sad tale . . . why, then I shall believe you.

"If you lose," it said, "then one of your number shall come to me, and pay the price of your defeat. Those are my terms, otherwise I shall hunt you down one at a time — for in truth, your present tale-telling has begun to lose my interest."

Ibn Fahad darted a worried look in my direction. Fawn and the others stared at the demon-shape in mute terror and astonishment.

"We shall . . . we shall give you our decision at sunset tomorrow," I said. "We must be allowed to think and talk."

"As you wish," said the vampyr. "But if you accept my challenge, the game must begin then. After all, we have only a few more days to spend together." And at this the terrible creature laughed, a sound like the bark being pulled from the trunk of a rotted tree. Then the shadow was gone.

In the end we had to accede to the creature's wager, of course. We knew he was not wrong in his assessment of us — we were just wagging our beards over the nightly campfire, no longer even listening to our own tales. Whatever magic had held the vampyr at bay had drained out like meal from a torn sack.

I racked my poor brains all afternoon for stories of sadness, but could think of nothing that seemed to fit, that seemed significant enough for the vital purpose at hand. I had been doing most of the talking for several nights running, and had exhausted virtually every story I had ever heard — and I was never much good at making them up, as Ibn Fahad will attest. Yes, go ahead and smile, old comrade.

Actually, it was Ibn Fahad who volunteered the first tale. I asked him what it was, but he would not tell me. "Let me save what potency it may have," he said. The under-vizier Walid also had something he deemed suitable, I was racking my brain fruitlessly for a third time when young Fawn piped up that he would tell a tale himself. I looked him over, rosy cheeks and long-lashed eyes, and asked him what he could possibly know of sadness. Even as I spoke I realized my cruelty, standing as we all did in the shadow of death or worse; but it was too late to take it back.

Fawn did not flinch. He was folding his cloak as he sat cross-ankled on the ground, folding and unfolding it. He looked up and said: "I shall tell a sad story about love. All the saddest stories are about love."

These young shavetails, I thought — although I was not ten years his senior — *a sad story about love.* But I could not think of better, and was forced to give in.

We walked as fast and far as we could that day, as if hoping that somehow, against all reason, we should find ourselves out of the gloomy, mist-sodden hills. But when twilight came the vast bulk of the mountains still hung above us. We made camp on the porch of a great standing rock, as though protection at our backs would avail us of something if the night went badly.

The fire had only just taken hold, and the sun had dipped below the rim of the hills a moment before, when a cold wind made the branches of the trees whip back and forth. We knew without speaking, without looking at one another, that the creature had come.

"Have you made your decision?" The harsh voice from the trees sounded strange, as if its owner was trying to speak lightly, carelessly — but I only heard death in those cold syllables.

"We have, " said Ibn Fahad, drawing himself up out of his involuntary half-crouch to stand erect. "We will accept your wager. Do you wish to begin?"

"Oh, no . . ." the thing said, and made a flapping noise. "That would take all of the . . . suspense from the contest, would it not? No, In insist that you begin."

"I am first, then," Ibn Fahad said, looking around our circle for confirmation. The dark shape moved abruptly toward us. Before we could scatter the vampyr stopped, a few short steps away.

"Do not fear," it grated. Close to one's ear the voice was even odder and more strained. "I have come nearer to hear the story and see the teller — for surely that is part of any tale — but I shall move no farther. Begin."

Everybody but myself stared into the fire, hugging their knees, keeping their eyes averted from the bundle of darkness that sat at our shoulders. I had the fire between myself and the creature, and felt safer than if I had sat like Walid and Abdallah, with nothing between the beast and my back but cold ground.

The vampyr sat hunched, as if imitating our posture, its eyes hooded so that only a flicker of scarlet light, like a half-buried brand, showed through the slit. It was black, this manlike thing — not black as a Negro, mind you, but black as burnt steel, black as the mouth of a cave. It bore the aspect of someone dead of the plague. Rags wrapped it, mouldering, filthy bits of cloth, rotten as old bread . . . but the curve of its back spoke of terrible life — a great black cricket poised to jump.

Ibn Fahad's Story

Many years ago [he began], I traveled for a good time in Egypt. I was indigent, then, and journeyed wherever the prospect of payment for a sword arm beckoned.

I found myself at last in the household guard of a rich merchant in Alexandria. I was happy enough there; and I enjoyed walking in the busy streets, so unlike the village in which I was born.

One summer evening I found myself walking down an unfamiliar street. It emptied out into a little square that sat below the front of an old mosque. The square was full of people, merchants and fishwives, a juggler or two, but most of the crowd was drawn up to the façade of the mosque, pressed in close together.

At first, as I strolled across the square,

134

I thought prayers were about to begin, but it was still some time until sunset. I wondered if perhaps some notable *imam* was speaking from the mosque steps, but as I approached I could see that all the assembly were staring upward, craning their necks back as if the sun itself, on its way to its western mooring, had become snagged on one of the minarets.

But instead of the sun, what stood on the onion-shaped dome was the silhouette of a man, who seemed to be staring out toward the horizon.

"Who is that?" I asked a man near me.

"It is Ha'arud al-Emwiya, the Sufi," the man told me, never lowering his eyes from the tower above.

"Is he caught up there?" I demanded. "Will he not fall?"

"Watch," was all the man said. I did.

A moment later, much to my horror, the small dark figure of Ha'arud the Sufi seemed to go rigid, then toppled from the minaret's rim like a stone. I gasped in shock, and so did a few others around me, but the rest of the crowd only stood in hushed attention.

Then an incredible thing happened. The tumbling holy man spread his arms out from his shoulders, like a bird's wings, and his downward fall became a swooping glide. He bottomed out high above the crowd, then sped upward, riding the wind like a leaf, spinning, somersaulting, stopping at last to drift to the ground as gently as a bit of eiderdown. Meanwhile, all the assembly was chanting "God is great! God is great!" When the sufi had touched the earth with his bare feet the people surrounded him, touching his rough woolen garments and crying out his name. He said nothing, only stood and smiled, and before too long the people began to wander away, talking amongst themselves.

"But this is truly marvelous!" I said to the man who stood by me.

"Before every holy day he flies," the man said, and shrugged. "I am surprised this is the first time you have heard of Ha'arud al-Emwiya."

I was determined to speak to this amazing man, and as the crowd dispersed I approached and asked if I might buy him a glass of tea. Close up he had a look of seamed roguishness that seemed surprising placed against the great favor in which Allah must have held him. He smilingly agreed, and accompanied me to a tea shop close by in the Street of Weavers.

"How is it, if you will pardon my forwardness, that you of all holy men are so gifted?"

He looked up from the tea cupped in his palms and grinned. He had only two teeth. "Balance," he said.

I was surprised. "A cat has balance," I responded, "but they nevertheless must wait for the pigeons to land."

"I refer to a different sort of balance," he said. "The balance between Allah and Shaitan, which, as you know, Allah the All-Knowing has created as an equilibrium of exquisite delicacy."

"Explain please, master." I called for wine, but Ha'arud refused any himself.

"In all things care must be exercised," he explained. "Thus it is too with my flying. Many men holier than I are as earthbound as stones. Many other men have lived so poorly as to shame the Devil himself, yet they cannot take to the air, either. Only I, if I may be excused what sounds self-satisfied, have discovered perfect balance. Thus, each year before the holy days I tot up my score carefully, committing small pecadilloes or acts of faith as needed until the balance is exactly, exactly balanced. Thus, when I jump from the mosque, neither Allah nor the Arch-Enemy has claim on my soul, and they bear me up until a later date, at which time the issue shall be clearer." He smiled again and drained his tea.

"You are . . . a sort of chessboard on which God and the Devil contend?" I asked, perplexed.

"A flying chessboard, yes."

We talked for a long while, as the shadows grew long across the Street of the Weavers, but the Sufi Ha'arud adhered stubbornly to his explanation. I must have seemed disbelieving, for he finally proposed that we ascend to the top of the mosque so he could demonstrate.

I was more than a little drunk, and he, imbibing only tea, was filled nonetheless with a strange gleefulness. We made our way up the many winding stairs and climbed out onto the narrow ledge that circled the minaret like a crown. The cool night air, and the thousands of winking lights of Alexandria far below, sobered me rapidly. "I suddenly find all your precepts very sound," I said. "Let us go down."

But Ha'arud would have none of it, and proceeded to step lightly off the edge of the dome. He hovered, like a bumblebee, a hundred feet above the dusty street. "Balance," he said with great satisfaction.

"But," I asked, "is the good deed of giving me this demonstration enough to offset the pride with which you exhibit your skill?" I was cold and wanted to get down, and hoped to shorten the exhibition.

Instead, hearing my question, Ha'arud screwed up his face as though it was something he had not given thought to. A moment later, with a shriek of surprise, he plummeted down out of my sight to smash on the mosque's stone steps, as dead as dead.

○ ● ○

Ibn Fahad, having lost himself in remembering the story, poked at the campfire. "Thus, the problem with matters of delicate balance," he said, and shook his head.

The whispering rustle of our dark

135

visitor brought us sharply back. "Interesting," the creature rasped. "Sad, yes. Sad enough? We shall see. Who is the next of your number?"

A cold chill, like fever, swept over me at those calm words.

"I . . . I am next . . . ," said Fawn, voice taut as a bowstring. "Shall I begin?"

"The vampyr said nothing, only bobbed the black lump of his head. The youth cleared his throat and began.

Fawn's Story

There was once . . . [Fawn began, and hesitated, then started again.] There was once a young prince named Zufik, the second son of a great sultan. Seeing no prospects for himself in his father's kingdom, he went out into the wild world to search for his fortune. He traveled through many lands, and saw many strange things, and heard tell of others stranger still.

In one place he was told of a nearby sultanate, the ruler of which had a beautiful daughter, his only child and the very apple of his eye.

Now this country had been plagued for several years by a terrible beast, a great white leopard of a kind never seen before. So fearsome it was that it had killed hunters set to trap it, yet was it also so cunning that it had stolen babies from their very cradles as the mothers lay sleeping. The people of the sultanate were all in fear; and the sultan, whose best warriors had tried and failed to kill the beast, was driven to despair. Finally, at the end of his wits, he had it proclaimed in the market place that the man who could destroy the white leopard would be gifted with the sultan's daughter Rassoril, and with her the throne of the sultanate after the old man was gone.

Young Zufik heard how the best young men of the country, and others

from countries beyond, one after the other had met their deaths beneath the claws of the leopard, or . . . or . . . in its jaws. . . .

[Here I saw the boy falter, as if the vision of flashing teeth he was conjuring had suddenly reminded him of our predicament. Walid the under-vizier reached out and patted the lad's shoulder with great gentleness, until he was calm enough to resume.]

So . . . [He swallowed.] So young Prince Zufik took himself into that country, and soon was announced at the sultan's court.

The ruler was a tired old man, the fires in his sunken eyes long quenched. Much of the power seemed to have been handed over to a pale, narrow-faced youth named Sifaz, who was the princess's cousin. As Zufik announced his purpose, as so many had done before him, Sifaz's eyes flashed.

"You will no doubt meet the end all the others have, but you are welcome to the attempt — and the prize, should you win."

Then for the first time Zufik saw the princess Rassoril, and in an instant his heart was overthrown.

She had hair as black and shiny as polished jet, and a face upon which Allah himself must have looked in satisfaction, thinking: "Here is the summit of My art." Her delicate hands were like tiny doves as they nested in her lap, and a man could fall into her brown eyes and drown without hope of rescue — which is what Zufik did, and he was not wrong when he thought he saw Rassoril return his ardent gaze.

Sifaz saw, too, and his thin mouth turned in something like a smile, and he narrowed his yellow eyes. "Take this princeling to his room, that he may sleep now and wake with the moon. The leopard's cry was heard around the palace's walls last night."

Indeed, when Zufik woke in the evening darkness, it was to hear the choking cry of the leopard beneath his very window. As he looked out, buckling on his scabbard, it was to see a white shape slipping in and out of the shadows in the garden below. He took also his dagger in his hand and leaped over the threshold.

He had barely touched ground when, with a terrible snarl, the leopard bounded out of the obscurity of the hedged garden wall and came to a stop before him. It was huge — bigger than any leopard Zufik had seen or heard of — and its pelt gleamed like ivory. It leaped, claws flashing, and he could barely throw himself down in time as the beast passed over him like a cloud, touching him only with its hot breath. It turned and leaped again as the palace dogs set up a terrible barking, and this time its talons raked his chest, knocking him tumbling. Blood started from his shirt, spouting so fiercely that he could scarcely draw himself to his feet. He was caught with his back against the garden wall; the leopard slowly moved toward him, yellow eyes like tallow lamps burning in the niches of Hell.

Suddenly there was a crashing at the far end of the garden: the dogs had broken down their stall and were even now speeding through the trees. The leopard hesitated — Zufik could almost see it thinking — and then, with a last snarl, it leaped onto the wall and disappeared into the night.

Zufik was taken, his wounds bound, and he was put into his bed. The princess Rassoril, who had truly lost her heart to him, wept bitterly at his side, begging him to go back to his father's land and to give up the fatal challenge. But Zufik, weak as he was, would no more think of yielding than he would of theft or treason, and refused, saying he would hunt the beast again the following night. Sifaz grinned and led the princess away. Zufik thought he heard the pale cousin whistling as he went.

In the dark before dawn Zufik, who

could not sleep owing to the pain of his injury, heard his door quietly open. He was astonished to see the princess come in, gesturing him to silence. When the door was closed she threw herself down at his side and covered his hand and cheek with kisses, proclaiming her love for him and begging him again to go. He admitted his love for her, but reminded her that his honor would not permit him to stop short of his goal, even should he die in the trying.

Rassoril, seeing that there was no changing the young prince's mind, then took from her robe a black arrow tipped in silver, fletched with the tail feathers of a falcon. "Then take this,'" she said. "This leopard is a magic beast, and you will never kill it otherwise. Only silver will pierce its heart. Take the arrow and you may fulfill your oath." So saying, she slipped out of his room.

The next night Zufik again heard the leopard's voice in the garden below, but this time he took also his bow and arrow when he went to meet it. At first he was loath to use it, since it seemed somehow unmanly; but when the beast had again given him injury and he had struck three sword blows in turn without effect, he at last nocked the silver-pointed shaft on his bowstring and, as the beast charged him once more, let fly. The black arrow struck to the leopard's heart; the creature gave a hideous cry and again leaped the fence, this time leaving a trail of its mortal blood behind it.

When morning came Zufik went to the sultan for men, so that they could follow the track of blood to the beast's lair and prove its death. The sultan was displeased when his vizier, the princess's pale cousin, did not answer his summons. As they were all going down into the garden, though, there came a great cry from the sleeping rooms upstairs, a cry like a soul in mortal agony. With fear in their hearts Zufik, the sultan, and all the men rushed upstairs.

There they found the missing Sifaz.

The pale man lifted a shaking, red-smeared finger to point at Zufik, as all the company stared in horror. "*He* has done it — the foreigner!" Sifaz shouted.

In Sifaz's arms lay the body of the Princess Rassoril, a black arrow standing from her breast.

○ ● ○

After Fawn finished there was a long silence. The boy, his own courage perhaps stirred by his story, seemed to sit straighter.

"Ah . . . ," the vampyr said at last, "love and its prices — that is the message? Or is it perhaps the effect of silver on the supernatural? Fear not, I am bound by no such conventions, and fear neither silver, steel, nor any other metal." The creature made a huffing, scraping sound that might have been a laugh. I marveled anew, even as I felt the skein of my life fraying, that it had so quickly gained such command of our unfamiliar tongue.

"Well . . . ," it said slowly. "Sad. But . . . sad enough? Again, *that* is the important question. Who is your last . . . contestant?"

Now my heart truly went cold within me, and I sat as though I had swallowed a stone. Walid al-Salameh spoke up.

"I am," he said, and took a deep breath. "I am."

The Vizier's Story

This is a true story — or so I was told. It happened in my grandfather's time, and he had it from someone who knew those involved. He told it to me as a cautionary tale.

There once was an old caliph, a man of rare gifts and good fortune. He ruled a small country, but a wealthy one — a country upon which all the gifts of Allah had been showered in grand measure. He had the finest heir a man could have, dutiful and yet courageous, beloved by the people almost as extravagantly as the caliph himself. He had many other fine sons, and two hundred beautiful wives, and an army of fighting men the envy of his neighbors. His treasury was stacked roofbeam-high with gold and gemstones and blocks of fragrant sandalwood, crisscrossed with ivories and bolts of the finest cloth. His palace was built around a spring of fragrant, clear water; and everyone said that they must be the very Waters of Life, so fortunate and well-loved this caliph was. His only sadness was that age had robbed his sight from him, leaving him blind, but hard as this was, it was a small price to pay for Allah's beneficence.

One day the caliph was walking in his garden, smelling the exquisite fragrance of the blossoming orange trees. His son the prince, unaware of his father's presence, was also in the garden, speaking with his mother, the caliph's first and chiefest wife.

"He is terribly old," the wife said. "I cannot stand even to touch him anymore. It is a horror to me."

"You are right, mother," the son replied, as the caliph hid behind the trees and listened, shocked. "I am sickened by watching him sitting all day, drooling into his bowl, or staggering sightless through the palace. But what are we to do?"

"I have thought on it long and hard," the caliph's wife replied. "We owe it to ourselves and those close to us to kill him."

"Kill him?" the son replied. "Well, it is hard for me, but I suppose you are right. I still feel some love for him, though — may we at least do it quickly, so that he shall not feel pain at the end?"

"Very well. But do it soon — tonight, even. If I must feel his foul breath upon me one more night I will die myself."

"Tonight, then," the son agreed, and the two walked away, leaving the blind caliph shaking with rage and terror behind the orange trees. He could not see what sat on the garden path behind them, the object of their discussion: the wife's old lap-dog, a scrofulous creature of extreme age.

Thus the caliph went to his vizier, the only one he was sure he could trust in a world of suddenly traitorous sons and wives, and bade him to have the pair arrested and quickly beheaded. The vizier was shocked, and asked the reason why, but the caliph only said he had unassailable proof that they intended to murder him and take his throne. He bade the vizier go and do the deed.

The vizier did as he was directed, seizing the son and his mother quickly and quietly, then giving them over to the headsman after tormenting them for confessions and the names of confederates, neither of which were forthcoming.

Sadly, the vizier went to the caliph and told him it was done, and the old man was satisfied. But soon, inevitably, word of what had happened spread, and the brothers of the heir began to murmur among themselves about their father's deed. Many thought him mad, since the dead pair's devotion to the caliph was common knowledge.

Word of this dissension reached the caliph himself, and he began to fear for his life, terrified that his other sons meant to emulate their treasonous brother. He called the vizier to him and demanded the arrest of these sons, and their beheading. The vizier argued in vain, risking his own life, but the caliph would not be swayed; at last the vizier went away, returning a week later a battered, shaken man.

"It is done, O Prince," he said. "All your sons are dead."

The caliph had only a short while in which to feel safe before the extreme wrath of the wives over the slaughter of their children reached his ears. "Destroy them, too!" the blind caliph insisted.

Again the vizier went away, soon to return.

"It is done, O Prince," he reported. "Your wives have been beheaded."

Soon the courtiers were crying murder, and the caliph sent his vizier to see them dealt with as well.

"It is done, O Prince," he assured the caliph. But the ruler now feared the angry townspeople, so he commanded his vizier to take the army and slaughter them. The vizier argued feebly, then went away.

"It is done, O Prince," the caliph was told a month later. But now the caliph realized that with his heirs and wives gone, and the important men of the court dead, it was the soldiers themselves who were a threat to his power. He commanded his vizier to sow lies amongst them, causing them to fall out an slay each other, then locked himself in his room to safely outlast the conflict. After a month and a half the vizier knocked upon his door.

"It is done, O Prince."

For a moment the caliph was satisfied. All his enemies were dead, and he himself was locked in: no one could murder him, or steal his treasure, or usurp his throne. The only person yet alive who even knew where the caliph hid was . . . his vizier.

Blind, he groped about for the key with which he had locked himself in. Better first to remove the risk that someone might trick him into coming out. He pushed the key out beneath the door and told the vizier to throw it away somewhere it might never be found. When the vizier returned he called him close to the locked portal that bounded his small world of darkness and safety.

"Vizier," the caliph said through the keyhole, "I command you to go and kill yourself, for you are the last one living who is a threat to me."

140

"*Kill* myself, my prince?" the vizier asked, dumbfounded. "Kill *myself?*"

"Correct," the caliph said. "Now go and do it. That is my command."

There was a long silence. At last the vizier said: "Very well." After that there was silence.

For a long time the caliph sat in his blindness and exulted, for everyone he distrusted was gone. His faithful vizier had carried out all his orders, and now had killed himself. . . .

A sudden, horrible thought came to him then: what if the vizier had *not* done what he had told him to do? What if instead he had made compact with the caliph's enemies, and was only reporting false details when he told of their deaths? *How was the caliph to know?* He almost swooned with fright and anxiousness at the realization.

At last he worked up the courage to feel his way across the locked room to the door. He put his ear to the keyhole and listened. He heard nothing but silence. He took a breath and then put his mouth to the hole.

"Vizier?" he called in a shaky voice. "Have you done what I commanded? Have you killed yourself?"

"It is done, O Prince," came the reply.

○ ● ○

Finishing his story, which was fully as dreadful as it was sad, the under-vizier Walid lowered his head as if ashamed or exhausted. We waited tensely for our guest to speak; at the same time I am sure we all vainly hoped there would be no more speaking, that the creature would simply vanish, like a frightening dream that flees the sun.

"Rather than discuss the merits of your sad tales," the black, tattered shadow said at last — confirming that there would be no waking from *this* dream, "rather than argue the game with only one set of moves completed, perhaps it is now time for me to speak.

CHILD OF AN ANCIENT CITY

The night is still youthful, and my tale is not long, but I wish to give you a fair time to render judgement."

As he spoke the creature's eyes bloomed scarlet like unfolding roses. The mist curled up from the ground beyond the fire-circle, wrapping the vampire in a cloak of writhing fogs, a rotted black egg in a bag of silken mesh.

". . . May I begin?" it asked . . . but no one could say a word. "Very well. . . ."

The Vampyr's Story

The tale *I* will tell is of a child, a child born of an ancient city on the banks of a river. So long ago this was that not only has the city itself long gone to dust; but the later cities built atop its ruins, tiny towns and great walled fortresses of stone, all these too have gone beneath the millwheels of time — rendered, like their predecessor, into the finest of particles to blow in the wind, silting the timeless river's banks.

This child lived in a mud hut thatched with straw, and played with his fellows in the shallows of the sluggish brown river while his mother washed the family's clothes and gossiped with her neighbors.

Even *this* ancient city was built upon the bones of earlier cities, and it was into the collapsed remnants of one — a great, tumbled mass of shattered sandstone — that the child and his friends sometimes went. And it was to these ruins that the child, when he was a little older . . . almost the age of your young, romantic companion . . . took a pretty, doe-eyed girl.

It was to be his first time beyond the veil — his initiation into the mysteries of women. His heart beat rapidly; the girl walked ahead of him, her slender brown body tiger-striped with light and shade as she walked among the broken pillars. Then she saw something, and

screamed. The child came running.

The girl was nearly mad, weeping and pointing. He stopped in amazement, staring at the black, shrivelled thing that lay on the ground — a twisted something that might have been a man once, wizened and black as a piece of leather dropped into the cook-fire. Then the thing opened its eyes.

The girl ran, choking — but he did not, seeing that the black thing could not move. The twitching of its mouth seemed that of someone trying to speak; he thought he heard a faint voice asking for help, begging for him to do something. He leaned down to the near-silent hiss, and the thing squirmed and bit him, fastening its sharp teeth like barbed fish-hooks in the muscle of his leg. The man-child screamed, helpless, and felt his blood running out into the horrible sucking mouth of the thing. Fetid saliva crept into the wounds and coursed hotly through his body, even as he struggled against his writhing attacker. The poison climbed through him, and it seemed he could feel his own heart flutter and die within his chest, delicate and hopeless as a broken bird. With final, desperate strength the child pulled free. The black thing, mouth gaping, curled on itself and shuddered, like a beetle on a hot stone. A moment later it had crumbled into ashes and oily flakes.

But it had caught me long enough to destroy me — for of course *I* was that child — to force its foul fluids into me, leeching my humanity and replacing it with the hideous, unwanted wine of immortality. My child's heart became an icy fist.

Thus was I made what I am, at the hands of a dying vampyr — which had been a creature like I am now. Worn down at last by the passing of millennia, it had chosen a host to receive its hideous malady, then died — as *I* shall do someday, no doubt, in the grip of some terrible, blind, insect-like urge

141

... but not soon. Not today.

So that child, which had been in all ways like other children — loved by its family, loving in turn noise and games and sweetmeats — became a dark thing sickened by the burning light of the sun.

Driven into the damp shadows beneath stones and the dusty gloom of abandoned places, then driven out again beneath the moon by an unshakeable, unresistable hunger, I fed first on my family — my uncomprehending mother wept to see her child returned, standing by her moonlit pallet — then on the others of my city. Not last, or least painful of my feedings was on the dark-haired girl who had run when I stayed behind. I slashed other throats, too, and lapped up warm, sea-salty blood while the trapped child inside me cried without a sound. It was as though I stood behind a screen, unable to leave or interfere as terrible crimes were committed before me. . . .

And thus the years have passed: sand grains, deposited along the river bank, uncountable in their succession. Every one has contained a seeming infinitude of killings, each one terrible despite their numbing similarity. Only the blood of mankind will properly feed me, and a hundred generations have known terror of me.

Strong as I am, virtually immortal, unkillable as far as I know or can tell — blades pass through me like smoke; fire, water, poison, none affect me — still the light of the sun causes a pain to me so excruciating that you with only mortal lives, whose pain at least eventually ends in death, cannot possibly comprehend it. Thus, kingdoms of men have risen and fallen to ashes since I last saw daylight. Think only on that for a moment, if you seek sad stories! I must be in darkness when the sun rises, so as I range in search of prey my accommodations are shared with toads and slugs, bats, and blindworms.

People can be nothing to me anymore but food. I know of none other like myself, save the dying creature who spawned me. The smell of my own corruption is in my nostrils always.

So there is all of *my* tale. I cannot die until my time is come, and who can know when that is? Until then I will be alone, alone as no mere man can ever be, alone with my wretchedness and evil and self-disgust until the world collapses and is born anew . . .

○ ● ○

The vampyr rose now, towering up like a black sail billowing in the wind, spreading its vast arms or wings on either side, as if to sweep us before it. "How do your stories compare to this?" it cried; the harshness of its speech seemed somehow muted, even as it grew louder and louder. "Whose is the saddest story, then?" There was pain in that hideous voice that tore at even my fast-pounding heart. "Whose is saddest? Tell me! It is time to *judge* . . ."

And in that moment, of all the moments when lying could save my life . . . I could not lie. I turned my face away from the quivering black shadow, that thing of rags and red eyes. None of the others around the campfire spoke — even Abdallah the clerk only sat hugging his knees, teeth chattering, eyes bulging with fear.

". . . I thought so," the thing said at last. "I thought so." Night wind tossed the treelimbs above our heads, and it seemed as though beyond them stood only ultimate darkness — no sky, no stars, nothing but unending emptiness.

"Very well," the vampyr said at last. "Your silence speaks all. I have won." There was not the slightest note of triumph in its voice. "Give me my prize, and then I may let the rest of you flee my mountains." The dark shape withdrew a little way.

We all of us turned to look at one

another, and it was just as well that the night veiled our faces. I started to speak, but Ibn Fahad interrupted me, his voice a tortured rasp.

"Let there be no talk of volunteering. We will draw lots; that is the only way." Quickly he cut a thin branch into five pieces, one of them shorter than the rest, and cupped them in a closed hand.

"Pick," he said. "I will keep the last."

As a part of me wondered what madness it was that had left us wagering on story-telling and drawing lots for our lives, we each took a length from Ibn Fahad's fist. I kept my hand closed while the others selected, not wanting to hurry Allah toward his revelation of my fate. When all had selected we extended our hands and opened them, palms up.

Fawn had selected the short stick.

Strangely, there was no sign of his awful fortune on his face: he showed no signs of grief — indeed, he did not even respond to our helpless words and prayers, only stood up and slowly walked toward the huddled black shape at the far edge of the clearing. The vampyr rose to meet him.

"No!" came a sudden cry, and to our complete surprise the clerk Abdallah leaped to his feet and went pelting across the open space, throwing himself between the youth and the looming shadow. "He is too young!" Abdallah shouted, sounding truly anguished. "Do not do this horrible thing! Take me instead!"

Ibn Fahad, the vizier, and I could only sit, struck dumb by this unexpected behavior, but the creature moved swiftly as a viper, smacking Abdallah to the ground with one flicking gesture.

"You are indeed mad, you short-lived men!" the vampyr hissed. "This one would do nothing to save himself — not once did I hear his voice raised in tale-telling — yet now he would throw himself into the jaws of death for this other! Mad!" The monster left Abdallah chok-

143

ing on the ground and turned to silent Fawn. "Come, you. I have won the contest, and you are the prize. I am . . . sorry . . . it must be this way. . . ." A great swath of darkness enveloped the youth, drawing him in. "Come," the vampyr said, "think of the better world you go to — that is what you believe, is it not? Well, soon you shall —"

The creature broke off.

"Why do you look so strangely, manchild? " the thing said at last, its voice troubled. "You cry, but I see no fear. Why? Are you not afraid of dying? "

Fawn answered; his tones were oddly distracted. "Have you really lived so long? And alone, always alone?"

"I told you. I have no reason to lie. Do you think to put me off with your strange questions?"

"Ah, how could the good God be so unmerciful!?" The words were made of sighs. The dark shape that embraced him stiffened.

"Do you cry for *me? For me?!*"

"How can I help? " the boy said. "Even Allah must weep for you . . . for such a pitiful thing, lost in the lonely darkness . . ."

For a moment the night air seemed to pulse. Then, with a wrenching gasp, the creature flung the youth backward so that he stumbled and fell before us, landing atop the groaning Abdallah.

"Go!" the vampyr shrieked, and its voice cracked and boomed like thunder. "Get you gone from my mountains! *Go!"*

Amazed, we pulled Fawn and the chief clerk to their feet and went stumbling down the hillside, branches lashing at our faces and hands, expecting any moment to hear the rush of wings and feel cold breath on our necks.

"Build your houses well, little men!" a voice howled like the wild wind behind us. "My life is long . . . and someday I may regret letting you go!"

We ran and ran, until it seemed the life would flee our bodies, until our

144

lungs burned and our feet blistered . . . and until the topmost sliver of the sun peered over the eastern summits. . . .

○ ○ ● ● ○ ○

Masrur al-Adan allowed the tale's ending to hang in silence for a span of thirty heartbeats, then pushed his chair away from the table.

"We escaped the mountains the next day," he said. "Within a season we were back in Baghdad, the only survivors of the caravan to the Armenites."

"Aaaahh . . . !" breathed young Hassan, a long drawn-out sound full of wonder and apprehension. "What a marvelous, terrifying adventure! I would *never* have survived it, myself. How frightening! And did the . . . the creature . . . did he *really* say he might come back someday?"

Masrur solemnly nodded his large head. "Upon my soul. Am I not right, Ibn Fahad, my old comrade?"

Ibn Fahad yielded a thin smile, seemingly of affirmation.

"Yes," Masrur continued, "those words chill me to this very day. Many is the night I have sat in this room, looking at that door —" He pointed. "— wondering if someday it may open to show me that terrible, misshapen black thing, come back from Hell to make good on our wager."

"Merciful Allah!" Hassan gasped.

Abu Jamir leaned across the table as the other guests whispered excitedly. He wore a look of annoyance. "Good Hassan," he snapped, "kindly calm yourself. We are all grateful to our host Masrur for entertaining us, but it is an insult to sensible, Godly men to suggest that at any moment some blood-drinking Afreet may knock down the door and carry us —"

The door leaped open with a crash, revealing a hideous, twisted shape looming in the entrance, red-splattered and trembling. The shrieking of Masrur's guests filled the room.

"Master . . . ?" the dark silhouette quavered. Baba held a wine jar balanced on one shoulder. The other had broken at his feet, splashing Abu Jamir's prize stock everywhere. "Master," he began again, "I am afraid I have dropped one."

Masrur looked down at Abu Jamir, who lay pitched full-length on the floor, insensible.

"Ah, well, that's all right, Baba." Masrur smiled, twirling his black mustache. "We won't have to make the wine go so far as I thought — it seems my story-telling has put some of our guests to sleep." ☐

WALPURGISNACHT

Like some gaunt skull wrapped in a rotting shroud
The dead moon peers through shreds of tattered cloud
To leer down on our revels. A cold wind
Awakes to prowl the lonely woodland, thinned
Of shrivelled leaves fallen from bare black limbs
That groan and creak like gibbets. The moon dims
To our impalpable and eerie flight
As witches gather from the edge of night.

Dark Lord Sathanas, help us celebrate
The midnight mysteries of darkling fate,
As we quaff babies' blood, foaming and red
From deep skull-goblets stolen from the dead
Of rifled sepulchres. The moon soars high —
Come, sorceress, embrace me! Dawn is nigh.

— Lin Carter

145

www.ingramcontent.com/pod-product-compliance
Lightning Source LLC
Chambersburg PA
CBHW070556180626
46817CB00005B/1869